The Angel Gang

Books by Ken Kuhlken

Midheaven

The Hickey Family Series
The Loud Adios
The Venus Deal
The Angel Gang
The Do-Re-Mi
The Vagabond Virgins

With Alan Russell
Road Kill
No Cats, No Chocolate

The
Angel Gang

Ken Kuhlken

Poisoned Pen Press

Poisoned Pen Press
6962 E. First Ave., Ste. 103
Scottsdale, AZ 85251
www.poisonedpenpress.com
info@poisonedpenpress.com

Printed in the United States of America

For Melissa

Many thanks to Martha Barbato, John Barbato, Ruth Cavin,
Judith Moore and Dan Thrapp.

Chapter One

On one of those days when nothing fit, when every damned screw proved too big or small, Tom Hickey tried to install a window in the new room he'd been adding to the cabin. He wanted to finish before the baby arrived, which gave him two weeks to plaster, paint, lay the tile. Once the baby came, he wasn't going to allow any fumes in the house. Nothing but the rich mountain air. Having to take his pipe outside would be a trial in winter. But this kid he'd vowed to protect a whole lot better than he had Elizabeth. Anybody granted a second chance, he believed, ought to learn from history.

At forty-four, he was bald at the crown. The mustache he wore to distract from his large nose had transformed to gray. Yet he still had the muscles to split foot-wide pine logs with one whack, the wind to climb in a short morning from the dock at Emerald Bay to the crest of the Rubicons, and the courage to dedicate the next twenty or so years to the kid. And to Wendy.

She stood in the doorway between the addition and their bedroom, wearing a quilt draped over her shoulders and squinting—still and watchful, as though expecting her husband to boot the jar of screws. In a couple steps, she crossed the little room. She reached for his shoulder and pressed the tight muscle. "Tom, what songs do you think you'll play tonight?"

He was booked to fill in on clarinet for Walt Ralston, who'd busted a finger when his skis got tangled and he plowed into a tree. Most of his life, Hickey'd played saxophone. He'd gotten the clarinet from Wendy for Christmas, a few months after the atom bombs hit Japan, right after the army cut him loose, the winter before they moved to Tahoe. Almost three years now, he'd been working fill-in on tenor and alto sax and clarinet for Charley Wayne's Orchestra, the house band at Harry's South Shore Casino.

"Search me," he said. "Never know what Wayne's mood's gonna be. You wanta come listen?"

"Every night you play I want to come, but I always get so sleepy."

"So we'll do like at New Year's. I'll shark Harry into giving us a room at the hotel. Only this time we'll make it a triple, an extra bed for Claire. Think she'll go?"

"I bet she will. Tom, maybe the green New Year's dress will fit me."

"Easily, babe." He turned and gave her a long hug, pressing against her belly, his favorite of all her curves. She kissed his shoulder and hummed her pleasure.

After they pulled apart, he reached for the jar of screws. He poured a handful and was sifting through when the phone rang. While Wendy hustled to answer, he stood quiet and listened, guessing it would be the bandleader asking him to show a half hour early to rehearse a new number. Though the phone was two rooms away and Wendy spoke softly, their cabin was small enough so he heard her say, "Just a moment, please."

He replaced the screws, met her in the doorway, gave her a kiss on the forehead. He slipped through the bedroom sideways, to fit between the bed and the dresser.

When he grumbled into the phone, the operator announced person-to-person long distance, from the law firm of Worthy, Wright and Wilcox. He flopped into his padded chair.

"Mister Hickey. Dick Wilcox here. Representing Cynthia Jones."

Hickey stiffened and glowered at the phone. The name Cynthia had walloped him like a sucker punch. He recovered by reminding himself that more than one person could use the same first name. "Cynthia who?"

"You might remember her as Cynthia Tucker. Ring a bell?"

"A cacophony of them," Hickey muttered.

"The lady needs your help. She's been arrested for murder."

Shutting his eyes, reaching around the chair, he fumbled on the table behind him for his meerschaum and Walter Raleigh. "Who'd she kill?"

"I take it you think she's capable of murder."

"Yeah. Who'd she kill?"

"They're holding her in the arson murder of her sister's husband. She denies the charge, and I believe her. She has a solid alibi and no apparent motive."

His pipe lit, he took a long drag, blew a smoke ring, noticed Wendy standing beside him. He reached up and laid an arm on her shoulder. "The motive's a feud going back twenty years, Cynthia and Daddy versus Mama and Sis. If she's got a tight alibi, why're they holding her?"

"Her alibi's a crowd of hophead musicians, one of whom has contradicted the others. The DA's sure he can discredit them."

Wendy rubbed his neck, and Hickey said, "Look, fella, I'm going to give you the number of my partner. Name's Leo Weiss. Anybody can fix things, he's the guy."

"She wants *you*."

"Tell her I'm flattered—and retired. Only investigating I do is security stuff for my neighbor's casino. Leo's your man."

"I doubt she'll accept that."

"Aw, darn."

"I hear your sarcasm. Mister Hickey. She said I might have to remind you that you owe her."

"Swell, tell her you reminded me. Wish her luck. Now I've gotta go to work." He gave the man Leo's number, hung up, and leaned into Wendy so his nose lay between her breasts and his chin rested on her belly.

She kissed his baldest spot. "Cynthia's the one you told me...in the hospital...with the baby?"

"Yeah." He lingered, getting comforted, and finally sat up. "Tomorrow I'll go to the hardware, find the right screws, put in the window easy."

"Okay.…Tell me about Cynthia?"

"Let's go for a walk, huh?"

She nodded happily and went for their coats and snow caps, her boots. While she dressed, Hickey stood at their lake-view window, watching pewter-colored shadows darken to steel gray, suppressing the urge to cuss viciously. Because he doubted a guy could hear Cynthia's name without trouble landing on him.

Outside, he grabbed the sled off the porch and tossed it down on the crusty snow at the foot of the stairs. Wendy settled onto it. He picked up the rope and towed. Halfway across the meadow to the beach, she asked about Cynthia.

"Looks like she torched a house," Hickey said dolefully. "Some fellow burned. She's banking on me to save her, on account of she figures I owe her."

"Money?"

"Naw. Remember, I told you, I stopped her from killing her mama's boyfriend, the swami. And if I hadn't snatched her out of TJ, that abortion joint, she wouldn't of had the baby."

"I remember. She doesn't like the baby, so her sister took it home."

"Yep. She wanted to kill the baby."

"Poor people.…Tom, how long will you be in San Diego?"

Hickey stopped and turned, knelt in the snow beside her and sank to mid-thigh. She was wearing the look that pierced his heart most deeply. Her sky-blue eyes glittering, her lips and chin pushed out a little, set firm—the look that exposed both how strong and how fragile a human could be.

"I'm not going, babe."

"But maybe they'll put her in jail forever."

"Yeah, and maybe it's where she oughta be."

"Maybe not, though."

"Hey, if she's innocent, Leo can spring her."

Wendy nodded, closed her eyes, thought a minute before shaking her head. "Leo's not you."

As he stood, he marveled at how blessed a guy could feel when somebody believed in him. He picked up the rope and towed her over a few low snowy dunes to the beach at the point where their property met the Blackwood estate. He ran her fifty yards up the beach and back, having to duck both ways passing under the Blackwoods' pier. The Blackwoods were descended from a fisherman who'd made his fortune off brown trout. Using ice-packed wagons and boxcars, he'd expressed the creatures to San Francisco, as if the Pacific didn't have enough fish of its own. After they'd netted the lake clean, the family had turned to banking and other respectable schemes. Their house was unstained cedar, like the Hickeys' place, only the Hickeys' cabin could fit in any one of a dozen of the Blackwood rooms. The estate lay on five acres, shaded and hidden by the pine forest. Surrounded by their stables, an arena big enough to hold bullfights, and a riding trail, it was the largest estate in the village except Harry Poverman's.

Poverman owned a swank South Shore Casino. Two years ago, he'd built a monstrosity on the other side of the Hickeys' place. The Blackwoods snubbed Harry in public. In private they pestered Sheriff Boggs about the gambler's houseguests: gun-packing LA and Vegas Jews, Greeks, Italians, who got drunk and raced Harry's speedboats, then chased painted dolls around the neighborhood at 3 A.M., shouting curses and strange propositions.

Living between a brood of snobs and a party house hadn't been one of Hickey's ambitions. But the gambler employed him and was a cordial fellow, so Hickey didn't complain. And the Blackwoods kept their distance. Except Claire, a daughter-in-law, the only Blackwood he deemed worth knowing. Wendy's best pal.

Hickey towed his wife along the beach to the tallest snowy dune at the south end of their property. On top, as he gave a push and watched her slide toward the golden water, her arms braced tightly against the sled so she wouldn't topple and risk denting the baby, he wondered if anywhere in any age had occurred a twilight so perfect. Crystals of snow displaced by the runners flew up to glitter in Wendy's hair. Her laughter resonated like bells. Beyond her, the lake's golden skin faded into silver, then darkened to a rich cobalt center. Toward the south shore, it turned flint gray, the same color as the only cloud in sight. Arrowhead shaped, pointed down. On its journey over the wilderness they called Desolation, the cloud appeared to have stopped about twenty degrees east of Mount Tallac. If it dropped, Hickey figured, it might splash into Sourdough Lake, where Hickey'd snagged a twelve-pound cutthroat last summer.

Wendy struggled to her feet but slipped, got her feet tangled, began to topple, but Hickey caught her. On the way down she'd grasped her quivering belly and laughed. Nothing enchanted Hickey so much as her happiness. Not a chance he'd desert her to fix things for Cynthia. Especially when he would've taken odds she lit the damned fire.

"I can pull you, Tom." Wendy swept thick blond-and-brown-mixed hair from her face and held it back in a short horsetail. She smiled and rubbed a snowflake from her rosy cheek. Kicking a step through the snow, she leaned her head on Hickey's shoulder. "Want me to pull you?"

"Naw. I'd bust the sled." Hickey rubbed his belly. Jiggled the ten or so pounds he'd stacked on during the year since his marriage. Not from his wife's cooking. They'd been sharing a house six years, since the war. He just moved a little slower these days, burnt less steam. His restlessness had fled once Wendy had cured him of the suspicion that either he possessed an uncanny knack for sabotaging every break he got or life was rigged against him.

He grabbed the sled rope and towed with his left hand while Wendy held the other, swung his arm a little, and shuffled her feet in the snow, walking more like a tomboy than a woman of almost thirty due to give birth in twenty-some days.

Rather than cutting back across their meadow, they kept hiking, toward the horse trail that passed through the redwood grove on Harry Poverman's land. To pass under Harry's dock, they had to wedge single file between two beached speedboats.

Wendy led the way. When Hickey'd gotten through, he said, "I oughta run over, ask Harry about the room."

She rubbed snow from her eyes and squeezed his hand. "Tom, you need to go to San Diego."

"Naw, darling. What I need is to stay here with you."

When she cocked her head to face him, her eyes glistened as if she were standing over a bonfire. "But maybe they'll never let Cynthia out of prison," she whispered. "Maybe she'll stay there until she dies. And you'll get nightmares."

Hickey dropped her hand, reached around, and pulled her so close they walked like tipsy people into the grove. Fifty yards ahead, in the clearing, he glanced up and saluted the bodyguard who sat smoking on the rear deck of Harry's place.

The Poverman house was a sprawling eyesore, single-story, white and burnt orange. A bunch of connected cubes, it looked as native to the forest as a herd of camels would've. Tyler, the bodyguard, waved back and threw his feet up onto the deck rail. The Hickeys cut between three lighted tennis courts and a drained swimming pool, into the meadow that led to their cabin.

According to most citizens of the village, the Hickeys' place, with its rough-hewn boards, miniature stature, and cheap asphalt roofing, should've been relegated to butler's quarters, towed to some logging camp, or burned. The Hickeys had built it themselves. All they owed was taxes. At least their lot was as foresty, with as long a beach frontage, as most anybody's.

Inside, around the wood stove, for an hour Hickey deflected his wife's arguments. That Clifford wouldn't arrive for three weeks. That she felt as strong as ever, and braver. Besides, Claire would stay with her, but poor Mrs. Jones might have nobody she could trust in such a jam except him. Tom was the best of anybody at saving people, she contended.

Finally he caught the notion that the strongest reason she loved him was on account of his always helping people. A minute later, he relented.

By 7 P.M., Wendy'd made a phone call and Claire Blackwood had joined them. She was tall and prim with a soft round face, bobbed hair, and pierced ears sporting baubles of silver and turquoise. A widow who lived in a guesthouse on the family estate of her late husband, who'd fallen on the march across Bataan, she wrote poetry, painted landscapes, and wore turtle-necked sweaters, embroidered Mexican blouses, and skirts to her ankles. In summer she'd go barefoot. She appeared as classy as Wendy looked ingenuous. The Hickeys loved her dearly.

Three times, Hickey got Claire's promise to stick by Wendy every minute. He worried that she might slip and fall on the ice, that her water might break or the baby drop suddenly into labor, that a nightmare might strike like they used to, catapulting her back into Hell, where he'd found her—a Tijuana dive where for a month during 1943 Nazis, Mexicans, and gringo soldiers had groped her with their fingers and damned yellow eyes. Where her brother had lain with half his head gone, splattered on the window and wall, on the night they'd freed her and Hickey'd stormed into her life.

He considered bargaining. If Wendy wanted him to help Cynthia, he could propose that she go with him to San Diego and stay at the bayside cottage with his daughter, Elizabeth. Except that before they moved up this way and ever since, on their few trips off the mountain, anyplace but here she couldn't lose the haunted expression, the flicking eyes, the tension that made her spook like a shell-shocked veteran. As though on the flatland demons surrounded her, but up here in the place she used to call heaven, angels gathered around.

He gave Wendy and Claire five San Diego phone numbers: the lawyer's, Leo's, Elizabeth's, and home and work numbers for Rusty Thrapp, his old pal, a captain with the San Diego police. He promised to stop and phone every few hours on the drive. The second she wanted him, he'd turn the Chevy into a jet and flash back up the mountain. No matter what, he promised to drive home Monday night. He'd give Cynthia forty-eight hours, tops.

Chapter Two

It might've been the wind that startled Wendy awake, a racket like somebody standing in the meadow tossing up armfuls of birch leaves. She wrestled her legs out of the sheets, hoisted her body around, and stood up. Before tiptoeing to the window, she bent to tuck covers around Claire.

A pale light radiated from a place between two of the thickest junipers, beyond the woodshed at the edge of the property line. Harry's guard dogs must've seen it, the way they snarled and the posts creaked as they tugged on their chains. The light was like mornings when the sun topped Mount Rose: beams refracting off the slopes, tinted pale green by the forest. Only it wasn't morning, and the light only fell that one place, an oval shape about the size of a doorway. Maybe it was a flashlight beam from somebody walking along the road peering into the woods. Wendy gave up the breath she'd been holding and gulped a deeper one, waiting for the light to move on.

It stayed put. Didn't even quiver. She folded her arms across her belly, rubbed them up and down.

Maybe it was a fallen star. A little piece of a star, egg-sized, could make that large a glow, she supposed. She wanted to ask Claire to tell her all about meteors, but Claire was sleeping so pretty with hair wrapped around her neck and her lips puckered like a whistler.

"Oh!" Wendy gasped and slapped a hand over her mouth to silence it.

She'd gasped from remembering the other time, a few years ago, when the same light appeared but she hadn't paid it much attention because those days most everything spooked her. Wind. Loud voices. Songs with violins. Ladies in tight necklaces. Spicy food. Stillness. Every surprise seemed rigged by the devil. Back then she couldn't sleep or take walks alone or sit on the beach without Tom. Every quiet time dared the pictures of Hell to return.

She remembered that the light appeared just after supper, on the night she ran away, just hours before she swiped the rowboat from Claire's beach and paddled out, thinking she could get to the middle, tumble into the darkest water, and drown. But the wind current pushed toward Sand Harbor and heaved against her rowing until it got her into the traffic lane where the excursion boat whacked her and the big fellow splashed in beside her and the other men rowed her to shore in a dinghy and Claire took her into the big house, gave her a cashmere sweater and baggy trousers, and got her all warm by the fire.

It's not a meteor, Wendy thought. Because the center of the light hovered about four feet off the ground. Meteors were rocks, they didn't float in the air. She turned to the chair by her bed, picked up her robe, slipped it on, stepped back to the window, and stood wondering why the most terrible nights could be the grandest ones too. The same night Clifford went to heaven, Tom appeared and carried her out of Hell. The night she decided to swipe the boat and drown, Claire arrived, to become her dearest friend. Except Tom. God did very peculiar things, she thought.

Wendy turned to her nightstand and squinted at the clock. 2:20 A.M. She reached for the California map she'd studied earlier. If the drive took about fourteen hours, Tom ought to be around Fresno by now.

◇◇◇

The last time Tom Hickey had seen Cynthia—maiden name Tucker, alias Moon—over seven years ago, she'd been nearly as pregnant as Wendy now. Two months short of the big day and still confined to the mental ward where he and Leo had deposited her a few weeks after she'd gotten raped. They'd driven her to Riverview Sanitarium the night they snatched her away from Charlie Schwartz's driver, after tailing her from San Diego to the Tijuana butcher shop where she planned to rid herself and the world of the seed planted by her mother's boyfriend, an Indian yogi and charlatan who'd been cashing in on his classic profile and his stunt of slinging blue fire out of his fingertips, and charming or duping the pants off a legion of females.

The last time Hickey and Cynthia had met, she'd screamed that for every horror this beast inside her would ever loose upon the world, Tom was to blame. He was the guy who wouldn't let her get scraped, she howled. The timbre of her voice had felt like icewater jetted into his ears.

The baby arrived prematurely, got incubated. By court order, before Cynthia could snap its neck, the kid went to Laurel, Cynthia's sister, whom she never called by name. Always "the Bitch." The same sister who'd finally drugged the swami and tied off his nuts with rawhide.

Hickey would've fought against the adoption. The wisdom of handing over to Laurel a child produced by the man she'd castrated and the sister who considered her a fiend seemed equal to asking a cat to babysit your goldfish. But nobody summoned him to the hearing. Cynthia was in hysterics and Hickey'd lost touch. Other quandaries had arisen.

The kid was a boy, about four pounds at birth and sickly, with a misfiring heart. Leo had brought Hickey the news. September in the navy brig where Hickey lay recuperating from the wounds of the vile and precious year when he'd lost his wife to a Cuban gangster, gotten drafted, and been condemned to stand guard at the border. An MP. From there, Wendy's brother Clifford lured him over the border and into the fray that won him the grand prize: Wendy.

A year later, Cynthia turned up again, singing for D. D. Drake's orchestra at the Mission Beach Ballroom. Hickey would've gone to see her, stood in back where she couldn't spot him. But she ran off to marry some flyboy. That was the last Hickey knew.

Through the San Joaquin Valley, he cussed the tankers and produce trucks that hogged the road. They stacked up like caravans, five or six deep. You needed a mile-long straightaway without a single northbound vehicle before you could pass. If not for the damned trucks, he would've gotten through LA before the traffic had jammed, stopped around Santa Ana and phoned Rusty Thrapp, caught him at home over breakfast, arranged for a meeting with Cynthia, and still made San Diego without losing much of the day.

Every time he passed a truck stop, he got an urge to phone Wendy but figured it'd be selfish, upsetting her sleep just to lighten his worries. Besides, waiting to call until he made San Diego would get him there faster. He eased his two-year-old navy blue Chevy coupe through the Bakersfield speed trap, then set the hand throttle at seventy-five, determined to climb the Grapevine before dawn when the truckers dozing along the highway would rouse and head out to jam the road. By first light he was halfway up the grade. He whizzed through the San Fernando Valley and Hollywood even before the churchgoers and folks on Sunday outings to the mountains or south coast beaches blocked his way. At half past eight he coasted around the bend in Laguna Beach where a strange old graybeard, long-haired and stooped as Father Time, stood waving joyously as though every motorist was the prodigal son he awaited to wrap in his arms.

Nearing San Diego, Hickey argued with himself about whether he'd visit Elizabeth. His only previous offspring, she was twenty-three years old, married to a drunken pretty-boy con named Stuart Crump, the black sheep of a bigshot New Jersey clan. The punk had started Elizabeth drinking, at first to keep him company, later on account of she was miserable living with the bum, who'd wheedled his folks into buying him a grocery in

Ocean Beach. It was the last payoff before they disowned him. Now Elizabeth was stuck running the damned store. Stuart showed up once or twice a day to loot the cashbox, on his way to the track or a saloon.

If Hickey stopped to see her, no doubt Stuart would rile him. He might finally thrash the bum. Better to wait until Wendy and the baby got strong enough, then drive them down for a week on the bay. Maybe early July, after the foggy season and so they could be there for the fourth, when the bay dwellers filled the sky with Mexican pinwheels and rockets. On that trip, he'd ask Elizabeth if she wanted to scram, go live in Incline with her dad, her little brother, and Wendy, at least long enough to give Stuart a jolt, maybe hard enough so he'd ditch the booze and the ponies.

Approaching Garnet, the cross street into Pacific Beach where Elizabeth and the bum occupied Hickey's cottage at the bayfront dead end of Fanuel Street, Hickey decided that for now he should leave his daughter be and attend to the most urgent business.

Sunday on the Coast Highway, the factories looked deserted. Only two Cessnas lifted off from Lindbergh Field while he passed. A single destroyer rested on the harbor, and a carrier loomed way down past the ferry crossing near the shipyards. Tuna clippers lined the docks where the warships used to load. From the looks of San Diego, you could've deluded yourself into thinking that people had melted their swords and cast them into plowshares.

The railroad-car front of the Pier Five Diner was tarnished, rusted along the floorline. The diner had a new cook, a Filipino. Bobo, the waitress said, had retired to a trailer in the Tehachapi mountains. The cabby at the counter next to Hickey remarked that this new guy slung elegant hash.

The hotcake batter, Hickey thought, could double as glue. The little he ate, he chewed and swallowed fast before it could cinch his teeth together. He washed it down with about two quarts of coffee, then hustled out to Market Street and up the block past a peep show arcade and a bar called the Blue Note where Negroes used to blow the town's hottest jazz. The faded sign hung askew. A wino sat leaning against the wall in a sunny place, scratching.

This part of town looked like a casualty of the war, as if it had gotten bombed or else contaminated by some dread chemical. The brick walls had darkened, the sidewalks and streetlamp poles turned a darker gray. The only hookers outside the Hollywood Burlesque were in glossy photos in the showcase. In wartime, any hour, this block would've accommodated a battalion of sailors, GIs, and jarheads and a company of females. Everybody on the make. You couldn't have decided who was the hunter and who the prey.

Hickey turned up Fifth and strode north across Broadway. Even the center of town looked old and lonesome. In Marston's windows, the mannequins stood naked. Only two buses sat idling in Horton Plaza, quivering as if half the spark plugs were fouled. A few people slept on the benches or inside the buses with their heads against the windows.

At the northwest corner of Fifth and Broadway, Hickey climbed the stairs to the second floor, above the Owl Drugstore, to the office he and Leo Weiss had shared from 1936 until Hickey got drafted in January of 1943. Across the hall, where the chiropractor used to moonlight providing abortions, Best Wholesale Eyeglass Frames had located. A redhead in spiked heels stepped out, wearing sequined, horn-rimmed specs. Nose aloft, she sashayed toward the stairs.

HICKEY AND WEISS, INVESTIGATIONS was still lettered on the door glass. The same old key fit the lock. Inside, the place looked as if somebody had scrubbed and dusted a couple of times since the war. Hickey walked to the Broadway window, threw it open, and stepped to the wall beside the desk where his and Leo's family histories hung. Sketches and watercolors Elizabeth had drawn before Madeline had stolen her off to New Jersey: a sailboat, ballerinas, a snowy forest scene. Photos of himself standing tall, arms around Madeline and Elizabeth. A shot of himself as a bandleader, baton in hand, circa 1927. As an LA cop somberly receiving a citation for valor. Studio photographs of Leo, Violet, and their two girls, Una and Magda. From 1943 until peacetime Magda had served as Wendy's sister. She and her folks had given Wendy a home. Beside the photos hung a poster copy of Magda's latest diploma: Bachelor of Science in Chemistry from Stanford.

Hickey stared a minute, then wagged his head and turned to the desk. He flopped into the rolling chair and grabbed the phone.

After two rings, Wendy said, "Hi, Tom."

"What if it wasn't me?"

"My face would get red, but only Claire would see."

"You okay?"

"Clifford's a naughty one. He kicks harder every day. Sometimes I think his foot's going to come out my belly."

"Babe, if the kid's a girl, are you still going to call her Clifford?"

"Funny man."

"You feeling good?"

"Sure am."

"Claire's sticking with you, right?"

"You bet. We were getting dressed warm for a walk up to the village. I'm going to buy some peanut butter and a button for my blue flannel shirt, and peas and a ham bone for soup tonight. Did you talk to the poor lady yet?"

"Nope. I just got in. Wanted to hear your voice and make sure you remember how crazy I love you."

"Same as I love you."

"Maybe I'll get home tonight, babe. I'm not wasting a second."

"Well, if you drive back tonight, there's a big storm coming. Be extra careful."

"Storm, huh?"

"Yep. Already the water's choppy and the clouds over Homewood look like dragons carved out of stone."

After he told her to watch her step and reluctantly said goodbye, in the desk's left top drawer he found Leo's phone list. Stashed under the crossword puzzle, the same place as ever. He dialed San Diego PD, detective division, asked for Thrapp. Waiting to get switched through, he filled and lit his briar.

"Tom who?"

"Tom the guy you promised to come mooch off and go fishing with but never did."

"I got five kids, old man. Want me to elaborate?"

"Naw. Tell me this summer when you visit. We'll make the kids stay outside, build 'em a wigwam or something. They'll think they're in heaven."

"You got a date. Last couple weeks in July okay?"

"That'll do fine," Hickey said.

"So, how's tricks out in the wilderness?"

"Swell. It looks as if spring and our kid'll arrive about the same time. Look, Rusty, I'm down here in a rush. Wendy's due in no time. You got my note about the wedding, right?"

"Hell, yes. I even sent a gift, a fancy spoon or something."

"Sure, that's right. Wendy hung it on the wall."

"On the wall? Good thing I didn't send an oil painting. You'd be lapping up soup with it. Speaking of soup, you busy for lunch?"

"Yeah. I'm down here in a rush."

"About an arson case, is my guess. Your client's a certain ex-songbird."

"How about you let me in to see her?"

"No sweat. I'll leave your name with the turnkey. You wanta look at the file, ask for Lieutenant Palermo. How about tonight? You still drink Dewar's?"

"If I'm still around and can spare a minute, sure."

"You wanta know what I think about the girl, after grilling her a couple hours myself on account of she's your old...whatever she was?"

"Yeah, tell me."

"I'd give twenty to one she torched the joint. The gal's not one of your better liars."

"Who's the dead guy, Laurel's husband?"

"Johnny Sousa. A fast talker outta LA. Checkered past. Two stretches in Quentin, for extortion. Produces a film now and then. Word is Mickey sent him down to cut in on the race track action, Caliente and Del Mar both, but the wops weren't budging. You know Angelo Paoli moved out here from Jersey?"

"I heard. And you're saying Laurel's husband was one of Cohen's boys?"

"That's what they say."

"Then it could've been one of Paoli's crowd that torched the place."

"Sure, Tom." The captain sighed. "If your Cynthia hadn't got to it first."

Chapter Three

By the time Hickey'd used the john down the hall, walked back across Broadway, past the lot where he'd parked near the Pier Five Diner, and arrived at the police station and jail on Market Street by the tracks that ran along Harbor Drive, it was nearly 11 A.M. Sunlight glared off the harbor. Hickey hadn't been this warm in months.

The station had archways and a patio, a shady Mexican design. There were potted cactus, climbing bougainvillea, a dwarf palm at the entrance to the women's jail. Hickey went in and slumped over the counter. The half gallon of coffee had lit his brain but enervated his muscles.

The sour matron who took his request reluctantly admitted she'd gotten a call from Captain Thrapp and showed Hickey the door to a visiting room, a lime-green cubicle with a wooden table and hard chairs, an aluminum shaded bulb hanging down. Waiting for Cynthia, he used a pocketknife to clean his fingernails and scrape his pipe. He wondered if she'd still be a beauty. When she sang at his club in 1942, she could've charmed Rommel into giving his tanks away. He couldn't imagine her changing. But here she came. Making her entrance, she looked like a barfly, her face caked in powder and a solid coat of eye shadow, as if she'd tried to fill in wrinkles or scars. Her waist, tied in a drawstring around the jail tunic, had thickened. Her arms looked softer, puffy. Her neck had widened and compacted, making her small mouth appear even tinier. Still, she could stop traffic. Tall, formidable as ever, she gazed straight and viciously into Hickey's eyes, her mouth twitching, too racked with fury to speak.

He got up and stepped close enough to touch her shoulder. As though his finger had hit the button, she snarled, "The Bitch has got Casey."

Hickey wagged his head. "You're already losing me. Casey who?"

"My son. My *real* son. The only reason I haven't jumped off suicide bridge. They gave him to the Bitch. Now she's got *both* of them. Casey's as good as dead." Her eyes looked like turquoise in the mask of a war goddess. "Unless you can save us, Tom."

He took her hand and led her to a chair, seated himself. He leaned toward her, across the table. "I hear you. Now, back up a ways. *Who* gave your kid, Casey—who gave him to the Bitch?"

"The cops did. She fixed it, Tom, don't you see? That's why she killed Johnny and framed me. Now she's got Casey. Without him, I'm dead. We're all of us doomed."

"All of who?" Hickey muttered.

She hissed, "Why in Christ didn't you let them scrape me?" She covered her eyes. Her chest heaved. As though from fatigue, she fell into the chair across from Hickey and buried her head in her arms on the table. When he tried to take her hand, she jerked it away, clapped it against her opposite shoulder.

"I could probably get your boy away from Laurel," he offered. "Most likely I can find a judge who'll assign him to Hillcrest Receiving. Then it sounds like you'd as soon I quit meddling and went home."

"But they're saying I killed Johnny. You've got to set them straight."

"Uh-huh. And the way you figure, Laurel torched her own place, right?"

"Don't speak her name," Cynthia snarled. "The Bitch."

"Yeah. And you're saying the Bitch torched her own place, right? Burned her own husband?"

"Sure."

"You got any proof?"

"It must've been her. She hated him, like she hates anybody who won't be her slave. Johnny was sharp, and his own man. She counted on breaking him, but she couldn't. So Johnny kept playing footsy with the Jew mob, after the Bitch got cozy with Angelo."

"Paoli?"

"Who else?"

"How cozy?"

"Cozy as it gets."

Hickey took out his pipe, Walter Raleigh, and a tamper, filled the bowl. "Give me a clue about the fire. A witness, maybe? A turncoat? Laurel have a confidante? Somebody she goes to the powder room with who might be the gossipy or jealous type?"

Burying her head in her arms, Cynthia muttered, "The Bitch hates women, and she wouldn't confide in anybody." She lay quietly a minute; then her shoulders heaved. "Get me out of here," she whined. "Go talk to Marty and the fellas. They'll tell you I was at the jam session all afternoon. Is today Sunday?"

"Yep."

"This'll be the first of Marty's jam sessions I've missed since last July, when Casey had chicken pox."

"Marty who?"

"Eschelman." She sat up, brushing the hair back off her face. "His place is number three, the cottages on the first ridge up the cliff from the foot of Newport in Ocean Beach."

"I oughta go see Laurel. Where's she live?"

"Dammit, quit using her name! Don't you see? It makes her sound *human.*"

Hickey lifted his hands a few inches, in surrender. "Where's the Bitch now?"

"Westwood, probably. She and Johnny got a place across the street from the botanical gardens at UCLA. The house down here they only kept for getaways and so the Bitch would have a hangout when she came to town to torment Casey and me.

You see how she plays cat-and-mouse? That's how the really evil ones do it, instead of just murdering you outright." She looked up pleadingly, streams of eye shadow tracking rivulets down her face. "Get me out of here, Tom, and I'll forgive you for everything."

"In lieu of dollars, right?"

"You want money, you'll get it." Burying her face in her arms, she gave in to sobs and moans.

Hickey patted her wild cinnamon hair. When her sobbing quieted, he rose and started for the door, but she flew up, snagged his arms, leaned close to his ear, and whispered, "If you're tough enough, you could beat the truth out of Charlie. Or maybe you wouldn't have to. He might come clean, to fix her for dumping him."

"Which Charlie's that?"

"Schwartz."

Hickey covered his eyes and rubbed his temples. "Charlie Schwartz?" he groaned.

"Sure. Where've you been?"

"In the woods, remember? And gossip's not on top of my list of failings. So the Bitch dumped Charlie Schwartz. Which means they used to be an item?"

"Charlie and the Bitch were tickling each other for years, almost since you locked me away. She got favors out of him, and he got a cheap imitation of me. Until the old slob bored her one time too many. Then she looked up Angelo. Charlie was one of the reasons Johnny socked her."

"Oh, yeah? When'd he sock her?"

"Lots of times."

Hickey suddenly recalled what it meant to fraternize with Cynthia. Like a gifted preacher, every meeting she'd lure you a step deeper into her bizarre world. For now, at least, he'd gone far enough.

"I'll pay Charlie a visit."

He stood up, pocketed his pipe and tobacco, gave her a peck on the cheek, and left. He crossed the patio to the detectives' office and found Lieutenant Palermo, a sleek fellow in a starched pin-striped shirt with suspenders, who ushered Hickey to a table and tossed him a file folder thick as the Bible.

Hickey skimmed the transcribed statements of eight jazz musicians, all of whom swore Cynthia never budged from Marty Eschelman's cottage between about 1 and 7 P.M. the previous Sunday. The ninth fellow told a different story.

A trombonist named Jack Meechum claimed Cynthia'd stepped out twice. One time a drummer was hogging the john, he'd stated, and she ran squirming to a neighbor's place. Later, she walked out to the cliff and stood a minute talking to a wino. Meechum claimed she gave the wino something.

After digging through the pile for Cynthia's statement, Hickey read twelve pages of her rage and denial.

The wino, she argued, was a beachcomber named Teddy who'd stood outside motioning to her, looking so pitiful she'd finally gone out, verified that he was starving, and fed him. A plate of bologna and potato chips.

The fire report was inconclusive, except that the investigator cited no apparent cause. He pointedly hadn't ruled out arson. The detective noted on the bottom of the page that the house was only two or three hundred yards up the cliff trail from Marty Eschelman's place.

Last, Hickey read the sister's statement. Laurel hadn't exactly accused Cynthia. She'd claimed they'd fought like demons that morning when they met outside the Spic 'n' Span Café on Bacon Street. Cynthia had raved for the hundredth time about Laurel's supposedly murdering Superman, meaning Cynthia's late husband, Carl Jones, who'd crashed during 1947 on a test flight over North Carolina. Her sister had rushed away swearing she'd collect an eye for an eye. Or so Laurel told the detectives.

Hickey jotted addresses and phone numbers: Marty Eschelman and the musicians, Laurel Sousa in Westwood. As he handed the file back to Lieutenant Palermo, he asked, "Where do I find Charlie Schwartz these days?"

"That'd be home, office, lunch, or dinner?"

"Yeah."

The lieutenant pulled a file, scribbled a list, and passed it over. "You going to visit Schwartz?"

Three young detectives besides Palermo had turned to stare. One was a smallish Mexican who'd been drumming on his desk with two pencils. "You plan to talk to Charlie like you did to Donny Katuolis," he said, "we'd as soon you didn't blab who told you where to find him."

Hickey walked out scowling. He wouldn't have figured the young cops to know who he was, let alone to remember the gunman he'd shot dead eight years ago. Charlie Schwartz's protégé.

Chapter Four

When he got to his car, Hickey's watch read eleven-forty. He wheeled a U-turn and headed west, made a right on Pacific Coast Highway, cruised past Lindbergh Field and a mile of armaments factories, turned left on Barnett. At the gate to the Marine Recruit Depot, where gangs of jarheads used to line up for taxis to speed them downtown or to Tijuana the last time Hickey'd driven this road, now only a pair of young women shoved baby carriages. Near the Loma Theater, an old haunt of his and Madeline's, he swung onto Rosecrans and headed downhill. The gate guard at the Naval Training Center had forsaken his post and marched to the curbside bus bench, where he rousted a sailor who lay sleeping.

At the foot of Dickens Street, he parked at the curb, three slots down from a silver Chrysler limousine—a machine Charlie Schwartz would own—next to the loading zone in front of Luisa's Seafood Mart.

A tattooed Negro carried bags of Guaymas shrimp over his shoulder into the rear of a wholesaler's truck. Hickey sized up the market and walked around to the rear, to a covered patio where tables and benches overlooked the sport-fishing dock and the pier of a yacht club. Women in bathing suits or scanty sundresses posed over cocktails along the yacht club end, opposite Charlie Schwartz and his companions.

Charlie's boys could've been identical twins except that one was gaunt while the other looked bloated. Both were sun-tanned, with freckles like squashed pinto beans and with thick carrot-colored hair that grew to within an inch of their eyebrows. The skinny one wore a checked sport coat. The other, in shirtsleeves, had his tie loosened, dangling like a neckerchief.

From afar, the gangster spotted Hickey. He reeled back a few inches, recovered, and folded his hands underneath his chin.

"Tom," he called out, as if they'd never exchanged a harsh word. As if Hickey hadn't knocked off Charlie's top gun and Charlie hadn't vowed to wreck Hickey's life. "You gotta try the clams. Say, Colin, go hustle up another plate of clams. Plant yourself, Tom."

As Hickey sat down, the fat twin rose, light as a ballerina. "What're you drinking, chum?"

"Coke. In a bottle."

Schwartz lifted his hand, holding a cigar, from where it had hung at his side. He puffed and let the smoke seep out between his teeth. His skin still looked jaundiced. His greasy black hair had gone monk bald in the middle. The mauve polo shirt, loose around the shoulders, appeared cinched at his middle. His voice sounded shallow, as if he possessed no lungs but carried all his wind in his mouth. "Come down off the mountain to see your kid? Or you just get homesick?"

"Aw, Charlie, you been keeping tabs on me."

"Sure. I don't wanta lose touch with the old crowd."

"You're not still planning to get even, huh?"

"Hey, you think I'm the kind to hold a grudge?" He tapped his forehead. "Naw. I'd have to be loony after all this time. Say, what's this I hear you been working for Harry Poverman?"

"Harry a buddy of yours?"

The gangster shrugged and cracked a little smile. "Same ol' inquisitive bastard. Ask a simple question, he spits one back at you." He'd focused on the center of Hickey's face, as though he were a student of noses, avoiding the eyes. He bent over his plate, dug a clam out of the shell, and slurped it. "Harry and me got mutual friends. What brings you to the tropics, Tom, business?"

"Yep. Same as ever. Nosing around in other people's affairs."

"That include mine?"

"Could be. I'm remembering how…fatherly you got with Cynthia Tucker. And didn't I hear about you taking her sister out for strolls? Hell, Charlie, you're like part of the family. Seems to me you would've got her sprung by now. I mean, there's not a chance she torched Johnny Sousa and Laurel's place. Everybody knows that, even the cops."

Schwartz devoured another clam, his jaw quivering as though it tickled going down. "You think I own the cops?"

"Who knows? It's not my town anymore. Maybe Angelo Paoli bought 'em. Came in with a higher bid."

"Paoli's a featherweight. Got chased outta Jersey, tail between his legs."

Hickey nodded. "Want to hear my surmise?"

"I do," the skinny twin muttered scornfully.

Schwartz gave his boy a scowl. "Go on, Tom. Paddy don't wanta miss a thing."

"See," Hickey said, "I expect the cops are toying with Cynthia to keep from having to fool with Mickey Cohen. The way I hear, Cohen sent Johnny Sousa down to butt in on Angelo's race-book action, only Mickey got suspicious that Sousa was playing both hands, doubledealing him with Paoli. So Mickey had him popped and fried."

The gangster chortled. His belly rattled the table. "This is rich. Your idea or the cops?"

"Everybody's. The thing is, the cops don't care to know which one of Cohen's stooges likes to play with matches. You know, who the hell'd wanta bring the guy in? Only some kid thinks he's the Lone Ranger, maybe. Besides, a mobster whacks one of his own, who loses?"

The fat boy returned with a plate full of clams, slid them in front of Hickey, and wedged into the chair beside his brother. "They're outta Coke."

"Get him an ice tea, then," Schwartz growled, pinching his eyes shut as if his patience had finally gotten overwhelmed. "What's this about Mickey? Hey, Mick don't need to play any games down here. Mick's got his hands full in LA. He's a pal of mine. I know how he thinks."

Leaning back, lifting his hat to scratch his head, Hickey assumed his most bewildered pose. "You're telling me Sousa and Cohen weren't associated?"

"Naw. Try those clams."

Hickey picked up a fork, toyed with a clam, set the fork down. "Maybe I'm a little outta touch. Yeah, now I see. The best thing I can do is, you being sweet on Cynthia, and on top of that a magnanimous guy—"

The redhead named Paddy snorted and wheeled his face toward the docks as though to cover a laughing fit.

"Magnanimous. I like that." The gangster pursed his lips and nodded contemplatively. "So what are you talking…you could do what?"

"I got a plan," Hickey said.

"Spill it, then."

"You bet. I'm gonna turn the job over to you, Charlie. You get her sprung, I don't ask who torched Laurel's place. I retreat back into the mountains."

Schwartz lowered his eyes, which had narrowed to a squint, and tried to cover his vexation with a wink, a grin, and a glance at a peroxide blonde careening on high heels as she chased a pigeon along the dock. Turning back, he smiled grimly. "You forgot to say 'or else.' "

"Oh, yeah. Thanks." Hickey stood, tipped his hat.

"Or else what?"

"Just I'll be disappointed. Get her loose. Today, Charlie. Meantime, I'll keep nosing around."

He met the fat boy bringing his tea, accepted the glass and took a swallow, then set it on an empty table and strolled out of the place, grinding his teeth, knowing he should've held his cards closer to the vest. He should've played dumb, at least not accused Mickey Cohen. Except he only knew two ways to fight. Shrewd, cautious, laying back with his guard up, waiting for an opening to jab. Or throwing the big punch every chance, which left you wide open. One way was sensible. The other could get you a first-round knockout. It could land him at home by tomorrow.

In the car he stuffed his pipe and fired up, stared at the dashboard, and thought about Wendy. Right now, after lunch, she was probably in the armchair by the wood stove, reading the Isak Dinesen book Claire had given her. For two years, most every day, she'd sat reading, the dictionary at her side, determined to grasp each word. Trying so heroically to make Tom proud of her.

Chapter Five

Hickey crossed the point and drove along Sunset Cliffs, admiring the foamy Pacific stirred by an onshore breeze. His eyes followed the white-capped rollers that hastened toward the beach looking serenely confident until the ebb tide slapped them silly.

In Ocean Beach he cut west down Newport Avenue, cruised slowly past Stuart's grocery, and peered inside to the check stand hoping to catch a glimpse of Elizabeth, but a Mexican fellow was clerking.

He parked at the foot of Newport Avenue in front of the Surfrider Motel, crossed the street to the beach, and walked in the sand a hundred yards south to the bluff. As he climbed the zigzagging steps etched in rocky dirt, from one place he got a clear view of a few charred beams and a chimney—all that remained of the house where Johnny Sousa had died. According to the police report, Sousa looked to have fallen asleep in the bathtub.

Atop the bluff sat eight dwarfish cottages in two rows. Sided in whitewashed plywood, with porthole-sized high windows, they slanted inland as though braced against a gale. Number three was second from the cliff in the north row. Red block letters above the door announced MARTY'S DIGS. Alongside it, in cursive of various colors, an inscription proclaimed, *Life without music would be a mistake.* Somebody inside played a bass run on the piano, repeating it like a chant. Hickey caught the scent of marijuana. He knocked and waited, listening to the hurried shuffle of feet and the scrape of a chair leg on tile.

The door opened a crack and a gravelly voice said, "Yeah, man. What's up?"

"Marty?"

"Who's asking? You look like a cop."

From inside, a man yelped, "Hey, cop, you figure you can bust us, think again. Last of the weed just gone up in smoke."

The man at the door laughed gruffly the way he used to when he played piano with Clyde McGraw's orchestra at Rudy's Hacienda, when Hickey owned the place.

"Weed's *your* problem, Marty. Mine's trying to spring Cynthia out of jail. Name's Tom Hickey, remember?"

"Yeah, hey. I see you now, boss." The door creaked open and a tall fellow appeared, his shoulders hunched and his neck crooked like a vulture's. Wispy gray hair, skin like crinkled paper. "Help me calculate, it's been how many years since Rudy's got boarded up?"

"Seven, eight. Still making noise with your fingers?"

"Hey, it's either that or work."

"I hear you. Clyde still around?"

"Naw, long gone, to Seattle or Portland, one of those green places, with Lady Gotrocks. How about—what was your partner's name, the spic dude that stiffed us a couple weeks' pay? Castillo."

"He must've stiffed the wrong guy. Got stabbed in New Jersey, a few years back." Hickey reached for his billfold, plucked out the hundred-dollar bill he always kept hidden there, folded into the coin pocket, for emergencies. He passed it to Marty. "Two weeks' pay and some interest."

"Whoa. Gracias, man."

"You going to let me in?"

"Soon as I fetch the red carpet."

The place was cluttered like a junk shop. Three sofas, one nearly hidden behind a drum set: snare, tom-tom, and cymbal. An upright piano, a stand-up bass leaning in a corner beside the window that overlooked the foot of Newport Avenue and Hickey's car parked at the curb. A man with pomaded wavy black hair sprawled on the couch behind the drums, wearing a cocky sneer. Curled into a tattered stuffed chair beside the piano, a tanned young fellow in an undershirt and boxer shorts dozed, his lips tooting like a kazoo.

Hickey sank into the nearest couch. It was almost 4 P.M. The sleepless night had finally caught up and walloped him. Marty took a seat on the piano bench. "How you going to spring the redhead?"

Hickey shrugged. "One thing, I could plug the holes in her alibi. Who's this character saw her go out and talk to the beachcomber? Jack Meechum?"

"Yeah, that's him. Plays trombone with the Undertakers."

"Why'd he shoot off his mouth?"

"Aw, he's been trying to pounce on Cynthia forever. Finally gave up, I guess, decided to pay her back the grief."

"So he's lying?" Hickey asked.

"Who knows? He probably saw her go outside. If anybody saw, it'd be him. Tags behind her like a caboose."

"How about you get him over here?"

"Gone, man. They're blowing a lounge act in Vegas."

"Vegas." In casinos you'd always find headbusters and gunsels making pals with the musicians, who usually had females to spare. "Ever known Meechum to run with any hard cases?"

"You mean tough guys or dames?"

"Anybody tight with Charlie Schwartz, Mickey Cohen."

"Yikes. Hey, I see a Jew with his hat pulled low, I hotfoot it like Seabiscuit. All I know is Meechum plays the ponies and takes a snootful now and then. If he misses a Sunday jam, you can bet he's on the road, flying high, or down at Caliente."

The man on the couch drawled, "Frankie Foster."

"Who's he?"

"Meechum's uncle or something. They say he used to work for Bugs Moran in Chicago. Now he's an old fart, lying low. They say."

"Around here?"

The man stretched, settled deeper into the couch, and grinned as though stalling Hickey pleased him tremendously. "*¿Quién sabe?* I seen him up in Santa Monica, at the Doubloon on the pier."

"How about this beachcomber? You guys see her talk to the beachcomber?"

Marty waved toward the man on the couch. "Rollo wasn't here. Me—maybe she stepped out a minute, could be, but that ain't long enough to burn down a house. All I know is, every time I looked up, she was around."

"So where do I find the beachcomber?"

"Nobody seen Teddy since the fire. If I was looking, I'd try Mexico. If he ain't there, he's six feet under or making like plankton."

"Somebody buttoned his lips, you mean?"

"Yep. Hey, you oughta stick around. An hour, cats'll show up and we blow. Bring the old tenor with you?"

Hickey thought, Be nice to these hopheads, Tom, no matter if they drift a little. "Who do you figure would've snuffed the beachcomber, Marty?"

"The guy that paid him to torch Sousa's pad."

"And that'd be?"

The pianist gave a mighty shrug. "Want a brew, Tom?"

"Naw. Where's the beachcomber live?"

"A shack down by the jetty."

"Show me."

Marty got up and stretched, wandered into the back room, and returned with a sweater he snaked into and a pair of huaraches he crammed onto his feet. He led Hickey outside, down the trail to the beach, and walked south toward the jetty, about a quarter of a mile from the bluff. As they passed a family picnic, a few sunbathers, and a trio of boys throwing a baseball, slinging long flies to each other, Hickey quizzed the pianist about Cynthia.

As far as Marty remembered, from the time she'd run out on her gig at the Mission Beach Ballroom nobody he knew heard a peep from the girl—until 1947, when a guitarist they called Mas Grande opened the door to his hotel apartment on Market

Street. Cynthia fell into his arms. Standing beside her was a rugged looking two-year-old. Her son Casey.

Cynthia flopped with Mas for a few months, acting wild and vicious. She hurled dishes. Tore sheet music into confetti. Screamed at her boy while she changed his diapers. Flung Grande's shoes and metronome out the window. Sometimes, like when he found her sharpening knives, Mas took the kid for safekeeping and locked Cynthia in the flat, to howl and weep alone about the flyboy, her husband Carl. During every tantrum, she'd threaten revenge against her sister, the Bitch, whom she believed had hired an army mechanic to sabotage her husband's plane.

Moving to the beach seemed to calm her. She would sit by the tide line beneath the bluff for hours watching the ocean while Casey ran, waded, dug for sand crabs. A few months of beach therapy and Cynthia was on her feet, auditioning. But something in her voice had gone scratchy and bitter, and her moves had transformed from a promise of savage embraces to a threat that she'd rip out your heart. The only job offers were for second billing, which Cynthia would never play. Three years now she'd been living off the army widow's and orphan's pensions, wandering the beach like a ghost in low-hemmed and long-sleeved dresses and a straw hat and singing at Marty's jam sessions every Sunday.

Where Abbott Street ended at the San Diego River channel, a court of bungalows slowly rotted. Adobe-colored paint flaked off in sheets like parchment. The French windows had more plywood panes than glass ones. A few stunted palm trees survived in the courtyard, surrounded by the five bungalows and a toolshed with an add-on room sided in tin: Teddy the beachcomber's shack. A few yards behind it, where the dirt gave way to sand, a ring of stones about six feet across framed a pile of ash from many large bonfires.

Hickey walked around to the courtyard side and rapped on a door that looked like the gate off a redwood fence. After he stood a minute waiting, Marty tapped his shoulder and cocked his head toward the courtyard.

A man with a hairy gray face, thick spectacles, and a crooked baseball cap was staring out the window of a bungalow. Hickey walked over and nodded cordially at the man, who lifted his window and bent forward to stick his head out.

"Let me guess," Hickey said. "The cops'll give you twenty or so if you call and report that Teddy or anybody's prowling around his shack."

"Could be," the man chirped.

"Yeah. Or could be it's somebody else, not the cops. Go on, call them. Make a few bucks. Tell them Tom Hickey's snooping around."

He walked back toward Teddy's place, past Marty Eschelman, who'd found a seat on the planter box around a palm. Hickey lifted the latch and stepped inside the shack. The floor was plywood with carpet scraps placed like throw rugs and scattered stacks of tabloids. Inspecting a few of the piles, he found several dozen copies of the *Racing Form*. There was scribbling, updated odds, and remarks about jockeys and trainers on every Agua Caliente page.

In a corner lay a single child-sized mattress with army blankets heaped on top. Pinup girls adorned the wall above the bed. One of them sported an extra pair of breasts. Beside the bed sat a large mason jar filled with one-, two-, and five-dollar tickets from Agua Caliente.

A threadbare sport coat, a jacket, and a few work shirts hung on a broomstick that angled across a corner above two cardboard boxes full of jeans, socks, and underwear. A pair of grease-soiled deck shoes sat beside them.

Behind a curtain that had once been a brightly striped Mexican serape, the add-on room was a merger of kitchen and bath: a toilet, a tin shower stall, and a miniature sink, cupboard, stove, and icebox unit, probably salvaged out of a trailer home. Next to the sink, in neat order, sat a toothbrush, a dish full of baking soda, a straight razor and shaving soap.

Hickey turned back outside and told the pianist, "Unless Teddy kept a spare travel kit and wardrobe, it doesn't appear he made vacation plans."

"He's shark feed." Marty turned to rolling a Bull Durham. They backtracked along the beach, talking music. Marty asked if Tom still blew sax, and why not. Hickey admitted that with swing, bebop, and jitterbug, playing sax got him jumpy. On clarinet, he could dream.

The jam session was on. A trio of drums, bass, and baritone sax droned a gloomy mood. Marty pointed the way up along the bluff to the Sousa ruins.

The sun appeared to sizzle behind a fogbank. Hickey maneuvered along the cliffside trail to the burnt house, a sidehill place with high block foundations. There were piers, and the blackened short lengths of floor beams, and plumbing that suggested a den or bar room downstairs. The upstairs alone would've measured twice the size of the biggest house Hickey'd ever occupied, five times as spacious as his Tahoe cabin.

He scanned the ashes and rubble, looking for nothing in particular except inspiration. A sudden gust blew soot that flecked his shirt and slacks, rasped his weary eyes.

Chapter Six

From a pay phone outside a curio shop, Hickey phoned the captain, made a date: five-thirty at the Café Milano. That would give him a few minutes to check on Elizabeth. Just time enough to get a hello-goodbye kiss and apologize for not staying longer. He walked up Newport the two blocks past the dime store, hardware, and resale shops, one Chinese and one greasy spoon café, to Stuart's grocery.

If Elizabeth wasn't around, on the off chance Stuart was at work instead of shooting pool or handicapping ponies around some lowlife's poker table, he'd grill the dear boy about the beachcomber and the trombonist—Jack Meechum. Both of them haunted Ocean Beach and Agua Caliente, like Stuart.

The produce in the bins beside the checkout counter looked wilted. With half the overhead bulbs burnt out, the store was dark as a movie theater.

After waiting for a pause between customers, Hickey asked the pudgy Mexican clerk for Mrs. Crump. The clerk said she had gone to the wholesaler's and might not return to the store until morning. Hickey didn't leave a message.

He drove the coast, up Abbott Street past the beachcomber's place, followed West Point Loma Boulevard to Midway Drive, and cruised alongside the wartime housing project of shoebox apartments and duplexes painted surplus gray. On the lawn, a team of Negro and Filipino boys faced off against a gang of whites. Somebody hiked a ball. They mauled and pounded each other while a giant, probably Samoan, charged through their midst. Young men lounged on the hoods of their jalopies assessing the girls who paraded down the sidewalk, past women in shapeless dresses hanging laundry on a wire that sagged so the cuffs of jeans scraped the lawn.

Hickey swung onto Barnett and turned into the parking lot in front of the Café Milano, where the Sons of Italy dined.

A square flat-roofed building of dark-stained planks, it looked about as swanky as the Midway housing project, except for the cars on the gravel lot: two Lincolns, a Jaguar, a Bentley, Cadillacs galore. Every one appeared spit shined. Hickey's mud-caked, bug-splattered Chevy fit among them like a mutt in a kennel reserved for purebreds.

As Hickey approached the door, a swarthy fellow ambled out, then stiffened and iced his gaze, as if Schwartz or one of the cops had passed the word that this snoop was on his way. When Hickey gave his name, asked if a guy was waiting for him, the maître d' leered as though at something he might roast for supper. He swept his arm toward the doorway.

Inside was mostly candlelit. There were trellised partitions between the booths and tables. Waitresses flashed around in short tutus, black net stockings, and heels like stilts. If a guy enjoyed spice on his privacy, this was the place. But Hickey got led to the most exposed location, a small table beside the swinging kitchen door, where the captain sat nudging the cherry around the surface of his Manhattan with a toothpick as though marveling that a cherry could float. In candlelight, the captain's face looked ruddier than ever, his thin brush-cut hair redder. He showed Hickey his bulldog smile, reached out his beefy hand.

"Scotch, Tom?"

A bargirl arrived wiggling her tutu, took Hickey's order, and wiggled off. The captain asked about Wendy. Through his first scotch, Hickey outlined Wendy's transformation from a crazy, terrified, dull girl everybody figured must've possessed only half a brain into a happy woman.

"How about you, Tom?"

"Better than ever."

"Leo tells me your bride cracks the whip, drags you to church every Sunday."

"Leo can make the Himalayas out of a dust mote. The truth is, whenever the choir's singing, Wendy goes to church. Sundays, Thursdays. I tag along sometimes. Your brood prospering?"

"Sure." He flagged the waitress.

Hickey bought a round and turned to business. "Any of your boys talk to Frankie Foster?"

"Nope. Should we?"

"You know him?"

"Uh-huh. A Jew from Cicero. Used to drive and who knows what else for Bugs Moran, until one Valentine's Day. Bugs's mob gets bushwhacked, Foster takes a powder. Last I heard, he was living up the coast, Laguna or Santa Monica. What about him?"

"Your witness, Meechum—the *only* one who noticed Cynthia gabbing with the beachcomber—he's some relative of Foster's."

Thrapp nodded. "Soon as Meechum gets back from Vegas, I'll bring him in, nag him all over again."

"Too late, Rusty. I mean to settle this business tomorrow. Maybe tonight."

"How's that?"

"First thing, I've been leaning on Charlie Schwartz."

"Aw, Tom." Thrapp groaned. "Besides that it's one of your favorite pastimes, why're you pestering the sorry old creep?"

"Because Cynthia isn't the firebug."

"Which you're presuming on account of you work for her."

"Yeah. I'm also presuming that marital problems could arise when one spouse is holding hands with the Jew mob, like Johnny did, and the other's playing footsy with the wops. That'd be Laurel. She's been having a ball with Angelo Paoli."

"So I heard."

"I'll bet dollars to pesos it wasn't Cynthia hired Teddy to torch the place. It doesn't fly, unless you figure she also disposed of the beachcomber, who's been gone a week without his toothbrush."

Hickey noticed fresh drinks in front of them but couldn't recall their arrival. He made a fist around the tumbler. "I stopped by Teddy's shack. Nobody home this week."

Thrapp leaned backward to fold his arms and scowl. "We've been dropping by the place. So Teddy's on the lam, so what?"

"So you figure Cynthia hired the guy for a firebug, what'd she pay him with, her pension check?"

"Hey, I never said the beachcomber torched the place. No reason Cynthia couldn't of done it herself. She's a big girl."

"So where's the beachcomber? Why's he on the lam?"

"Went to visit his maiden aunt in Lodi, for all I know. You ever heard of coincidence?"

"Yeah, but I haven't got time to consider it, so I'm pinning the fire on the Italians or the Jews."

Thrapp plucked the cherry from his fresh drink, slapped it into his mouth, and made a face as if some joker had switched the cherry for a lemon. "Okay, Tom, you win. First thing tomorrow I'll call Mickey and Angelo, tell them to gather their boys, go on down to the nearest precinct, surrender, make their confession."

"Don't trouble yourself, Rusty. Just introduce me to somebody belongs to Angelo. I'll take it from there."

Thrapp grimaced and rubbed the back of his neck. "Explain, pal."

"The way I figure, either Charlie, Mickey Cohen, or Angelo— one of them set up the girl. She makes a topnotch patsy, having threatened her sister a couple hundred times. Now, if Angelo did it, Mickey or Charlie got no love for him and vice versa."

"So?"

"So, like I reminded Charlie, I can be a pest. But as soon as anybody spills enough to make you wise up and cut the girl loose, I disappear. Back to the woods and outta their hair. A bargain all around."

"Damn clever, Tom," the captain snarled, and sullenly watched a smoke ring float by. "I got a wild idea. Suppose I tell you, before I'll let you risk toying with Mickey or Angelo, I'll buy the DA a fat steak and libations, see to it the girl's sprung?"

Hickey spread his arms in mock satisfaction. "Sure, Rusty. That'd work just fine. You tell me that, tomorrow noon I'm back home."

"Sorry, Tom." Thrapp killed his Manhattan and stared into the glass as though making sure it was dry. "Here's the deal. I make an introduction. You stir the caldron, for about five minutes tops. We'll take it from there. See, you gotta promise to scram. Tonight."

Hickey sipped, licked his lips, and pondered. "Deal. Soon as I catch a few hours' sleep and get breakfast with Elizabeth. But if you're still holding Cynthia in a couple weeks, after the baby shows up, I'm coming back to stir the caldron again."

The captain rolled his eyes, nodded irritably. "How about we eat first. They got exquisite lasagna."

"Naw. I'll grab a sandwich at Leo's."

Thrapp reached for his wallet, slapped down a tip. "Drink up, before I change my mind."

Sucking an ice cube, Hickey stood and followed the captain around a trellis to a booth where two young Latins and one about Hickey's vintage sat nibbling antipasto.

The fellow on the outside closest to Hickey looked barely of age. He wore his hair in a pompadour and had a pinstripe mustache, probably for the same reason Hickey had one, to distract from his prodigious nose. Thrapp introduced him as Pete Silva, then rushed through the other introductions while Silva rose and shook Hickey's hand familiarly. The older man nodded curtly at Hickey and turned to swabbing salad oil off his plate with a hunk of bread. The other young fellow refolded his napkin, leaned back, and lit a smoke.

"Funny name, Hickey," Pete Silva drawled. "Say, you must be Lizzie Crump's old man. I heard about you. How about you tell her to dump that juicer? Best thing could happen to Lizzie is you kick Stuart's ass down the road. I'll take it from there."

Hickey rubbed his head, futilely attempting to put out the sparks. "Let's talk about it outside."

"Sure thing."

The boy hoisted his shoulders back and swaggered ahead of Hickey and the captain. He passed behind two waitresses, gave each a swat in the tutu. Out on the gravel he turned and shrugged for directions. Hickey motioned to the right and nudged Silva ahead of them to a dark place at the corner of the building. As they stepped into the shadow, Hickey grabbed the boy's shoulders, shoved them against the wall, pinned them hard.

"You getting tough with me, Pop?"

"Not yet. That'll come soon as you make another crack about my daughter."

"Hey, no offense, huh? She's a dish, that's all." He reached up to brush Hickey's hands away, but the hands didn't budge until Hickey let go, in his own time.

The punk straightened his coat while Hickey stepped back, pulled out his billfold, peeled off a ten, and folded it into Silva's coat pocket. "I need to hire a message boy. You look like the type."

Silva's hand jerked from his lapel to his side: waist high and fisted. "That'd be an insult, right? You make me for a dope, like I'm gonna slug you with the cop standing by, so you can run me in and put on the thumb screws. That it?"

"Yep. Make your move, Pete."

"Maybe I will." Silva managed a fusion of snarl and smile, as though he'd practiced in front of the mirror for weeks. "First, what's the message? To who?"

"Angelo. Tell him Charlie Schwartz figures to pin the Sousa fire on him."

"That so? Where do you come in?"

"Pretend I'm Cynthia's guardian. She got stung. It oughta be Angelo or Charlie taking the fall, you know as well as me. Either's okay, as long as the girl walks."

Silva's grin looked touched with genuine delight. "You a crazy man?"

"Could be. Make your move, Pete?"

"Yeah, yeah. That'll come around."

He plucked the bill out of his breast pocket, tossed, and let it flutter to the ground. With a chuckle, he turned and swaggered past the captain, who was leaning on a Jaguar.

The boy disappeared inside the café and Thrapp hustled over, clutched Hickey's arm, then crossed the lot to Hickey's Chevy.

"Silva's got insight," the captain said.

"Meaning I'm crazy?"

"Sure enough. Now get moving. I'll tail you awhile, until I make sure I'm the only one."

As he cruised alongside the flood channel, Hickey watched the fishermen, conjuring memories that softened his head, which allowed him to think about Wendy, to miss her, worry, and forget to look over his shoulder. He'd stopped across from the ballroom at the end of West Mission Bay Drive to make a right onto Mission Boulevard when he spotted a giant white car as it crested the bridge behind him, so fast it launched itself into the air. The instant he saw it, he jumped on the gas and shot around the turn, goosed the Chevy up to 45, and held steady, one eye fixed on the mirror the entire mile or more to Leo's place. The big car didn't appear. He swung the left turn into Pismo Court and onto the gravel of Leo's carport, beside the old Packard.

As he climbed out, spooked by a screech and rumble, he jumped to the rear of his Chevy and looked back up Pismo just as the Cadillac roared across Mission from the alley that parallelled the boulevard on the bay side.

His gun was in the suitcase locked in his trunk. By the time he got it out, they could drive this far idling and perforate him a dozen times. He dashed for the house, grabbed the screen door, yanked it off a hinge. He groped at the entry door and wrenched the knob. It wouldn't turn. He kicked, pounded, dropped to his knees. Tried to disappear behind the Packard.

"Open up! Leo!"

A bullet cracked, sparked the concrete walk, ricocheted into the door. Behind the Packard, feet hit the gravel and skidded.

Another bullet sparked off the concrete, then glass shattered. A shotgun boomed. A man yelped. Pellets rang against metal. A car door slammed and the Cadillac squealed away, spewing gravel that peppered the carport and the Packard.

Hickey turned and lay frozen against the doorjamb, his heart on triple time like a string bass jamming boogie-woogie. When the door whooshed open, he barely cocked his head to look.

Warily, Leo Weiss stepped out. Over the past few years, his walrus mustache had grayed and his chest finally sunk to his belly. His shoulders looked like pillows. But from Hickey's angle, and as he cradled a shotgun, Leo appeared a titan.

"Now can I come in?" Hickey mumbled.

"Sure, for a minute. Then I'm chasing you and your car off my property. What a guy. Doesn't even tell us he's coming to town. This your idea of a grand entrance?"

"Yeah. The actors cost me a bundle."

Leo reached out his free arm. "Stand up like a man, will you? Tom, anybody ever point out you've got a gift for aggravating people?"

"Nope."

"Must be everybody's scared to offend you. How long you been in town?"

"All day. I would've called soon as I got a minute, but I didn't get one."

"We'll let it pass. So, who all did you rile today?"

"Lots of guys. What'd they look like?"

"I only saw the shooter. Tall, tailored suit. Hair like one of your classier pachucos."

"Angelo's boy," Hickey said. "Vi home?"

"Last I looked she was diving into the kitchen, behind the counter. Going to make cocoa, I guess."

Chapter Seven

Before he followed Leo inside, Hickey got the short-barreled Smith and Wesson .38 out of his suitcase in the Chevy's trunk.

Inside, he flopped onto the threadbare velvet love seat that used to be elegant, when Leo'd bought it for his wife in 1943—after he and Hickey and a gang of Indians liberated a half million in gold from the freaks who'd enslaved Wendy in Tijuana. Leo spent the rest of his share, over thirty grand, on Magda's first four years at Stanford and on a hospital and private nurse for their older daughter, Una, who had gotten beaten by Nazis in Vienna in 1937 and never quite healed.

Leo occupied the matching sofa. Both men faced the door, guns beside them. It was the only door, all the place needed.

The Weisses used to own a bigger house, until Charlie Schwartz and his brother Al got the city to condemn a string of oceanfront homes, claiming some rare and voracious breed of termites had infested them. Charlie and Al owned Coast Construction. The Schwartzes bought the homes cheap, paying just enough so Leo and Vi could cover the mortgage, which they'd borrowed to send Magda to graduate school, and buy this dollhouse where the kitchen and living room were only separated by agreement and coats hung on a hat rack because their modest wardrobes bulged the walls of the single closet.

Since Hickey's last trip off the mountain, Vi had become a henna girl, lost twenty pounds, and either gotten sickly pale for a half-Mexican and developed the huge eyes of a prayerful invalid or gunfights on the doorstep spooked her. While she gave Hickey a hug, a kiss, then made cocoa for herself and the men and spiked it with coffee liqueur, and while she served and sat next to Leo and sipped, she never took her eyes off the door.

She asked about Wendy, the baby, Elizabeth, and who the hell was shooting. After boasting about the virtues of his wife and lamenting his daughter's circumstances, Hickey briefed them about Cynthia and her alleged crimes and confessed his rough talk to Charlie Schwartz and to Angelo Paoli's gunman.

Vi studied the two men as if they were naughty boys she regretfully had to scold. Finally she asked, "You two ever think about giving it up? Most fellows retire from playing cops and robbers at about your age, Tom." Turning to Leo, she wagged her head mournfully. "And he's a whole generation younger than you, dear. Tom, at least do us a favor?"

"Sure."

"Tell the old coot he oughta retire. Next year he'll turn seventy. A septuagenarian has got no business consorting with guys like you. I mean, you're sweet as any man alive, but you're a magnet for trouble."

"Yeah, Tom," Leo grumbled, "tell me I oughta retire. Then, while you're leaning on Charlie Schwartz, squeeze him for the twenty grand he sharked us out of."

Vi made a clucking noise. "Aw, you'd just spend the money trying to send Schwartz and Mickey Cohen to Alcatraz. What do you think, Tom, about a Jew who hates the Jew mob twice as bad as he hates the Italians?"

"I think he oughta give it up, like you say. He oughta rent this place out summers while you stay with us at the lake, in a trailer house."

"Sure, summer rent and his pension, we'd be fine."

"Aw, nuts, why retire?" Leo said. "The work's a romp. Only time I dodge bullets is when Tom's around."

"You plan to stay here tonight, Tom? Should I make up the couch?"

"Naw. I'll go up to the Surf and Sand. Who could sleep here, the way we're all watching the door?"

"What about the gunmen, you think they went home?"

"Undoubtedly," Leo grumbled. "They're probably gathered around the hearth, singing hymns. Or else they're cruising Mission, waiting for Tom to poke his head out so they can make it look funny. I'll follow down to the motel, Tom, just in case."

"Might as well," Hickey said. "Everybody else is tailing me tonight."

Vi offered them more cocoa, but Hickey said he wanted to spin by Elizabeth's just to check on things, then get to the motel, call Wendy, and log about ten hours of sleep. While Leo went for his overcoat, hat, and shoes, Vi ordered both men to be careful. Several times each.

Hickey drove north on Mission Boulevard. The sidewalks bustled with wanderers from bar to coffeehouse to pool hall, but the street was vacant—nobody behind except Leo. He cut east on Pacific Beach Drive, sailed along the newly paved road beneath palms that disappeared into the fog, past a dozen whitewashed bungalows and a few low-slung ranch-style houses, the latest architectural blight. He slowed as he neared the intersection of Fanuel. At the bayside dead end, parked against the trellis of bougainvilleas across from the cottage where Elizabeth and the bum lived, a white Cadillac attempted to hide in shadow.

Hickey jammed the pedal, braking enough so he wouldn't screech making the turn onto Gresham. He raced up to Garnet Avenue and wheeled into the corner Texaco. A man in a fringed western coat stood gabbing on the pay phone. Hickey pulled out two dollars and waved them in front of the man, who gladly handed over the receiver. As Leo's Packard wheeled into the station, Hickey was already plunking his nickel into the slot.

"Hi there."

"Elizabeth."

"Dad?"

"Yeah, babe. You okay?"

"Sure. Where are you?"

"Close," Hickey said. "Stuart there?"

"Uh-huh. How come you're breathing hard?"

"I rode a bicycle down from Tahoe."

"Smart aleck. Come on over, Daddy."

"Not now. Listen, darling, tell Stuart to go peek out the carport window, see if two guys are sitting in the white Cadillac."

"Okay." She called to Stuart, gave him the instructions, and repeated them testily. "Who are they?"

"Bad guys," Hickey said. "Maybe pals of Stuart, all I know."

"Dad, just because he knew Paul in Jersey and he drinks, doesn't mean—Okay, Stuart says there're two guys in the car."

"You got a pistol?" He glanced toward the noise of Leo's skuffing feet. The old man flashed a salute.

"A what?" Elizabeth demanded.

"Pistol."

"Yeah, Stuart's got a couple."

"You take one of them, slide out the garden door, and run up to Eva's place. If anybody follows you, just shoot the damned thing and run into the nearest house. Make a world of noise. Soon as you get to Eva's, phone Vi, give her the number. I'll call you back soon as I can check into a motel."

"Why? What is this? Tell me it's a party game."

"You guessed it. I'll tell you more when you're at Eva's."

"What about Stuart?"

"Put him on the line. Then you get going. Babe, in case Eva's not home, keep running, up to the Crown Point grocery. Call Vi from the pay phone. I'll get there in a flash."

"Okay, Daddy."

Hickey got her promise to follow his directions, then asked her to put Stuart on. He caught his breath, shut his eyes to gain a moment of quiet, commanded himself not to scream at the bum.

"What's up, Pop?"

"Plenty," Hickey growled. "I've got a job for you."

"Name it."

Five words and already Stuart's brash, throaty voice had pinched Hickey's nerves. "Make yourself a pot of coffee. Sit up all night, if you have to, until those boys in the Cadillac give up and vanish. You got a shotgun, right?"

"Brand-new Remington."

"If one of them gets near the house, give him an appendectomy with it."

"Aren't they Angelo Paoli's boys?"

"Yeah. Friends of yours?"

"Naw, but I've seen one of 'em around."

"Silva."

"Yeah. What goes? They after you?"

Hickey shut his eyes, rolled his shoulders, tried to speak softly. "It's business. *My* business."

"Don't worry, Pop. I can handle things."

"Right, Stuart," Hickey snarled. "Enough gin, a guy can handle anything."

"You got me wrong, Pop. I been cutting back on the juice."

"Yeah, well, you get the shakes, dash a little into your coffee. Don't screw up, you hear? Anybody hurts Elizabeth—" Hickey bit on his lower lip to cinch his big mouth closed. Already he'd endangered Leo, Vi, and Elizabeth by threatening creeps. If he didn't tread lightly on Stuart, his daughter might have to pay.

Stuart gave assurances. Hickey muttered thanks, slapped down the phone book, plunked in another nickel, and dialed. He asked the kid who answered to put her father on.

Thrapp yawned into the receiver. "Who's this?"

"The guy you quit tailing too soon. Angelo's pretty boy caught up at Leo's, made splinters out of the door."

"Pete Silva, you mean?"

"Yeah. Now he's sitting outside my place on Fanuel. Him and a driver. Get 'em picked up, Rusty. Leo saw. He can finger the punk." He told the captain where to reach him, then hung up.

Leo chucked Hickey's shoulder. "Say, you always that impolite to Stuart?"

"A no-good," Hickey snapped, starting for his car. "Worst of it is, Elizabeth thinks she's gotta climb down to his level. She could be a painter, teacher, a singer like her mom, something fine that'd please her. He's got her making like a grocery clerk while he blows the receipts at Caliente."

"Yeah, I know how it is. Magda picked a no-good too. What is it with these kids? Meet a good guy, they stick up their nose. Something crawls out from under a rock, they act like it's Prince Charming."

Leo gave Hickey a block head start down Garnet, before he followed, past Oscar's Drive-In where the boys with ducktails and T-shirts, girls in pedal pushers, sleeveless sweaters, bobbed hair, sat on the hoods and seat backs of their hot rods, half of them frantically pawing each other as though any second the bell would ring. His eye on Hickey's Chevy, Leo almost clipped a trio of pedestrians who'd rushed into the street from the crowd that milled outside the Roxy Theater, beneath the marquee that announced *Battleground*—Van Johnson.

Hickey swung onto Mission Boulevard and drove north a block to the Surf and Sand Motel. He rushed into the office, tossed down a ten, and asked the dowdy woman to hurry on account of he needed to powder his nose. She scooped up the bill, slid a key across the counter.

"Hey, wait for your change and receipt, mister."

He was already gone, climbing three stairs per stride.

In room 21, overlooking Mission Boulevard, Hickey pounced on the phone and called Vi, who gave him the number at Eva's place, which Elizabeth had given her a minute before. He memorized the number, then collapsed onto the bed and rested a moment. Leo came in and sat beside him. "All's well?"

"Yeah." Hickey sighed. "Elizabeth's okay. Now what?"

"About what?"

"Cynthia. It looks like I threw the knockout punch and missed. What's next?"

"First thing, I sneak across the road and bring us a nightcap."

Leo heaved himself up, went to the door and opened it a crack. He peered both ways and made his exit.

Hickey reached for the phone and dialed. A muffled voice said hello.

"That you, babe?"

"Of course it's me. I live here. You wanta tell me what's all the intrigue about?"

"Eva, anything I tell you'll spread like the radio news. By nine A.M. it'll circulate all around the bay."

"So?"

"There's a couple guys trying to scratch my name off the roster, on account of I'm snooping into the cause of a fire in Ocean Beach a week ago."

"The Sousa fire. Who you gonna pin it on?"

"Anybody but the one they're holding. Look, Eva, I'm fatigued, so let me talk to Elizabeth. We can all gab in the morning when I pick her up at your place."

"She's right here. Don't be a stranger, Tom."

The door swung open loudly and Leo appeared, holding out a pint of Dewar's. "This mansion got glasses?"

"Hi, Dad," Elizabeth gasped. "I'm here."

"Now you're the one sounds like she's been running a mile. Any trouble?"

"Nope."

"Sorry, babe. I never figured you'd get mixed up in this game."

"What's it about?"

Hickey said Eva could give her the capsule version. Tomorrow he'd fill in the blanks. He got her promise that she'd spend the night at Eva's, and he asked how things were going.

"Same as last week, pretty much. Stuart dropped a bundle at the track this afternoon. I was reading him off all night, till you called, getting him awful riled. Another minute he could've belted me. You might've saved our marriage, Dad."

"Thanks, babe. That puts the cap on a swell day. Now I'm gonna expire."

"You mean retire."

"Sleep. You too, huh? Think you can sleep?"

"Anytime, anywhere. Should I be worried for Stuart?"

"Naw. The cops are on their way to roust the creeps in the Caddie."

"Who *are* they?"

"Just a fella I got nasty with. He wants to thump me, is all. I'll be by for you in the morning, first thing. We'll find some hideaway that's got waffles, and I'll elaborate."

They wished each other good night. Hickey dropped the receiver and accepted the glass Leo held out. He took a gulp big enough to make him grimace. "Needs ice."

"You asked, I would've booked you at the Bahia. They'd bring you ice, bar service. Next time, don't be a tightwad."

Hickey reached for the pipe and tobacco in his coat and lit up. He propped both pillows behind him, lay back on the bed, and asked Leo for any insights or schemes. Where to go from here.

"Fine time to ask," the old man grumbled, "after you already jumped in the ocean, opened a vein, and hollered, 'Here, Mister Shark, come and get it.' Not particularly subtle, Tom."

"Yeah, and it didn't work, either."

"Well, at least you set balls rolling all over the place. Now you got a baby to see born. And supposing you owed Cynthia—which you didn't—you paid her back today, in spades. So I'm taking over, and you're gonna hit the road tomorrow, first thing."

Hickey pondered a minute. "I don't know. Who's to say, you take over, they won't come shooting at you?"

"It's different, Tom. I'm gonna use my brains, not just guts like you did. I've got a larger brain, remember, and plenty of time. Besides, anymore I know my way around town better than you. How about it? You snooze awhile, then drive off into the sunrise."

"Maybe. After I get breakfast with Elizabeth. Maybe not. I'm gonna sleep on it, partner."

Leaning back in a squeaky chair tipped against the wall, jotting notes onto a pad, Leo quizzed Hickey about Charlie

Schwartz, Pete Silva, Teddy the beachcomber, the police report. Soon they both fell to yawning. After a second round of scotch, Leo said good night.

Hickey rolled across the bed for the phone and dialed long distance, gave the operator his home number. At nearly eleven, Wendy'd be asleep. But Hickey needed to assure himself that she and his life on the lake were more than a beautiful memory. He needed to hear her voice, to feel it inject him with wonder and innocence.

Claire answered, and asked for a report. He lied, said everything was falling his way. As she passed the phone to Wendy, during the moment of silence, Hickey pictured the two of them lying side by side in the double bed. They were so lovely, the room glowed.

"Hi, Tom."

"Sorry to wake you, darling."

"Well, I'm sure not sorry."

"Even if I'm just calling to say good night and remind you I'm leaving here tomorrow by dark, anyway?"

"Yep. Even so."

"You feeling okay?"

"Swell. Except I'll be happy when the storm's over."

"Lots of snow?"

"No, but so much wind it makes the trees crack and moan. One time it got—the lake had waves so high, splashing so loud, it sounded like the ocean. Made me think about you, down there. Is the ocean pretty?"

"Sure. The wind scare you, babe?"

"Hardly any. But I wish the clouds would go away so we could have a little starlight. It's awfully dark."

"Is Claire sticking with you?"

"You bet. She won't leave me be. She watches me like any minute Clifford will want out. But don't worry. We're waiting for you. Did you get the poor lady out of jail yet?"

"Nope. Probably tomorrow. You go back to sleep now, before you're wide awake."

"Okay, Tom. You love me, huh?"

"Oh, God, yes. If I could say how much, I'd put Shakespeare outta business."

After he gave up the phone, downed another taste of scotch, and brushed his teeth, Hickey slipped out of his trousers and shirt, dove into the bed. Flushed with warmth, he felt himself drifting toward heaven.

A salesman or tourist banging his suitcase along the railing startled Hickey awake. He rolled to the window side of the bed, reached for the curtain, and pulled it aside enough to see the first glints of daylight on dusty tiled roofs. He rolled back the other way, out of the bed, and stumbled into the bathroom.

When the phone rang he had to cut short his business and tug up his shorts. He caught it on the third ring.

"Tom?" The voice stammered so timidly, dread washed through Hickey so swiftly, his pulse lunged into a gallop.

"Claire?"

"Tom, somebody kidnapped Wendy." Her breaths sizzled against his ear. "Tom, are you there?"

"Yeah," he said, but not into the receiver. He couldn't see it or anything. A zealous black light filled his skull and throbbed spasmodically at the temples, as if some doctor using forceps had seized him.

"Tom!"

"Yeah, I hear you!" he yelped.

"I called your pal Leo, got this number. It wasn't more than ten minutes ago."

Hickey'd drawn his shoulders together to press on his ribs, to hold in his heart, which pounded like a bass drum imitating thunder. He found the hand holding the receiver, pressed it to his face. "Who grabbed her? You see them?"

"It was dark as hell. They couldn't even see us. Only way they could tell which of us was Wendy was her belly. They knew about the baby. One of them shoved a note at me. Maybe if I read it, you can guess who they are."

"Yeah, read." The receiver shook in his hand, belting his ear.

"It says, *Greetings, snoop. At the moment, we don't figure to hurt the doll. If you want to see her and the kid one of these days, shag your nosy ass back to the sticks and plant it there. We'll be in touch, one of these days.*"

Hickey's throat felt jammed shut, leaving only passage enough for puny breaths. When he tried to speak, he couldn't breathe. Gulping breaths, he couldn't speak. He dropped himself onto the bed, slid off it to the floor.

"I'll call the sheriff, Tom."

"Yeah." He sucked down a mouthful of air. "I'm on my way." In a sudden fit, he slammed the receiver onto the mattress and yowled, "God, no!"

As though from a block away, he heard Claire shouting. "Hurry, Tom!"

He jumped up and tugged on his pants, grabbed his shirt, hat, shoes with yesterday's socks, and bolted for the door. When he got to the car he checked for his billfold and keys, found them in his pockets.

He wheeled out of the motel, leaving rubber on the turn.

Chapter Eight

Even rigged with chains and on a plowed dirt road, the Oldsmobile's tires spun climbing the grade. The driver yanked the steering wheel, trying to wrestle the tires out of ruts. He was slender and so tall his sandy hair scraped the headliner. He cussed and grimaced. His face was all angles, as though sculpted out of wooden blocks.

"She talking to herself or what?" he snapped.

The man in back next to Wendy leaned forward, to make his whispery voice heard over the clatter of chains and springs. "Praying, I think. Don't that beat all?"

He wore a hat pulled low, almost touching his thick wire-framed glasses. Though his hair showed gray at the temples, his skin was smooth as a pampered woman's and his lips appeared molded into a permanent, boyish smirk.

"We got us a real character, Tersh. I'm not so sure she's got eyes. All I've seen so far is eyelids. Say, you ever notice how pretty eyelids are? Prettier than legs, I think."

"Depends on whose legs and whose eyelids, don't it?"

"Could be."

Near the crest of the grade, the driver commanded, "Shut her up, Bud. This drive's bad enough without her squealing. How far we got to go?"

"How far've we gone since the pavement?"

"Damned if I know."

"It's right over the hump, I think," the man in back said, "then a ways around the pond. Mile or so, I guess." He fell back into the seat, reached over, and touched Wendy's lips with a finger. "Keep it to yourself, cutie."

Wendy sat wrapped in the patchwork quilt Claire had given her and Tom last Christmas. When the men had bashed through her door and she'd sprung from the bed, she'd dragged the quilt with her and thrown it around herself.

Even though she'd burrowed her feet into the quilt, they'd gone numb, except her toes burned. Every few seconds, the cramp in her belly pinched tighter. Her ears felt hard as ice. When the man touched her lips, she pressed them tightly together and continued her prayer in silence, asking God for a pair of warm socks and for the men to hurry to wherever they were taking her, out of this freezing car. She thought about Claire, rushing around the cabin aimlessly, her hair disheveled, her face bruised because one of the men must've smacked her. Something had made a noisy thump just before the time Claire screamed loudest.

The baby kicked. Wendy laid both hands on her belly and drummed her fingers. She pictured the baby listening intently, his hands cupped at his ears. Big hands like Tom's.

She imagined Tom in his car, pounding the dashboard like he did when they drove to San Francisco last summer and got stopped on a bridge by a line of cars, when he needed to use a toilet awfully. He was chewing on the stem of his pipe and lighting the tobacco even though it already burned. A truck going the other way whizzed past, bellowing its horn. Because Tom had crossed the white line.

She prayed he wouldn't cross the white line again. What if he couldn't think about driving straight while he worried so awfully over her and Clifford? She asked God to hold the steering wheel for Tom. And to steer other cars out of his way.

The Olds made a leap and tossed Wendy into the air. Slamming back down, a pain shot across her middle, front to rear, as she hit the seat. Clifford must've socked her bladder or something.

"Our Father," she murmured, "maybe you could make me a little softer inside." She caught her lower lip between her teeth and sat still, feeling God's spirit wash through her like a fever, chilling her skin and heating her blood until the cramp loosened. "Thanks so much," she whispered, then silently begged God to hold Clifford safe inside her until Tom came and rescued them like before, when he'd snatched her away from the Nazis and the devil. Her blood seemed to thicken and seep like molasses; her spine hardened from its base to the top of her skull, as she realized that these men might be servants of the devil named Zarp, the Nazi who'd sworn that she and him would live and die together. This road didn't look like the way to Tijuana, but tonight or tomorrow they might drive her there, and lock her upstairs in the bar called Hell.

The past eight years dissolved. As though the earth had gotten yanked from beneath her, she fell through a blizzard of lights into the room where the devil had made her stab George and pour blood on the *penitentes*. Once again, she sat with her arms bound and a sack over her head, cinched around her neck.

A rumbling started in her belly. In her throat it became a low growling noise. By the time it escaped through her constricted throat, it had turned to the squeal of a tormented pig.

"Knock it off!" the driver shouted.

The other man clapped his paw over her mouth. "Hush, sweetheart."

When she opened her eyes, the window beside her glittered with dew. Dim morning lights and shadows through the cedar forest looked subtly glorious. The needles glimmered dark green under the shelves of new snow. They passed a clearing of logged stumps. The ground sparkled as if the whole earth were a black diamond. A wolf with dark bluish fur streaked across the clearing. Wendy smiled in admiration.

"Get a load of this! One second she bleats, now she's grinning like a chorus girl. I think we got us a real screwball here, Tersh."

Chapter Nine

Twenty minutes out of San Diego, Hickey had realized that chartering a plane might've got him home faster. Yet he wasn't about to backtrack. Besides, the fog was soupy enough so he might've wasted the morning finding a plane, even a charter. Had he been called to stand still for an instant, he might've turned to ashes. Movement felt like his only salvation.

As he neared LA, the fog broke. Again he thought about flying. But the nearest airport to his place was an hour off, on the south shore, out highway 50. Anyway, it might be closed on account of the storm. And he'd risk losing hours if he cut across the city to the LA airport or passed the highway 99 merge and tried one of the airports in Burbank or Ventura.

So he jumped red lights through LA and Hollywood, rolled through stop signs. He clocked eighty topping the hill past Griffith Park. Through the groves of the San Fernando Valley and up and down the Grapevine's switchbacks, past fire-blackened hills and a half dozen wrecked and abandoned cars, he kept the hand throttle wide open and panned the horizon for cruisers. He only had to back the speed down twice. One patrol car lay hidden behind a boulder, the other in a cluster of oaks. Hickey's gaze felt so intense he could've spotted them through a ridge of granite. His brain seemed supercharged, as though he'd made up for years of lost sleep, only it kept firing arbitrarily until the San Joaquin Valley, when the explosions of fear and anger had quieted enough to let him reason.

He didn't figure the kidnappers to be Angelo Paoli's boys. Not a chance they could've gotten up north so fast, at night anyway. Charlie Schwartz might've sent some punks directly after lunch. Except, from all Hickey'd seen of the man, Charlie didn't think that fast. It was hardly brains that'd made him top dog. Meanness was Charlie's weapon.

More likely they were hired guns, out of San Francisco or maybe from around the lake. If they were locals, that'd make them fellow employees of his, since his neighbor and boss Harry Poverman had his fist around the Tahoe action.

He thought of pulling over and calling Poverman but nixed the idea. That'd be like a burglar ringing the doorbell. He sped on until his gas ran dry. From a Sinclair station in Bakersfield, he phoned Leo at the office and got lucky.

"Another minute, I was gone," Leo said. "Got any news?"

"Claire told you, right?"

"Sure. I hopped in the Packard and blazed up to the motel, just in time to miss you. Had to pay the tab before they'd give me the stuff you left behind."

"I paid it up front."

"Well, she stiffed us. Where you at?"

"Bakersfield."

"You're making time, all right. Tom, don't lose your head, will you?"

"Anything happens to her and the kid, I'm done." Hickey wanted to explain how it felt, that if he lost Wendy his soul would flee, leaving nothing but the carcass, the withered heart and vanquished mind. But he choked on the first word.

"Don't think about losing her, Tom. Think about next year, you and Wendy on a second honeymoon, taking the kid on a whirlygig at the Pike. Think about how that lousy valley you're passing through stinks like fertilizer. Think about revenge or anything you please except losing her."

Hickey opened his mouth, found it mute. The second attempt he managed a sigh; the third time he forced words out. "Claire read you the note?"

"Yeah, when I called her back. She's staying put at your place, in case the punks call. Look, you're doing like they say, getting outta town. They're liable to cut her loose soon as they find out, which they're gonna in about a half hour."

"How's that?"

"I'm meeting Schwartz at that fish place."

"And saying what?"

"Haven't rehearsed it. One thing, I'll tell him you backed off, let Cynthia fry if she's gotta."

"Yeah? Only problem I see is the ten times better odds it's Angelo had her grabbed, judging from the guys that shot up your house last night."

"That could've been Silva on his own. My guess is you dented his pride. He wasn't shooting to hit you, the way he binged it off the ground."

"The ground where I was lying low, behind your car."

"Yeah, why'd you pick my car?"

"Don't," Hickey mumbled. "I've got no heart for wisecracks right now."

"Tom, you'll get her back. I'm not gonna snooze anymore down here than you will up there, till she's back home."

"Sure. Thanks."

"You wanta know how I figure it's Charlie?"

"Yeah. Make it quick."

"First off, since the war, he's been frothing over one or the other of the Tucker sisters. Both threw him over. Sousa, like you said, was probably two-timing Mickey Cohen, double-dealing with Angelo.

"Mickey gets wise and tells Schwartz, Go ahead, knock off Sousa, and Schwartz decides to burn the place with Johnny in it. All he's gotta do is pin the fire on Cynthia, he gets the last laugh all around. The two-timer's rubbed out. One Tucker sister's a widow and the other's busting rocks."

If Hickey'd felt able to stand still another minute, he'd have asked his partner, If Charlie's as vindictive as all that, how come he's never popped me for wasting Donny Katoulis? In 1942,

Hickey'd finished Katoulis, Charlie's best gunman and pal. Maybe all these years, Hickey thought, Charlie's been waiting for the perfect opportunity. Or he'd written Hickey into this whole arson deal. Maybe Charlie was shrewder than he seemed.

"Or maybe you're just wishing, Leo. You *want* it to be Schwartz and Cohen. If you could pin the fire on Mickey, you'd be dancing with glee. Mickey and Schwartz weren't teamed up, I guess you wouldn't be so damned sure."

The operator came on, squawking for another fifty cents. Hickey plunked in the quarters, though he only had a few words left. "Tell Schwartz, without Wendy I'm a goner. And if that's what I am, so is he."

"Yeah, Tom. I'll talk sense to the lard-ass."

Chapter Ten

Leo arrived at the seafood mart twenty minutes early. He walked around back, past the sportfishing dock, and up to the yacht club, where the sun-wrinkled dolls who noticed him either crimped their noses, disappointed again, or practiced the coquettish smile they figured to use on richer, younger guys.

He strolled out past the day sailors and small cabin cruisers rigged with marlin gear, to the longer sloops and schooners that he and Tom used to mutually admire, especially when they'd owned the Chris Craft dealership together—the reason they'd both given up the LAPD and moved south. In 1935, sure the depression was about to lift, they'd bought the dealership cheap. Summer of 1936, they'd sold out even cheaper.

Leo stood gazing at a white Newporter, about forty feet, plenty big enough for himself and Vi. Maybe they could swing a trade with some old salt finally ready to forsake the sea. Their house for the boat, straight across. They could sail through the islands off British Columbia. Visit Magda in Seattle, Una in Berkeley. Follow the gray whales south. Drift around the cape into the Sea of Cortez. Or cut across Panama.

After he leaned on Charlie Schwartz.

He strode back up the dock, along the wharf past the sport-fishers, turned into the patio behind the seafood mart. He took the first seat inside the gate. The waitress swept over haughtily, dressed like a flamenco dancer.

"I'm meeting Charlie Schwartz," Leo said.

He suspected she muttered, "*Lo siento mucho,*" as she ushered him across the patio, into the corner closest to the yacht club. He sat down, checked the menu, ordered a sweet rum drink called a mai tai, and wondered if the doctor who'd hounded him into giving up cigarettes could be a quack.

When his mai tai arrived, he swilled the top half and was sipping when Charlie and the freckled brothers showed. All three were in shirtsleeves with open collars. Leo slipped his jacket onto the back of the chair. A sudden breeze tickled his ribs, damp from sweating.

"Mr. Weiss," Charlie said cordially.

Leo rose, shook hands. Charlie used the finger-pinch grip, like most guys trying to keep their edge.

"These here are my protégés," Charlie said, pronouncing the last word as if there were a hyphen between each syllable. "The brothers McNees." They nodded glumly and perched on the two end seats across from Leo. Schwartz took the seat between them. "Mr. Weiss, we got something to talk about? You bring an apology from your pal Tom?"

"Not exactly."

"That's a shame. I had one coming. Then, maybe you're thinking, at our age it's time to make new friends outta old foes. That it?"

"Yeah. You're a mind reader." Leo tapped the menu. "Any recommendations?"

"Clams. Nothing but clams. Perfect with the sissy punch you're drinking. Clams it is?"

"Sure."

Schwartz nudged the skinny brother, who got up slowly and meandered across the patio on a line to intercept the waitress. Leo raised a finger and crooked it at Schwartz. The gangster leaned closer.

"Now that we're friends," Leo whispered, "you wanta tell me who grabbed Tom's wife and where they got her?"

Schwartz leaned back, wrinkled his brow. "Tom's wife? The dimwitted gal? When'd this happen?"

"Sometime after Tom and you talked."

"Who grabbed her?"

Over the rim of his mai tai, Leo stared daggers into the gangster's smoky eyes, thinking there ought to be something different, if you looked close enough, between the eyes of humans and those of a ghoul.

"They asking for ransom or what?"

"Just to get him outta town, Charlie. Who'd want him outta their hair, do you think?"

"Angelo Paoli, could be. I heard Tom was trying to hang the Sousa fire on Angelo."

"Damn, Charlie, you're confusing me here. Way I understood, Tom was trying to hang the fire on you. Matter of fact, that's why I figured we oughta be pals, you and me, on account of then I could do your chum Mickey Cohen a favor, and in turn you'd see that Cynthia gets sprung and Tom's wife shows up at home by tonight."

The gangster had clenched his jaw so tight it made his jowls tremble. "Supposing I had the power to fix all this crap—this whatever you could do for Mr. Cohen'd have to be a whopper."

"Yeah. That's the kind I mean."

"Spill it, then."

"The Guns for Israel scam. There's a guy on the *Herald* knows all about the phony stories. The ship sailing. The ship sinking. This guy, there's a little voice in the back of his head shouting he's gotta pass the truth on. If the cops don't want it, and the FBI don't, he gives it to the newsreels, *Life* magazine, Mr. Ben Gurion. No way he's gonna let Mickey off the hook on this one. The guy's a fanatic, I hear. Thinks God's talking to him, saying, 'Clip ten million off my people, you burn for it.' " Leo smiled, thinking he could hear the gangster's teeth gnash.

"That so? Gimme a name."

"Yeah, I will. You know when."

Schwartz bunched his fists together, braced his elbows on the table, leaned his chin on the fists. "Listen up. I get around, hear things. Nothing you'd like better than to watch me and Mickey take a fall. How about that?"

"I might've said that once or twice. Blowing off steam, is all, Charlie." He offered an ingenuous smile.

"Okay, now let's suppose it's like you say and Guns for Israel wasn't exactly on the level. How come you'd sell out this fanatic, and the Holy Land to boot, for one stinking goy?"

"You oughta know. Hey, I've got my excuses, same as you. Twenty years we been best pals, Tom and me."

"So, when he hears you been playing games with Mickey, and Mickey had to send a couple boys to squeeze this fanatic's name outta you before they cooked you on a spit, he'll send flowers. I bet he'll send a truckful."

Leo sat panting through his nose. He lifted the drink, gave himself a double dose. "What's the advantage in knocking me off? Why would Mickey wanta do it the hard way? Why not just spring the two girls and pin the fire on some other chump, if the cops need a fall guy? Pin it on Angelo, say."

"On account of Mickey ain't got Hickey's wife, and I ain't got her, and maybe can't anybody spring the Cynthia dame, if the cops are holding her dead to rights. That's why." Charlie whipped his head around to the rail and spat onto the dock, a step in front of a prim tourist zeroing her camera at a pelican. "Mr. Weiss, you oughta give me the name of this fanatic, save a lot of grief. Suppose, before Mickey hears you're trying to pin a bum wrap on him and sends for you—suppose before that you get lost or fall over dead or something? Now Mickey's gotta slap around every pinhead that works for the *Herald* to figure which one's spreading lies about him."

"That's a lot of slapping," Leo said.

Charlie's boy and the waitress crossed the patio, each of them carrying two plates of clams. The boy was in the rear, his eyes beaming down on the waitress's prancing hips.

When the plate landed in front of him, Leo picked up his fork, pricked a clam, grimaced, and stabbed the thing. Slowly he lifted and placed it on his tongue. He rolled it around his mouth a minute, finally bit, and swallowed. His face crimped in revulsion.

"Hey, Charlie," he said. "Want my clams?"

"I got plenty."

"Put 'em in the bait bucket where they belong, then." Leo heaved himself up, slipped into his coat. "Oh, yeah, I got a message from Tom. He says, without the girl, his life comes to a screeching halt, and so does yours."

"Hey, pigface, how is it I'm getting blamed for everything?"

"Pigface?" Faster than the eye, Leo snatched up a fork and pronged the gangster's neck, on the jugular vein. Charlie only sat frozen, sneering, while the skinny boy wedged between the table and the patio rail, jumped behind Leo, and got him by the throat. He wrenched the old man up and out the dockside gate, kneed him around to the alley alongside the seafood mart and a drydock. He shoved Leo's face down onto a stack of cardboard that was slimy and reeked of fish guts. A cat yowled and squirted out from between layers of cardboard.

By the time Leo rolled over, the redhead was turning the corner, out of the alley. "Hey," Leo called after him. "This mean you're picking up the tab?"

He dragged himself up and around the fish mart to his car, worrying about which hotel in LA he should check into, and where he might sequester Vi, and if some innocent folks that worked for the *LA Herald* were about to get squashed by Mickey Cohen.

Chapter Eleven

The storm had blown down trees all over the Sierra Nevada, but the snowfall had been light. Plows and sun, a high of near 50 degrees, had cleared the highway up from Sacramento, across Donner Pass, and along the Truckee River, which cascaded out of Tahoe's north shore. All the way down, the Truckee was rapids that flooded its banks. Rivulets cut every hillside, unsettling roots, felling trees, emptying into the river.

The lakeside highway was clear and slick. Hickey reached the village at dusk and skidded his Chevy down the hill toward the shore, to his place. Ten feet into his driveway, mud stopped him. He left the car and ran through the slush. He slammed the door open.

Claire sprang up from the easy chair next to the phone. She'd been dozing. Her exquisite, regal face looked battered. The whites of her eyes were bloodstained pearls. The pupils had faded to milk chocolate. Tangled black hair jutted in all directions. Her willowy body seemed aged, brittle. Beside her stood an easel holding a half-finished portrait, the eyes, forehead, and hair of a Reno banker. Claire made her living with portraiture.

"I'm sorry, Tom."

"Nothing new?"

"Nothing."

With a groan, he strode over and hugged her. While she wept with her head on his shoulder, Hickey wished to God he could join in. But even if he were capable of weeping, now it would feel like giving up. Giving in. As if Wendy were already lost.

"I've been here every second," she sobbed. "In case they called."

He helped her back to the easy chair and took the wooden chair beside it. "Cold in here."

"I fell asleep."

Hickey got up and went to the wood stove, stirred the coals, and threw in a couple of small logs. He filled and lit his pipe, returned to the chair, and noticed, on the coffee table, Wendy's stack of *Saturday Evening Posts*, her Bible, her dictionary, and the stories of Isak Dinesen. He choked on a breath. His brain smoked and crackled.

"The sheriff came, right?"

"Uh-huh. He looked for stuff they might've dropped. Nothing. A fellow dusted for fingerprints, even though I told him they were sure wearing gloves. The one was, I know, and coming in out of the cold....Sheriff Boggs looked at their prints in the snow, said one of them had awfully big feet, size thirteen or so. And a deputy asked around, all the neighbors. Only one who said he might've noticed anything at that hour was Harry Poverman's cowboy, Mac. He said there was a dark blue Oldsmobile passed by. That's all."

Hickey gazed around at the half-knitted blanket thrown over a chair back, at the fur-collared woolen coat he'd bought Wendy for Christmas, and at the snow cap and muffler, all on hooks beside the door. "They drag her out in her nightgown?" he snarled.

"She had a blanket. They wouldn't let her freeze, Tom. I'll bet they wouldn't."

Hickey needed to scream, curse, or weep but, stuck between impulses, he sat pounding his fists together. Claire leaned and touched his knee. "The sheriff said you ought to call when you get in. Left his home number, for after six."

"He phone Leo, ask what this is all about?"

"I passed on what Leo told me, about the two gangsters you threatened."

Hickey nodded, checked his watch: five-twenty. He reached for the phone, put it on his lap, looked at the card Claire held out, dialed the Washoe County sheriff's north shore station, and asked for Sheriff Boggs.

"Yeah, Tom. I didn't expect you this early. You holding up?"

"Fair. You got anything?"

"Not a damn one. Those boys slipped in and out like ghosts, except one of Harry's guard dogs saw an Olds driving away, could've been them."

"Mac saw the Olds. He give you any descriptions?"

"No. Said he couldn't tell if there were two men or a brass band inside the car, dark as it was."

"Let's don't bet on Mac. It might've been a couple of Harry's boys that snatched her. Suppose you're a mobster down south who wants to fix somebody here, who'd you call?"

"Poverman. I'm with you. Fill me in, though, would you? I only got pieces from Mrs. Blackwood. Give me the whole story."

Starting with the phone call from the lawyer, Hickey explained that he'd raced down to San Diego, in a hurry to do the job and get back to Wendy. He admitted his carelessness, that he'd pissed off the wrong guys: Schwartz, Paoli, possibly Mickey Cohen. He confessed that, even after Angelo's stiffs had fired on him, he still hadn't considered that a phone call, maybe to Harry Poverman, could stop him cold. Stop him good as dead.

"Let's try it this way, Tom. S'pose it's Harry's boys, all right. That'd indicate the instigator was this Schwartz fella, or Cohen. Since Harry's a Jew."

"Except you've got Jews shooting for Jack Dragna, Italians knocking off their cousins for the Jews. You've got Greeks, Hungarians. Forget race or creed. These guys aren't patriots."

"I'm saying Poverman's thick with the Hollywood Jews, no matter if he's an Eskimo. You oughta know, Tom, working for him, living next door and all."

"He doesn't take me in his confidence."

"Look, you sit tight, don't pull any more boners, huh? I'll make some calls to South Shore. They got a list of Harry's boys that'd fit this kinda action. If a couple of 'em are outta touch, maybe we got something. Meanwhile, think you can muster some patience?"

"If I had any patience," Hickey muttered, "or sense either, I wouldn't of blown this game, and Wendy'd be home right now."

"Sit tight, Tom. Have a few drinks. Read a good book."

Through the phone call, Claire had leaned close with a hand on his arm. The instant he hung up, she said, "What?"

"The sheriff's got an angle."

"Harry?"

"Yeah."

"Do you think he's that evil?"

Hickey shrugged, got up, and walked into the kitchen. All day he'd been groping for answers about what to do when he got here, without a single inspiration. So he'd kept dreaming that, if a miracle hadn't delivered Wendy, at least a clue might await him. Besides a dark Oldsmobile and Harry Poverman, he'd found nothing, except a house full of reminders that his carelessness might've cost him everything. All he'd gotten from Claire or the sheriffs were questions and comments that deepened his shame.

Some thirty hours had passed since his last meal. He considered a plate of crackers and cheese or something, decided he couldn't force it down. He reached to the cupboard above the sink where he used to keep whiskey before he cut back, almost a year ago. He thought there might be a little left out of the fifth they'd bought when Claire and her cousin visited on New Year's Eve. It was gone. He must've used it to spike coffee once or twice, coming in from the cold.

As he passed through the living room, Claire asked, "You want a bowl of soup, Tom?"

"Naw."

He walked into the bedroom, opened the linen closet, and reached behind a pile of sweaters for a bundle, out of which he unwrapped his .45 Colt automatic. His .38 could drop most guys, except wild men, if you hit them square. The Colt could've felled Goliath. He went to the closet, got his heavy woolen coat with big pockets, and stuffed the pistol into the one on the right at hip level. After returning to the living room, he backtracked again to the linen closet, dug behind the sweaters for two seven-round clips, and pocketed them.

Claire had returned to dabbing oils on the portrait she'd been painting. The dabs looked like liver spots on the forehead. When she turned and saw Hickey wearing the coat, her eyebrows furled. "Where you going?"

"Over to Harry's."

"Do you think that's smart, Tom? What can you do there, except yell and get beat up?"

"Borrow some whiskey." He stepped over and patted her cheek. "Thanks, Claire. You're tops." He kissed the summit of her head, at the part, then turned to the door. On the way, he picked up his pipe and tin of Sir Walter Raleigh off an end table.

Outside, he set out trudging in ankle deep snow through a stand of lodge pole pine, and across the meadow where the snow had melted into crunchy layers. As it deepened, he kicked it aside.

Harry's place was five cubes, each nearly thirty feet square. All four outside cubes attached to the middle one, in a lopsided wheel pattern. Each cube had at least one chimney, making eight chimneys in all. Smoke poured out of two of them, one in the center cube, another in one of the bedroom wings. Tyler, Harry's daytime bodyguard, stood watch on the deck that led off the center cube on the lake side, his arm around the shoulder of a blonde in a maid outfit, pointing toward the lakeshore where, in moonlight, a tall, meaty, five-point buck stood gazing back toward the mountains as if he'd lost his way.

Hickey crossed a swampy expanse and sank calf deep in frosty mud. Cussing, he plodded out and picked up his pace across the meadow, keeping to the shadowed, icy places along the tree line.

The maid, Frieda, nudged the bodyguard. He turned from viewing the buck, spotted Hickey, and waved. They'd first met a few years ago when Tyler was a bouncer at Harry's casino. A Kansas farmboy, he'd played two years of college football, same as Hickey. He wore a Russian hat and a hayseed smile. He met Hickey at the steps.

"Problems, huh, Tom?"

"Yeah. You see anything that could help me out?"

"Nope. Talk to Mac. You won't catch me up at dawn."

"Smart man. The boss in?"

"Yep. Wait here a minute."

Tyler and the maid went inside, shutting the door behind them. Hickey watched the moon ripples on the lake, felt the pounding in his temples increase each time he got a vision of Wendy. In every frame, she was turned aside. He only could see her profile. She wouldn't look him straight on.

Frieda poked her head out the door. "Come on in, Mister Hickey."

The place reminded Hickey of an ice cream parlor. Floored in ceramic tile in neapolitan colors, chocolate, strawberry, and vanilla, like Claire's sorry eyes. The walls matched the floor, except the lakeside wall around the picture windows was the pastel of lime sherbet. Each wall had a sliding glass door leading to a deck that connected the bordering cubes. In the southwest corner was a stainless steel sinkboard and bar polished to gleam like chrome. The fireplace, beginning ten feet east of the bar, beyond the sliding door, was of brick painted neapolitan strawberry.

The furniture was all Formica, cast iron, and dyed leather. There were seven couches: two each of strawberry, chocolate, and vanilla, one black. In the room's dead center, between a strawberry and a vanilla couch, sat a large glass tank, home to a rosy boa and a pair of sidewinders. Harry claimed he kept the damned things because they got women all giddy.

The man of the house lay sprawled on the black couch, which faced the lakeside window. Slow as a dreamer, he got up to greet Hickey.

He stood at least six feet three inches, an inch or so taller than his neighbor. Several years younger. The tight polo shirt showed off his long, lean, muscular arms. He strutted like an Olympian. His skin was olive, his dark hair curly, his nose a classic. He had a slightly cleft chin and full lips. His voice was a rich and confident bass that charmed women so profoundly, those who didn't nearly swoon at least fluttered. "Hey, Tom. I heard, pal. Give me the latest."

Hickey walked over and shook hands. "Nothing new."

"Drink?"

"Scotch."

"Hey, Tyler. Ale for me, scotch for Tom. Tall one."

Tyler stepped out through the doorway near the bar. It led into the northwest cube. The kitchen. After a few visits, Hickey'd come to know the layout.

He and the boss sat on the black couch facing the lake. Harry seemed to understand his neighbor's silence. He leaned back, hands folded on his neck, and sighed ponderously.

The buck was gone from the beach. A lighted party boat chugged near shore, over the dark glassy water striped with foam. Hickey caught a shiver. As soon as it passed, the throbbing in his temples came so hard he went blind for a moment. When his sight returned, he glimpsed what seemed the outline of a huge person reflected in the window, for an instant before it disappeared and the shiver began to fade.

Tyler served the drinks, threw a couple of logs on the fire, and wandered back into the kitchen wing beyond the bar, while Hickey knocked down his scotch in three swallows. He set the glass on the floor, got up, shoved a strawberry leather chair into the corner between the fireplace and the lakeside picture window. From there, he could view the entire room and the doors that led to every deck and cube.

He sank into the chair and spilled his confession. All the bad he'd done yesterday. The guys he'd accused and threatened. The new enemies he'd made.

"One of these guys put the snatch on Wendy," Harry drawled. "That's what you're telling me?"

"You got it." Hickey reached into his coat. Plucked out the automatic.

The boss's arms jerked out like wings, then dropped slowly until they touched down lightly on his knees. "Look here. A new toy?"

"Naw. It's a few years old. From the army. They invented the things to knock down crazy Filipinos the thirty-eight wouldn't stop. You heard that story?"

"I heard. You wanta tell me a war story? That it?"

"Nope. What I want is, either you find out who's got Wendy and where, or it goes boom."

"You're gonna *shoot* me?"

"Depends what happens to Wendy."

Harry braced his arms on the couch beside him. "That simple, huh?" He cocked his head sideways, pursed his lips. "I get the message, Tom. This thing's bowled you over."

"You bet. Now, tell me where they've got her. You don't know, then pick up the phone and start asking."

"Hey, I didn't snatch her."

"Don't," Hickey snarled. "No games. You didn't snatch her, then you know somebody who knows somebody who knows who did. Now, the phone."

His eyes fixed on Hickey's, the boss inched along the couch to the far end, where a phone sat on a Formica table. With his hand on the receiver, he said, "Thing is, you didn't need the toy. You and me are pals, is what I thought. All you had to do was ask."

"Swell," Hickey muttered. He raised and jerked the gun.

Chapter Twelve

Hickey pointed toward the far wing, from where he'd seen another smoking chimney. "Who's back there?"

"Mac and a gal."

"Anybody else around besides Tyler and Frieda?"

Harry wagged his head, gave a pensive scowl. For a minute he tapped the phone receiver against his shoulder. Then he dropped it back onto the cradle. "Tom, let's cut the jive. See, I know you're not gonna pop me."

"Uh-huh," Hickey muttered, peering into the shadows of corners and doorways.

"You wanta know how I know?"

"Yeah, sure."

"You're not the kind who could pop a guy just because he won't take orders. You know how I know?"

"I don't have to. You're gonna tell me."

"I know because I'm the kind who could." He flashed a wan smile. It looked tainted by regret. He picked up the receiver, dialed, and a moment later said, "Pauline, give me some phone numbers. Charlie Schwartz. Sal Randazzo. The guy they call the Jockey, what's his name—Schweidel, something Schweidel." He cupped a hand over the receiver and hollered, "Tyler, bring me a paper and note pad."

Instantly, Tyler came strolling from the kitchen. Halfway across the room, between the snake tank and the Formica desk, he stopped cold, staring at Hickey's gun.

"Don't get all hot and bothered, Tyler," Harry drawled. "Tom just needs some, whatta you call—security. Like a guy falls asleep holding his dick, that's all the rod's for."

Tyler shrugged and opened the desk, fished out a steno pad and pen, delivered them. With a quizzical look at Hickey, he turned back toward the kitchen. The boss uncovered the receiver.

"Okay, hon. One more time." He jotted on the pad. "Yeah.... Check....Okay. Yeah, see you tonight. Late, probably. How you dressed?...Ooh, that red angora with the poofy sleeves? I'd climb Mount Everest to see you in that."

Frieda poked her head out from the kitchen, long enough to verify the story Tyler must've given her, about the loco neighbor who'd probably get snuffed any minute now.

"Who're Randazzo and Schweidel?" Hickey demanded. "I never heard of the guys."

"You been outta touch, Tom. Sidekicks of Angelo and Cohen, respectively. They oughta know what's up. Paoli and the Mick don't take calls straight from a nobody like me. To them, I'm a nickel-and-dime hustler from the boondocks. How about I ring Charlie first?"

Hickey nodded. The boss dialed the operator, gave her a San Diego number. He reached one of Schwartz's errand boys, left a message that Charlie should call him on urgent business. He pestered the operator again, got forwarded, gave a similar message to a Mrs. Randazzo.

Arnold Schweidel he caught at home. After gabbing a minute, Harry pardoned himself, muffled the phone, and asked, "How about it, Tom? Ought I tell him you're threatening to plug me? Give him a laugh?"

"Tell him whatever you want."

"So, Jock," Harry said, "the deal is, a neighbor of mine stopped by here a while ago, pulled a heater, waved it around. Then he ran off someplace." He listened a moment and reared back chortling. "The Jockey asked can I change my will," he told Hickey. "Bequeath him one of my speedboats."

Harry told the man that persons unknown had snatched his neighbor Tom Hickey's wife, on account of Tom was a snoop and had got a little arrogant, trying to push guys around to deliver some female from an arson rap, for which behaviors Tom was sorely ashamed and willing to make amends anyhow he could. All he wanted was his wife back. The wife being pregnant, Harry figured Mr. Cohen might take pity, ferret out whoever put the snatch on, and persuade them to reconsider.

Or else, he said, this lunatic was apt to waste somebody and get the yokels all flustered, just when there's already talk of Washoe County putting the screws on gambling.

"I could take him out, but the thing is, I like the guy, and he does good work when he's not off his rocker. Talk to Mickey, will you?"

He told Schweidel they'd wait for a call. He hung up, slid to the middle of the couch, picked his ale bottle off the floor, and leaned back contentedly. "Now we relax, huh? Don't wanta tie up the line." He sipped, sighed. "You know why I didn't tell him you were pointing a gun at my ear?"

"It would've made you blush."

"Close. What kinda reputation'd it buy me, getting stuck up in my own parlor? You're compromising me, Tom. I don't like that."

A wiry fellow with flyaway black hair, shirtless, wearing jeans and a silver cowboy belt buckle had appeared in the doorway to the northeast cube, leaning on a rifle as if it were his cane. A Latin woman stood behind him, peering over his shoulder.

Raising his gun to where the cowboy could see it angled in his direction, Hickey said, "Get Mac over here."

The boss hollered and Mac obeyed, letting his rifle drop to the floor. The stock landed on the woman's instep. She yipped and jumped from the doorway into the dark. Mac ambled through the maze of couches to stand beside the hearth, about five feet from Hickey. He sucked a deep breath as though to expand and exhibit his furry chest. "Problem, boss?"

"Don't sweat it," Harry said. "Tell Tom what you saw this morning."

"Big blue four-door, looked like an Olds. About six. I was making the rounds. It came clunking out from behind the trees out front of your place."

"Clunking?"

"Yeah. Had chains."

If they were flatlanders, Hickey thought, if they'd driven up from the coast, they must've stopped in a gas station to buy the chains. "You get a number, see anybody inside?"

"I look like a cat? Hey, last night was so dark I couldn't see the tip of my nose."

Hickey stared hard.

Mac yawned, wrinkled his nose. "Hey, I'm sorry. That good enough? You want me to keep a watch on your place, you gotta tell me ahead of time."

"I'm telling you now. Bundle up and go over to my place. Claire Blackwood's there. Send her here and wait till she gets back. Stay by the phone."

Mac turned to Poverman, got a nod, and strolled off toward the cube from where he'd appeared.

"Another drink?" the boss asked. Hickey declined. "So, while we're sitting by the phone, how about a card game?" When he got no response, Harry clapped his hands for attention. "Cards?"

"No."

"Tell me something, then. How's it feel, being a family man after playing the field all those years?"

Hickey sat glowering, at the fire for one long moment, another at Harry, a third scanning the room. He didn't want to talk, didn't believe he could muster the heart to sit conversing. Besides, talk would shift his mind off business. Off Wendy. But the tempest inside him had to find some release, or else it might blow him apart at the seams. He filled and lit his pipe, smoked awhile, watching Harry and wondering about the man. Sure, he was a gambler, probably had his finger in some other rackets. But Hickey'd known a few mobsters who had a decent side. If he had to make book on the roster in heaven, there were mobsters on whom he'd put shorter odds than on plenty of churchgoers he'd met. At least on one churchgoer he'd known intimately: his mother.

When Mac came out dressed and started for the north door, Harry shouted a command. "Hey, not a peep to anybody! One yokel laughs at me, whoever spilled the beans gets crucified." Mac waved his assent and left.

"Look, Tom. I don't mind you holding that piece. Just don't bore me to death. How about it? Talk to me."

"Give me a topic," Hickey muttered.

"You and the wife. What else?"

"You wanta hear about me and Wendy?"

"Yeah. Give me the scoop. I been wondering a long time. When I first saw you and her, with the Blackwood dame always hanging around, I figured you and Blackwood were smooches. Wendy I made as your kid, maybe the Blackwood doll's niece. How much older are you?"

"Plenty."

"Yeah, well, young's just fine. Young's magnifico. Only she's…you know. What keeps you stuck on a gal like that?"

"Like what?" Hickey growled.

"Aw, how do you say it? Sweet. Pure. One of those. What'd you think I was gonna say?"

"Lots of people think she's stupid," Hickey muttered.

"Hell, Tom, if I spurned dames on account of their intellect, I'd be a horny guy. She stupid?"

"No," Hickey said adamantly. "Claire's got her reading these books—I'd guess she's brighter than me, only she never went to school."

"Why's that?"

"Her ol' man wouldn't let her."

"I get it," Harry said. "Must've been a German. So the tale I heard, you and a gang of pachucos stormed the old Agua Caliente Casino, swiped a ton of gold, and massacred about a thousand Nazis who were holed up there scheming an invasion. The way the yokels tell it, the girl was some Nazi honcho's sweetheart. That story pretty accurate?"

"That'd be the Hollywood version."

The north door flew open and Claire ran in, looking robust as if in the past hour she'd taken a magic elixir. In the entryway, she halted and gawked at Harry's decor. Then she hustled through the maze of dyed leather couches, pulling the snow cap off her head and shaking out her hair, pausing for a glance at the snakes.

"Quite a layout," she remarked flatly, just before noticing Hickey's gun.

Her cheeks flushed, and her eyes flashed darkly. She strode past the gambler to the fireplace side of Hickey's chair, leaned over him, and demanded, "What the hell are you doing, Tom?"

Hickey smiled bitterly. "You got any smarter ideas?"

"No. But I can't match this one for ignorance, either." After scalding him with her glare, she turned it on the boss.

"Miss Blackwood," Harry drawled, in his silkiest bass. He rolled his hand toward the .45 and shrugged. "Never mind the prop. Tom and I are having a swell time, chewing the fat. Say, I don't recall our being properly introduced, and I'd remember if we had." He stood and offered his hand.

Claire stayed beside Hickey long enough for the gambler's arm to tire, yet he resolutely held it out. Finally she stepped to meet him halfway and awarded her hand for a second. As he started lifting it toward his lips, she yanked it away and hustled back to kneel beside Hickey's chair, scowling.

"Sit down," Hickey snapped at the boss.

With a mock servile nod, winking at Claire, Harry retreated and sat primly on the sofa's edge. "Drink, Miss Blackwood? Hors d'oeuvres?"

"Look, you wanta put the make on Claire, you had the last two years and maybe you'll get a few more. It's not what I called her over here for."

"Why *did* you send for me, Tom?"

"A couple chores. How about you call every gas station, starting from here, to Truckee, over the pass, all the way to Auburn if you have to. Ask did anybody in a blue Olds buy chains last night. Somebody says yes, get all you can. Maybe there's a receipt with a license number. Maybe an attendant can describe the guys. If nothing turns up that direction, start back here and go south, off the hill at least to Placerville. Got it?"

"Sure."

"Call from your place. That'll leave my line clear. Stop on the way and tell Mac to stay put, would you?"

"Okay. Is that all?"

"Yeah. Thanks, babe."

"For the record, Tom, you're acting like a dope." Sorrowfully, she gave him a peck on the forehead and hustled off.

"A pleasure, Miss Blackwood," Harry called after her.

Chapter Thirteen

Hickey paced in front of the picture window: five steps, wheel, and back. He shot glances at the boss and at the doorways to the other cubes, in case Tyler, the maid, or Mac's brunette had a rifle sighted on him. He listened to his breath, to the heart drumming his ears.

"So you whipped the Nazis, won the girl. Then what?"

It took a minute for the gambler's question to cut through Hickey's trance. "She was a mess," he muttered, and got a sudden rush of joy, in which he realized that talking about Wendy would deliver him out of the present, and for now memory was the closest to her he could get.

"A couple years, till winter after the big boom in Japan, when I finally got discharged, Wendy stayed with my partner, Leo, and his wife and daughter. Only family she had was some aunts she didn't know, in Oklahoma, and she wasn't having any of them, people she'd never met. Anyway, they belonged to her old man. A sicko."

"What kinda sicko?"

"The worst kind," Hickey said as though issuing a curse. "The thing was, her brother Clifford was all she had left, and he didn't make it. We got into a scrape in TJ. A Nazi blew his skull in half. And after the Tijuana business, the army wanted me long gone. They shipped me out to the desert: Tucson. Two years handcuffing drunks, slinging them into a panel truck.

"Now and then I'd get a day or week's leave, drive home, and see Wendy. Every week, I'd drop my wages into the pay phone, calling her up."

"What was left after you visited Nogales, right? Made friends with the señoritas?"

Hickey sat glowering.

"Hey, you don't like interruptions, shoot me," the boss quipped. He chuckled and clucked as though awed by his own wit. "Naw, I'm just ribbing you, Tom. I'll zip it up. Go on."

"See," Hickey said, and reached for his pipe, "the Nazis messed her up bad. The first year, no telling when she'd bust out weeping or howling. It was all Leo and Vi could do to keep her from casting herself into the riptide. One time, they left her in the kitchen with Magda, their kid. Magda got careless, stepped outside, came back, and found Wendy with a knife aimed between her ribs, the tip already bloody. Most often, though, they could lift her spirits by promising in a week or two I'd visit, and reminding her that soon as the war wrapped up, I was going to take her up here, to heaven."

"Whoa. Cut. You lost me."

"See, when she was little, they lived down by Reno. One time they brought her up here, and she got the idea this place was heaven. So, after my discharge, I kicked the renters out of my house on Mission Bay, gave her my daughter's old room. All winter, on account of I told her about blizzards and avalanches to keep her from coaxing me up here before spring, she worried about whether the angels had houses, slippers, and things."

"Angels, you say?"

"If it's heaven, there's gotta be angels, right? She figured the place was infested with angels. Matter of fact, she still does."

"I'll be damned." The boss leaned forward as though thinking intently. He touched his fingers together and worked them like twin Siamese spiders practicing knee bends. "You're telling me she sees angels?"

"Nope. Only believes they're hanging around."

"How can she believe what she can't see?"

"You believe in anything? Luck?"

"Naw. So, your wife's got a screw loose?"

"Not anymore. Back then, after the war, she was a mess."

"Yeah, but she musta been a tiger in the sack, or you'd have stuck her in a nuthouse."

Hickey gave the man a contemptuous glare. "You're a piece of work."

"Huh? Why're you giving me that look, like a snooty dame at some guy with lousy table manners?"

"Get this through your head: a man can keep his pistol in the holster if he wants to. I never more than gave her a squeeze till last year."

"Naw."

"Yep." Hickey sighed wistfully, for a moment losing sight of the truth that right now some freak could be drooling on Wendy or rolling her into a grave. When he remembered, he wheeled and glowered savagely at the phone as if he could intimidate it into ringing.

"How long you kept her around like that?"

"About five years."

"Five years!" Harry groaned. "And you're calling me a piece of work. You're gonna tell me she cooked and cleaned. So what? Meantime, you're checking into the motel every time you wanta score."

"I *didn't* score."

Harry flashed a grin that meant he'd finally caught on, seen how badly ol' Tom was ribbing him. "Get lost. I've seen you at the club, overheard the dames chatting. Hardly a one doesn't think you're hot stuff."

"Did I tell you I didn't have offers?"

"What're you saying here? That you're such a lame you get an offer from a piece of fluff like Ruby the croupier and you tell her to hit the road?"

Hickey stood up, turned sideways, stepped a couple of paces to where he could see out the window while keeping Harry and the doors to every cube in sight. "I say, 'No, thanks, babe. There's somebody at home. If she knew it'd break her heart.' " His vision had blurred, his temples throbbed fiercely. For a minute, all his will got spent to keep from grabbing the closest Formica and hurling it through the picture window.

Moonlight cast a greenish, fan-shaped stain on the water. Thousands of stars pulsated like the headlights of spaceships nearing earth. From a tourist lodge across the lake beneath the silvery, jagged Rubicons, lights blinked like someone in distress dispatching a signal. Hickey got elated with hope, for a second, until his heart received the news that lights from over there always seemed to blink. He groaned and flopped back into his chair.

"Okay," Harry said. "You telling me you did without, all those years?"

"Yeah."

"Naw. I don't buy it." The gambler had stiffened and begun shaking his finger like a scolding grandma. "I mean, you take some hermit, stick him out in Death Valley for five years, maybe he don't go crazy, long as he's got a fist and a couple pinups. But you're over there all this time, sleeping how far—how far can anybody get from each other in that shack of yours? Either you're giving me the business, Tom, or you're from Mars."

"Let's drop it," Hickey said sharply, and checked his watch. "Get back on the phone. To Charlie Schwartz. By now he's at the Golden Lion."

"Yeah, soon as you come clean."

"Do like I say," Hickey snarled.

"Sure. Just one question. Okay, let's suppose you're giving me the straight dope, that you managed five years or so rooming with a doll before you wised up—what I wanta know is how you did it? And *why*?"

"You do what you've gotta."

"What's that mean?"

Stressing most every syllable, Hickey said, "It means I couldn't risk shoving her back into hell. I had to wait till she grew up some, forgot some things, forgave herself for others. And till she quit wondering if every fella was a Nazi at heart." Scowling viciously, Hickey waved his .45 toward the phone.

"Chrissake." Harry groaned. "Five years!"

The aroma of baking bread wafted from the kitchen. Tyler stepped out and asked if anybody needed a drink or something. Hickey declined. The boss called for another ale; then, still wagging his head in consternation over Hickey's five years of celibacy, he slid to the end of the couch and dialed the operator, who switched him through to San Diego information. He got the number of the Golden Lion, a downtown supper club with a lounge where, according to Lieutenant Palermo, Charlie Schwartz held court most evenings.

After giving his name to the maître d' and waiting a couple of minutes, the boss growled, "Yeah, well, it's about time, Maurice." He turned to Hickey. "They're bringing him a phone....Yeah, Charlie, it's me. You got my message?...And you figured urgent meant something like tomorrow. I'll tell you what urgent means. There's a chump up here thinks he's gotta beef with you so he's threatening to whack me....Sure it's Tom Hickey. He's saying you sent some boys up to snatch his wife—who's my neighbor and a personal friend, by the way—and I'd appreciate you cut her loose....I ought to fix Tom, you say? How do I fix him when he's hiding out someplace? I only got a call from him, is what I told you."

Hickey caught himself biting his hand to restrain it from snatching the phone, so he could tell Schwartz what would befall him if the freaks didn't bring Wendy home. Except Schwartz should've already gotten that message, through Leo. Besides, Poverman could talk and deal without throwing a tantrum, and his lying might save Hickey's neck, if Schwartz's boys were speeding this way, cleaning and loading their machine guns.

The boss sat rubbing his eyes. "Yeah? Well, do me a favor. Tell whoever oughta get told that Tom damn sure left San Diego already. He's up here someplace....What old guy?"

As Harry sat listening, he wheeled on Hickey and rapped his knuckles on his forehead. "Yeah, Charlie. I'll pass it along, next time he calls."

Harry slammed down the receiver, missed its mark, hit it on the second try. "I just figured out why you live in a shack, Tom, why you gotta toot a horn to make change. You got no brains. Hell, you had me fooled. All along I took you for a sharp one."

"What'd he say about an old guy?"

"Some partner of yours name of Weiss. He pulled a move so crazy it makes your strategy look shrewd as one of Eisenhower's. He goes to Charlie, says there's some jerk works for the *LA Herald* is gonna rat on Mickey Cohen about a dirty deal he might've ran. Guns for Israel. Where Mickey set up that charity, raised a bundle. Your partner buys the rumor there wasn't any ship set sail, no ship went down at sea, only some *Herald* reporter scribbling what Mickey tells him to say. This what's-his-name …"

"Leo."

"…says to Schwartz, 'You get Wendy cut loose and this other dame sprung from the arson charge, I'll hand over this fink's name, you pass it on to Mickey.' Who's the old guy think he's messing with?"

Hickey sighed and rubbed one of his throbbing temples. "Leo's hated Mickey ever since back when. On account of he figures Jews more than anybody oughta play it straight, that whatever any one of 'em pulls gets pinned on the whole race."

"Yeah, well, he ain't the only Jew thinks that, but he might be the dumbest, going up against Mickey. Aw, hell, and I was dreaming another half hour, the Olds'd come rolling in with Wendy, let me get on over to the club. I got a business to run and a doll to meet."

"What else did he say?"

"Number one, you're screwy thinking he lit any fire or snatched the girl. Number two, it don't appear like you're backing off, as long as you're threatening me and sending the old guy around to put the squeeze on him and try to pin a bum wrap on Mickey." Harry flung up his hands in dismay. "Son of a bitch, I'm going stir crazy here. Hey, Tyler!" he shouted. "It's suppertime. Tom, how about a T-bone? Potato, salad?"

"Nothing," Hickey said. "Bring me the phone."

While Tyler appeared, walked over, and took the boss's order, Hickey called the operator and asked for Leo's number. The phone rang long enough for a tortoise to run a dozen laps around the tiny beach house. When the operator returned, Hickey gave her Leo's office number, which connected him to the answering service, a new girl named Susie who told him Mr. Weiss was out of town.

"Who's calling?"

"Tom Hickey."

"Ah-ha. Mister Hickey, I have to ask you a few questions. First, what was the name of your last captain on the LAPD?"

"Pepper. What is this?"

"Mister Weiss's orders, sir. And what kind of dogs does your sister breed?"

"Poodles, damn it. Ugly ones."

"Please, sir. Be patient. What's your daughter's birth date?"

"May ninth, nineteen twenty-eight."

"Bravo. Mister Weiss is waiting for your call. He's in the Los Angeles area, at Brentwood four-five-oh-five."

Hickey grumbled thanks and hung up. Repeating the number out loud, he rose and sidestepped to the Formica table, .45 in hand. He picked up the note pad and pen, jotted the number. He took the phone and sat back down. Holding the receiver between his shoulder and chin, he dialed O, got connected to the Las Palmas Motor Court in Los Angeles, and switched to the line for room 6. Midway through the third ring, Leo gasped hello.

"You been out sprinting?"

"Singing in the shower. What'd you think of my quiz game?"

"Never mind your quiz game. How the hell you figure you're gonna survive throwing beanballs at Mickey Cohen?"

"Survival ain't everything, Tom."

"Big talk. What're you doing in LA?"

"Disappearing, mostly. Keep from getting more bullets lodged in my front door. And tomorrow I got an appointment to see a guy."

"Who's that? Not some reporter who plans to snitch on Mickey?"

"There's no such guy, Tom. Wise up, will you? I'm going to see a fella named Gomez, FBI agent. You remember Arturo?"

"Yeah."

"His kid's a G-man. I figure he might shed some light on the action up your way, know some mob hideouts up there, give us a hand finding Wendy."

"Swell," Hickey said. "Now, you phone Charlie at the Golden Lion, tell him you're full of crap up to the eyebrows, and you were just blowing steam about this person who's gonna snitch on Cohen. And give him scout's honor that you're outta the whole deal, that Tom Hickey ordered you out, and that's where you're going. Got it so far?"

"I hear you."

"Don't go home. Stay hid. You put Vi somewhere?"

"Sure."

"Okay, then call Thrapp. Talk sense to him, how the shooting at your place and Angelo's boys waiting outside my place and Wendy getting snatched oughta make it a breeze for him to talk the DA into releasing Cynthia. Only make damn clear that Cynthia can't get sprung till Wendy's home. Cynthia walks, whoever grabbed Wendy'll get so steamed he'll ..." Hickey's jaw locked tight, of its own will.

"Yeah, Tom. I know what Charlie'd do."

"So you gonna lay off Mickey Cohen?"

"You got most at stake. You call the shots."

"Okay. I'll do that. Soon as you talk to the Gomez kid, get yourself up here. I need somebody to spell me, give me a chance to sleep, maybe do some legwork. How about it?"

"Soon as I talk to Gomez, I'm on my way."

"You driving?"

"Yeah."

"Call from Sacramento. I'm at Harry Poverman's place, Homewood six three three four."

As Hickey placed the phone on the tile floor beside him, Mac's Latin friend stepped out of the northeast cube, wearing a floral print dress that looked to pinch her everywhere and an ermine wrap. After shimmying halfway across the room, she stopped abruptly as if twenty feet was out of range of Hickey's gun. "So Harry, you send Mac to China?"

"Tokyo. Hey, Gloria, you're looking *fine*."

"Thanks. Only what am I supposed to do about it? Me and Mac was going on the town."

"How about you take the Jag, go on over to the club, and tell Pauline I'm indisposed. Tell her, any trouble, Big Steve can handle it. Tell her no phone calls to me. For nothing."

"Ain't the Jaguar gonna be freezing, Harry? Being a ragtop?"

"Naw. It's got a heater big enough for the Taj Mahal. Go on. Tyler'll give you the keys."

"Okay. When you see Mac, give him a big smack on the face for me."

"I'll do that, and you keep thinking, If word gets out Harry Poverman's letting a guy boss him around, Gloria had better hop a plane to Brazil."

Gloria shimmied and tugged down the hem of her dress, tossed her hair, turned, and swished toward the kitchen.

"Tyler," Harry shouted. "Give Gloria the Jag keys and get my dinner out here!"

The bodyguard poked his head out of the kitchen. "We figured you wanted the potato cooked, boss."

"Skin the damned thing and fry it. I'm starving."

Hickey gave up fretting about Leo, quit wishing the old man were here to make him laugh and breathe easier, to slap him around if he couldn't convince him with words that our fears are usually a whole lot worse than the plots our worst enemies devise.

He put the phone on his lap and dialed. On the fourth try he got a ring instead of the busy signal.

"Claire Blackwood."

"Any luck?"

"None so far, Tom, and I'm almost down to Placerville. Have you heard anything?"

"Only my partner Leo's on his way, first thing tomorrow, to give us a hand, in case we haven't got her back already."

"Tom, I've been thinking. Wendy's made it through so dog-gone much, I just know she'll come through this one too."

"Yeah. Sure, babe."

"Have you said your prayers?"

"Think that'd help, do you?"

"I don't know, except I believe sometimes people can talk to each other, heart to heart, even when they're distant. Maybe, if you said a prayer, Wendy'd feel it."

"Yeah, she'd get a kick outta seeing me on my knees."

"That would please her, all right. Only thing, Tom—remember to keep one eye on Harry while you're praying."

"Yeah. Claire, I got another errand. You holding up?"

"Just fine."

"Could you run to Stateline for me? In the Cal-Neva, talk to a bartender. He goes by Speedy. He's most always got rolls of Mexican benzedrine. Sells to the all-nighters. I'm gonna need the bennies sooner or later. And a couple sandwiches, and a thermos of black coffee would sure hit the spot. Oh, yeah, and a tin of Sir Walter Raleigh."

Chapter Fourteen

The few clouds over the lake were small puffs marbled black and gray. They kept shifting around like pods in a shill game. Hickey stood sideways at the window, glancing at his neighbor—asleep on the couch—and back outside. His lungs and head ached from smoking half a tin of tobacco and consuming nothing else except water from the pitcher he filled himself at the sink behind the bar. Several times he'd almost broken and ordered Harry into the kitchen where they could watch Frieda brew and pour him coffee without doctoring the stuff. But then Harry's boys might creep into the main room to hide and wait.

Hickey's mind skittered around so fast, it seemed all at once he was charged for action, about to collapse in fatigue, both heartsick and stalwartly hopeful. He needed to keep one eye on Harry and to spot Tyler if he came tiptoeing across the room, or Mac if he tried to sneak in one of the eight doors that led to decks or cubes. He kept staring at the lake. Always before, the sight of glassy water had slowed his brain, allowed him to focus. But tonight it was no use. His nerves sparked and quivered. At least every minute, a new vision of Wendy appeared. In one, she beamed like the day she learned they'd conceived. In another she lay dreaming or dead. Far too often, she lunged at him, screaming, her eyes bugged and teeth bared in fright. Like he hadn't seen her in three years, since the last, worst nightmare.

He turned back to the chair, slumped into it, and remained the way he fell, limp and awry as a tossed-off scarecrow, wondering how he could manage if the freaks knocked off Wendy or spooked her so bad her wits defected again, this time for good. Every life or death he imagined without her looked equally vile.

He could chase after the freaks or Charlie Schwartz, if he was the man. He could go berserk, swear vengeance against the whole Jew mob, team up with Leo against Mickey Cohen, either succeed or get smoked in the act. No matter which.

In the past, visions of revenge might've slightly appeased his distress. But no more, since Wendy had shaken his disbelief, gotten him crediting the idea of heaven and hell just enough so his bones chilled at the thought of serving an eternity in hell when he might've landed someplace else with her. Maybe this God of hers could forgive his rage. Probably not.

Forgive, he'd read somewhere, and you'll get forgiven. Then what? Dwell in a hammock on the back porch of his place on the bay? Mooch off Elizabeth and the bum? Walk the sand, swill wine, fall onto his knees in whatever alley he wandered at 2 A.M. and wait for the street sweeper's machine to run him down?

One thing sure. He wouldn't start again at forty-four years old after getting his guts kicked in twice. At some point, he mused, you've got to throw in the towel, figure it's no sense to keep punching, getting clobbered, heaving yourself off the mat and making your chin a target all over again, once you've decided it's a rigged fight anyway.

With his brain fervently engaged elsewhere, it took him a while to figure the cause of the sharp pain in his gut. Finally he realized and stood up, over the stockpot he'd gotten Frieda to bring. He unzipped and pissed loudly, the stream clanging on the metal. Harry rolled over, socked his pillow, doubled it over, wedged it back under his head, and muttered, "I'm waiting for one of us needs to crap. It's gonna be a sight. How about we get Frieda to immortalize it with the Kodak?"

"Sure. Make a blowup, hang it over the bar in the casino."

"I like that, Tom. Getting your sense of humor back?"

"Not a bit of it." While Hickey zipped his trousers and flopped into his chair, the gambler sat up. Hickey growled, "I'd as soon you went back to dreamland."

"Not a chance, now I caught a nap. I'm a light sleeper, especially when there's some dick pacing around, noisy as a tap dancer. Besides, guns make me edgy. I keep some of mine locked up in the closet, back in Tyler's room."

"I get it. Any second Tyler could pop me."

"Bingo! So why don't you give it up? You being unmolested eight, nine hours now—that oughta tell you I'm on the level."

"Or else you don't figure it's worth the risk crossing me, on account of you got nothing to lose by playing along, making some phone calls."

"Nothing to lose?" Harry's voice ascended to tenor. His fist shot up, then unclenched, leaving his palm out as though he were passing a candy. "I got nothing to lose if Cohen figures I'm siding against him?"

"Depends if you're a front man. Are you?"

"Hell, no! The club's *my* action. Nobody else's." Harry lowered his eyes, rubbed his brow, and said quietly, "I got a little help in the start. Not a dime from Mickey, though. Only thing, I don't treat him right, he buys the lot next door, builds a place ten times as swanky as mine. Or else he puts me outta business a faster way. See, Tom, it's why I don't vote Republican. A big boy can take out a little guy any time he wants. Nothing to lose, you say."

"Okay, you got that hand."

Harry sighed, gazed around. "Wanta play rummy or something?"

"Naw."

"Tell me a bedtime story?"

"Read a book."

"I hate books. I hate radio. I gotta *see* stuff. Soon as they build a station we can tune in from the basin here, I'm buying a television. You ever seen a television?"

"Sure."

"I know a guy down in Oakland, puts cellophane over the screen, it looks like it's in color. Swear to God."

Hickey nodded glumly, reached for the pitcher of water.

"Okay," the gambler said, "you don't wanta talk, I'm gonna pick your brain. What I wanta know is, how's a fella get so stuck on one doll that he's willing to give up fresh pussy for all time. Think about it, Tom—for all time! Awful. The whole idea sounds nuts to me." Staring at his fingers, he wagged his head like a scientist pondering a new and disturbing cosmology. "The way I figure, you treat the broads great. Give them stuff. Tell 'em they're gorgeous, mysterious, delightful to gab with and all. You make 'em feel like queens. Smart. Sexy. The whole deal. You even let them push you around, make like they got a ring through your nose. Give 'em a few months if you want. Four's tops. I mean, four months of your life is a big hunk. You gotta draw the line." He slashed the air with his hand, leaned back, and stared intently out the window.

Hickey stood up, looked outside, in case whatever had caught the boss's attention meant danger. All he noticed were moonbeams skittering across the lake, tree shadows rippling, a skyrocket that zoomed from the deck of a cruiser that chugged across the entrance to Crystal Bay.

He stood awhile marveling that a fellow could live as long as Harry without ever looking closely enough at a woman to notice the spirit that captivates a guy more even than a darling face or luscious figure can.

"You don't get married," Harry proclaimed. "It's a sucker's game. If nothing else, it ain't ever gonna last. One of you's gonna go fooling around. Somebody'll get bashed good. You ever married before?"

"Yeah. Sixteen years."

"Then what?"

"She ran off with my business partner," Hickey snapped.

"Bingo. Does Harry P. know what's up? How long ago?"

"Eight years."

"And you still got a case for her."

"A case *against* her. She took my daughter to New Jersey, introduced her to the country club set. That's where she met this no-good she married a couple years ago."

"You got a kid already, huh? She still in Jersey?"

"San Diego."

"You pals?"

Hickey shrugged. "She doesn't much like me hanging around on account of I'm nasty to the bum she married. He's a gin hound. She still figures she can reform him."

"Thinks she can love him off the sauce, huh?"

"Yeah. Same old story. How many reformed juicers you know?"

"Maybe one in a hundred."

"Meantime, she could've been a painter, a dancer. She always wanted to make stuff beautiful. She's sad, though. Real sad. Can't find a way to pull herself outta the garbage heap."

"See what you're doing, Tom?"

"What's that?"

"Why, you're making my point for me. So where do you get off thinking this marriage of yours is gonna endure?"

"Lay off," Hickey growled.

"Naw. I'm on a roll. Gotta play it out. See, on top of the fact marriage *always* stinks, you got other factors. Fifteen years from now, you're pushing sixty, your dick's in traction, she runs off with the preacher. You gonna tell me that can't happen?"

"Let's say I'm betting against it."

"Or else she finds a guy with a real house, while all you got's a log cabin. Betting against that too?"

"Yep."

"Why? Something peculiar about the gal. Tell me that—what made you so stuck on her? I mean, don't get me wrong. She's a dish and all. But we got no scarcity of dolls around here."

Hickey's eyelids felt heavy as theater curtains. His nerves and brain were on overload, flashing signs that warned any second the plant could shut down. Talking might at least help him disregard the signs until Claire showed with benzedrine, or coffee, at least.

"See, you know somebody awhile, or maybe you just met her. What she says, or a look she gives"—Hickey snapped his fingers—"just like that you see you'd never get tired of her, because no matter how much you learn about her, you're never gonna do more than scratch the surface. She goes too deep to ever fathom, but you wanta get as deep as you can. Like some explorer. Buck Rogers. It looks like she's got more mystery than you'd find if you climbed on a rocket to Mars. You never got that feeling, right?"

"Naw, but it sounds like a kick. So what'd she look like?"

"Who?"

"Wendy."

"When?"

"Like you said, when you first saw her this way you're talking about."

"Oh, yeah. It was just after my discharge. Fall of 'forty-five. We were driving up here on vacation to survey the lot, so over the winter I could do some sketches, make plans for building the cabin. Out of Sacramento, there was this gal talking on the radio. A Jap that spoke English just fine. She was telling about Hiroshima, day of the big boom. She said there was a flash, it felt like thick paint thrown at her. She figured heaven was falling. Said she ran for cover, pulling her son by the arm. And then her clothes were burning, and her son's too. They started ripping clothes off and their skin turned bright yellow. And her right arm was flaming at the root. And her kid was blind.

"I heard this whimper, looked over. Wendy was sobbing, real quiet, but hard all the same. I switched the radio off. But she flipped it back on."

"She change the station?"

"Nope."

"Why'd she switch it on?"

Hickey shrugged. "I've got an idea, that's all."

"Hey, I'll bet you figured half of her was a softy, but the other half was a ghoul. Makes her real complex. I know broads like that."

"You got it wrong, Harry. I figure she switched it on because she wanted to know the truth, no matter what."

For minutes, Hickey sat still, pictures of Wendy flashing like the frames of an old nickelodeon—as soon as he focused on each, it would vanish. Finally he caught one and held it: Wendy as she prayed, her hands folded and crooked under her chin, her head cocked a little, her eyes not quite shut, the lashes barely fluttering. Her face got so radiant, it stirred him as though seas had parted or a new star materialized before his eyes. Knowing Wendy, you didn't long for omens or signs. She was a daily miracle. Her hands unfolded and reached down to cradle her belly.

Hickey jolted up stiff. "This kid," he yelped. "I'm gonna do it right. This kid's gonna grow up straight. Happy."

"Take it easy, Tom. You fall dead of a stroke, somebody's gonna pin it on me."

"Go to sleep."

"Can't do it, pal. Mind if I use your pissoir?" Chuckling, Harry got up, walked over, stretching, unzipped, and half filled the stockpot. He requested permission to take it to the bar sink and dump it. Hickey shook his head. "Chrissake," Harry growled. "You got a clothespin, then?"

"You want it moved, wake up Frieda or Tyler."

"I get it. You suspect, when you follow me over to see I'm not grabbing a heater from behind the bar, Tyler's liable to dash out the door over here, plug you from behind."

"For all I know, Tyler might've rounded up his sidekicks and he's got one waiting at every door."

The boss chuckled grimly. "You think Tyler's that smart? Hey, Tyler!" he yelled.

In a few seconds, the bodyguard came bounding out of the northwest cube where he and the maid slept. In flannel pajamas. Rubbing his eyes with his fists. "Yeah, boss?"

Harry motioned to the stockpot. "Dump that mess in the john. Bring the pot back. Rinse it out first."

Tyler wrinkled his nose, grabbed the thing, and hustled off.

"Damn." Harry groaned. "We gotta keep this under wraps. I mean, people start talking about some guy can waltz into Poverman's own damn house, stick him up, boss him around like his name was Sachmo, make him piss in a tin can—you ever had a business, Tom?"

"Yeah. A few."

"What kind?"

"Chris-Craft dealership. Nightclub."

"Chris-Craft, no kidding. I've got four of those babies."

"Yeah. I've seen them."

"Well, then you know how it is. You wanta run a business, you gotta have respect. This gets around …" He drew a finger across his throat.

"I don't plan to go out bragging."

The gambler inspected his thumb and gnawed a hangnail. "Nightclub, you say? Same place I got started. Wanta hear about it?"

"Not particularly."

"Too bad for you. See, I was a waiter, this basement gin mill in Saint Paul, nineteen twenty-three, -four. Couple times a week, me and a fella called Bucky, on account of his teeth—pointed; they oughta called him Dracula—Bucky and me, we'd drive up to the border, make a pickup out in the woods, and …"

The first time Hickey caught his head nodding, he snapped it back upright and sat vaguely feeling like a louse because he didn't give a damn about the man's history. Only once every few minutes did his own concerns make way for a part of Harry's tale.

"… we headed for the coast, Bucky and me, bought a fish and grog joint on Battery Street, three blocks up from the Embarcadero. Bucky wanted to stay clean, strictly legit. We could've done it, made a go, all right; there wasn't much heavy action around, nobody stepping on us. But making a go's one thing. Cleaning up, hauling in enough to lavish it on the dames and speedboats, that's something else, I'll tell you. ..."

The second Hickey's eyelids fell, the brighter circuits of his brain switched off. For an age, it seemed, he floated in the bliss of forgetfulness. It looked like inside a rainbow.

A figure hovered over him. His eyes sprang open. The boss leaned toward him, his hand creeping out. Reaching for the gun.

Hickey's right foot flew up, sprang out. It launched the gambler backward, stumbling over his feet. He landed on the couch.

Collecting himself, impaling Hickey with his eyes, he snarled, "You shouldn't of done that, Tom."

Chapter Fifteen

A tamarack that rustled in a gusty wind kept slapping the wall of the cabin, directly outside from the corner where Wendy sat near the stove, wrapped in her patchwork quilt. On the other side of the stove, next to the bin of logs, the blond man lay sprawled on a bunk. He was so tall his legs from the knees down hung over the end. Beyond him, out the frosty window, the middle of the lake appeared dark and thick as oil. In the center, like a bull's-eye rose an island of pale gray boulders. The shoreline all around was fringed in ice.

The man about Tom's age, with the soft, pretty voice, stood washing a pan. Since they'd arrived, he'd been cleaning things. Mopping the floor and dusting the shelves. Sneezing a lot.

He set down the plate and turned around. Light from the hanging lantern sparkled off his bottle-thick glasses. "Goddam wind," he said. "Why don't you get off your can, Tersh, go out and hack down that branch?"

"Shut up. I was just nodding off."

"Sleep with that noise? Goddam wind, sounds like another lousy storm blowing in. How about this: we get snowed in. Two, three weeks, we're outta food. What do we do, cook the broad on a spit?"

"Sure," Tersh muttered. "I get the breast, you take the rump roast."

"Yeah, and a month goes by without a thaw. Foster's pal don't send an expedition to rescue us. With us and the doll starved to death, he saves a bundle. Suppose we already ate her, it's gotta be you gets cooked up next. You're twice as meaty as me."

"Shut up, Bud. What kinda dreams you think I'm gonna have, you talking that way?"

"You? How about the doll?"

Bud turned back to the sinkboard and picked up another dish, while the tall man rolled over, gave Wendy a leer and a wink. "Come on, join me, cutie." He patted the bunk, beside his hip. "Plenty of room. Hey, Bud, how about she wants some more of that tea, or hotcakes, she's gotta smooch for it. I mean, she oughta have to pay for her keep. It's only right."

"How do you feel about pregnant gals, Tersh?"

"Whatta you mean, how do I feel?"

"I mean do they get you hot, what else? Personally, I think they got a special kinda charm. You ever had one of 'em?"

"Not yet. Maybe soon as I wake up."

As long as Wendy kept praying, she didn't get too afraid. Her belly didn't cramp too hard. The chills didn't shoot down her arms or legs. Her eyes didn't blur.

Having already prayed a lot for Tom, baby Clifford, and Claire, she prayed for some people at church, ones she knew were sick or troubled. After those, she prayed for dead people. Her brother, Clifford. Their mama. Their beastly father, who needed forgiveness most of all. For Mr. Poe, whose stories had haunted her since last summer when she chose a book of his from the lending library at Pederson's store in the village. She often prayed for Mr. Poe, figuring he must've dwelt in torment, or else how could he write those things?

She sent off a prayer for the poor lady Tom had gone to rescue. When he learned that his wife and baby were in trouble, Tom might've left the poor lady in jail and come speeding to the mountains. Wendy knew Tom was searching, because the third or fourth time she'd asked the men why they'd snatched her, Bud said, "Hey, all I know's your ol' man got his nose stuck in somebody's affairs. And this somebody's the kind, you tweak his ear, he rips your head off. You wanta win, that's how you play the game."

Her mind struck up a hymn. It came loud, as out of a radio.

> *Far away in the depths of my spirit tonight*
> *rolls a melody sweeter than psalm.*
> *In celestial strains it unceasingly falls*
> *o'er my soul like an infinite calm.*

While she listened, she grew deeply sorry because wherever Tom was, he wouldn't be sleeping very well, because she hadn't been there to kiss him good night or rub his tight shoulders. He wouldn't sleep enough, she thought. He'd get too angry. His face would turn red. Blue veins would cross his brow. He might sock the wall—or somebody.

> *Peace, peace, wonderful peace,*
> *coming down from the father above.*
> *Sweep over my spirit forever I pray,*
> *in fathomless billows of love.*

When Tersh began snoring gruffly, Wendy sighed and felt her muscles loosen. He was the one who frightened her, the way he stared icily as if she were a page of numbers he needed to cipher. The way the Nazis used to stare. Ever since she'd gone to Hell, tall blond men most always spooked her.

The tree slapped louder against the wall. She gazed out over the lake to see if the wind had foamed the water, but it still looked flat and oily. Only along the far bank there were spots that gleamed on the ice, as though fishermen had arrived, with lanterns. Except lanterns ought to throw sharper beams. These were soft, as though from a light wrapped in gauze.

She didn't dare get up to look closer, or else Bud would shout and wake up Tersh, who'd yell and threaten and maybe smack her. Besides, her legs were numb, and one foot was sound asleep. She leaned forward, squinting toward the lights. The center of each beam seemed to hide behind the manzanita that lined the shore, on the bank about five feet up from the waterline.

Her heart thumped so loudly, she wrapped her arms in front of it to muffle the noise. The lights might be campfires, she tried to believe, though they didn't flicker. It could be Tom out there. Maybe with a gang of Mexicans like the ones that helped him snatch her out of Hell. She counted nine lights along the far shore. They might have the lake surrounded: Tom, and a bunch of Mexicans, and Clifford. Like before.

Her eyes flooded, because Clifford and two of the Mexicans were in heaven. Looking out through her tears, she narrowed her vision to the light straight across the water. It quavered and sent out ripples like the moon did after rain; then it took a shadowy form. First it became a thunderbird—Wendy had seen plenty of those in clouds. Suddenly it changed to an angel, flying sideways, its wings tucked as though for a dive.

Oh, God! Wendy's heart sang. Maybe Tom had rounded up a gang of angels.

Chapter Sixteen

Waiting felt like a crime against nature. It pressurized Hickey's brain, made it crackle and flare. If he could run around showing Wendy's picture to motel clerks and gas station people, roam the casinos bribing or slapping around tough guys in hopes they might spill something—all he needed was to feel that now and then he got a step closer to Wendy—he'd be okay.

But he couldn't drag Poverman to those places. The first chance, Harry'd thump him. Besides, the minute they stepped out, Angelo Paoli or Mickey Cohen might call with a deal. Or a pair of sharp-shooters, Harry's boys, might be hiding in the woods across the driveway to knock him off before he reached the car.

Too damn bad, he thought. I'm getting out of this prison.

The gambler was snoozing. Hickey got up and started to lap the room. Fatigued as he was, it looked like a quarter mile around.

He hadn't seen Tyler or Frieda in an hour. Out the picture window, the junipers swayed like hula girls and the lake rolled as though coming to a boil. A mass of black clouds had blotted the heavens. Hickey imagined hordes of evil warriors sweeping across the Rubicons.

He was startled by a sudden rumble; then two strokes of lightning blazed. A double blast of thunder rattled the window. Hickey'd never seen such lightning in winter.

The doorbell sounded. Harry sprang to life. Before he could shout for the maid, Frieda came shuffling out of the northeast cube, in a bathrobe, hair tied with a bandanna. She peered through the peekhole and opened the door. Claire rushed in. She stopped for a moment in the entryway and scanned the room, squinting into the dim light. There was only one lamp on, beside the couch where Harry sat, and some glowing coals in the fireplace.

She flicked a wall switch that brightened the entryway and crossed the room. "Sorry it took so long. I finally caught up with the benzedrine guy." She passed Hickey a small paper-wrapped cylinder, a thermos and a paper sack, and dropped into the couch, at the far end from the boss. "God, I'm beat. Aren't you?"

"Sure," Hickey said. "These oughta help. Thanks a million." He peeled the wrapping off the cylinder, tossed it onto the floor, and dropped all but two of the small white pills into his shirt pocket.

"Any news?" Claire asked.

"Not a word." He gulped the two pills and reached for the water pitcher, washed them down. "You see the lightning?" He opened the sack, grabbed one of the egg salad sandwiches and chomped it ravenously.

"I'll say. It scared the dickens out of me. How about you?"

"Woke me up a little."

"You okay?"

"Not so good," he admitted. "I'm going stir crazy, nothing to do except try and fool myself into thinking we'll get her back in one piece."

"We'll get her back," Claire said earnestly.

"Suppose we do. What chance she won't be loony again? I'm seeing her in a rocking chair, with big spooky eyes and scabs on her head from banging it against the wall. If I listen close, I can hear her bawling."

Claire sighed, folded her hands on her knees, and sat watching tenderly while he devoured the sandwich and carrot sticks.

"Last year when I wrecked the car," she said, "we were climbing out of the ditch....I thought Wendy'd be scared to pieces, the way she'd bounced around when we skidded off the road. I mean, she smacked into the roof and the dash and all, landed upside down with her head on the floorboard, between the seat and the gearshift. I thought sure she'd be screaming, but she was fine. Even laughed about it. And remember what I told you she said? She believed we would've flipped head over heels and tumbled into that gully, if the angels hadn't stopped us."

"Sure, I remember."

"As long as she doesn't give up believing in angels, Tom, she'll be all right."

Hickey tried to conjure a vision. The best he could dream up were cherubs and ghosts, just enough to lighten his heart for a minute. Until he remembered that angels don't always come to rescue people. Sometimes they carry people away.

The boss still sat looking sleepy and bewildered. Finally he slapped his face and rubbed it and asked Claire what she wanted to eat or drink. She declined anything, got up, went to the fireplace and tossed on a fat log, came back, and knelt beside Hickey.

"I might as well go out snooping around the casinos. I asked two palookas at the Cal-Neva what they'd heard about the kidnapping. Snuggled up close, batted my eyes, and still couldn't get a damn thing out of them. How about I go try South Shore, Harry's place, first?"

The boss gave her thumbs up and nodded. "Toss me the pad, Tom. I'll write a note that'll get Miss Blackwood all the drink tokes she needs and a couple boys to keep an eye on her, in case some jerk gets rude."

Hickey tossed the note pad and pen. "While you're at it, nose around some of the motels and lodges. Keep an eye out for the Olds, maybe show Wendy's picture around. There's a good one on the bookshelf by the hat rack." He fished in his pocket. "Want some bennies?"

"No, thanks. I'm wide awake and allergic to every pill ever invented. You want me to call, keep you posted?"

"You bet. Every hour or so. And keep checking in with Sheriff Boggs, see what they've got, keep 'em honest. If they ask about me, say I'm out snooping. Maybe the sheriff wouldn't be pleased about this." He lifted the .45, motioned it toward Harry.

"All right. Photo, motels, sheriff. I've got it." She rose, patted Hickey's skull, then bent and kissed it lightly. "Don't take too many of the pills, Tom. Just what you've got to, huh?"

Hickey squeezed her hand before she hustled across the room and out the door. He screwed the cup off the thermos, pried out the cork and poured the cup full, took a swallow, then leaned back, stuffed and lit his pipe, and sat blinking his eyelids so they wouldn't stick together before the benzedrine took hold.

The boss had sprawled lengthwise on the couch again, staring malevolently at the ceiling, as though he'd spotted a wasps' nest. "If you weren't spooked I'm gonna poison you," he grumbled, "I could give you prescription stuff, better than those Mexican jumping beans. I keep it around. You never know when some dame'll want to lose a few pounds quick."

"I'll keep it in mind," Hickey muttered.

"Say, what's with all the blab about angels?"

"Wendy believes in angels. Like I told you."

"How about that." The boss wagged his head pensively. "I've seen you two stepping out Sunday mornings. You go to that church up in the village?"

"Yeah."

"What's it get you? You sing in the choir, toot your clarinet?"

"Nope."

"What the hell's it get you then? You shout and stomp, figuring you're gonna land in heaven while the rest of us no-goods fry?"

"You wanta sit here and argue religion?" Hickey growled.

"We got something better to do? Tell me what's the point of this churchgoing, I'll shut up and snooze."

"Go to church, it makes you feel different, that's all." He caught the boss starting to object, raised his hand for silence. "Hold on. I'll tell you how Wendy explains it. She thinks we don't live with both feet in the world. Either the right one's gonna be in hell and the left on earth, or the right's on earth and the left in heaven. You go to church, it's like you shuffle your feet, that's all."

"You a believer?"

"Now and then. I'll tell you something, though. Wendy's not famous for her brain. Hardly one of your top intellectuals, and she hasn't got around as much as you or me. But I'd bet the pot she knows ten times more about God than either of us do. If she says there's angels around, you won't find me calling her a liar."

Suddenly he felt like a drunk, awash in self-pity, desperate for a lap to cry on. "She wants me to go to church, I go. See, I've known a lot of swell women, Harry. Seen them at their best. Dancing, dressed fit to kill, undressed. I guess I've seen 'em from most every angle. But I've never seen anything half so beautiful as Wendy when she lays her cheek on her hands and prays." He swallowed hard. "That by itself'd get me to church any day."

The boss stretched as though to brace up the ceiling. He almost reached it. "Hmmm. So, what about the Blackwood gal? She a churchgoer?"

"Not a regular."

Harry sat up and leaned on his hands, rubbing his chin and smiling pensively. "Claire," he mumbled.

Chapter Seventeen

Leo woke to the banging of garbage cans in the alley outside his bathroom window. He cussed and for a minute or so tried to muffle his ears with the pillow, but strategies for the day ahead already had chased off sleep. By the time he tossed the pillow, rolled across the bed, and grabbed his watch off the nightstand, his brain had slammed into second gear: 6:35 A.M.

He rolled to the other side of the bed, reached to the floor for a box of tissues, and took a couple out. After he blew his nose, he gathered the tissues he'd discarded during the night, rolled each one into a tiny ball, and sailed them across the room, into the trash can under the floor lamp. Seven for seven. Five swishes and two caroms.

The old man stretched his legs. Groaned. Heaved himself up and staggered into the bathroom just as the trash men slung the cans off the truck so they banged on the pavement, rattling Leo's head. He yanked down the window and tugged the curtains together. While the water ran to hot, he splashed his face, got out his shaving brush and soap. He lathered, brushed. Picked up his Gilette and began scraping while he reviewed the day's itinerary.

Breakfast at the Spring Street Café, near the Federal Building, where Preston Gomez, the son of his old partner, Arturo, had promised to meet him at the entrance, eight o'clock sharp.

Talking Preston into running a scam against Mickey Cohen was going to require a slick pitch, though all he planned to ask was that they drop a word on the street about how the G-men had gotten handed new evidence in the Guns for Israel fraud.

Gomez would pry. Refuse to budge until Leo'd spilled the whole story. So Leo'd have to decide between the truth and a whopper, if he could dream one up by then. At lying, he'd never rank better than amateur. On the other hand, he'd spun quite a yarn to Charlie Schwartz.

If he gave Preston the truth, he could already hear the kid's rebuttal. If he admitted the lie he'd fed Schwartz—that there was a *Herald* employee who'd deduced that the stories about the Guns for Israel ship sailing and sinking were crap, and nothing but, and said employee was about to go public—"Oh, swell," Preston would say. "Mickey chooses a *Herald* writer who's called him a louse once or twice, decides he must be the guy. Knocks him off."

While he made the second pass over his stubble, Leo rehearsed his counterargument. Cohen, he'd contend, would realize that the only way they could pin the fraud on him was if the reporter who'd gotten Mickey's lies committed to newsprint—confessed that Mickey'd bribed or muscled him into writing the tall tale. So, rather than knock off every *Herald* employee, from editor to paper carrier, Mickey'd hit his own stooge. The G-men would be shadowing the reporter; they could nab Mickey's boys in the act. Maybe this time one of them would rat on the boss. Anyway, by now the reporter's prepped to sing like Caruso, since he's on Mickey's goodbye-card list.

No doubt Preston would argue, "Yeah, and suppose Cohen's boys sneak up and pop this reporter before we can grab them? It leaves him paying damn high for writing a couple phony articles."

"Nope," Leo'd say. "What he's paying for is throwing in with Mickey." In Leo's book, Cohen was page one. If Leo had gotten to choose between skewering the gangster or Hitler, Adolf would've been pleased. "See," he'd tell Gomez, "if you collar Mickey's boys doing the reporter, they're left standing with their dicks in the meat grinder. One of 'em's liable to get more spooked of the Rock or the gashouse than of Mickey."

If that didn't win Arturo's son over, Leo thought, the kid was a bonehead.

He brushed his teeth, rubbed down his scalp, ran a comb through his short wiry hair, and stuffed all his gear into a drawstring pouch. He left the bathroom, stood in the open space near the front door, and bent to see if he could still touch his toes. The third try he got within a few inches. He changed his underwear and put on a clean shirt, his brown trousers and coat, and a tie covered with stars and tiny half moons.

He sat on the bed, gazed around to check if he'd forgotten to pack anything, and ruminated about whether to fly or drive to Tom's place. The eight- or nine-hour drive would be cheapest, but he might cut off three, four hours by flying to Sacramento, then renting a car for the trek up the hill. Besides, that way if he skidded on ice and crashed, he wouldn't dent his Packard, which lately had been puffing like it was on the homestretch. If he made it climb the Sierra Nevada, he might have to send the old workhorse out to pasture.

There was a phone booth next to the motel office. He still had time to call Tom; maybe Schwartz had bought his yarn and cut Wendy loose already. Then, Leo wondered, should he still try to burn Mickey? "Yeah," he muttered. He'd already barged into the lion's den. They couldn't kill him twice.

He felt a little traitorous for lying to Tom about why he'd set up a meeting with Gomez. How he'd claimed Gomez might pass him some dope on mob hideouts around Tahoe, places worth looking for Wendy. That'd been an ad lib. He wasn't thinking about Wendy, not when he called Preston. He was trying to bag Mickey. Although squeezing Cohen *might* save Wendy's neck, keep her alive until Tom located her. With the pressure on, so Mickey or Schwartz might have to use her, say for a phone call to Tom, more likely they'd keep her alive. Release the pressure, they finish her off.

He might've spelled that out for Tom, except Tom couldn't see straight, disturbed as he was. When he got this agitated, like eight years ago in TJ, Tom didn't listen to reason. He got fanatical and bossed you around.

Leo put on his hat, checked its angle in the mirror, grabbed his satchel, and stepped outside.

An old acquaintance sat waiting, chin on his fist, elbow on his knee. On the right front fender of Leo's car.

His real name was Gregory something. You only called him Bass when you were out of range. He'd gotten tagged with the nickname when a mercury-based medicine for some disease tinted his flesh, gave it a scaly grayish sheen. Framed by that skin, his eyes looked yellow. His nose was round and dark, like a bonbon. He slid off the fender, hand in his overcoat. Sauntered over to Leo. His lips hardly moved, only quivered as he said, "Lemme carry your suitcase."

"Where to?"

"The car. Around the corner. Go on, you'll see it. Big pea-green Lincoln." He bent and swept his free arm like a matinee butler. "On second thought, you carry the suitcase. It ain't so far."

"Tell you what," Leo said. "I'll throw the satchel in my car and pull around the corner. Wherever it is we're going, I'll follow you."

"Step on it, wise guy."

"What you got in the pocket, hardware?"

"Yeah. Wanta see?"

"Sure," Leo said, hoping to God somebody would be watching, notice the gun, scribble the green car's plate number, and call the law.

Without lifting the gun from his pocket, Bass jammed the barrel into Leo's gut. "See it? Now move along, Pancho."

Leo walked ahead, slowly, hoping for a break: an open doorway he could duck through or somebody he could flash a hand signal to. Bass nudged him along, around the corner and toward the long green two-door Lincoln.

The shotgun door flew open. The man who stepped out looked dressed for a ball: a pin-striped black three-piece suit, tie of rich maroon, black shoes glossy as patent leather. His hair matched the shoes. Sleek and lush, it cascaded straight back into a ducktail. He stepped aside. Bass grabbed Leo's bag, dropped it on the sidewalk, gave Leo a nudge, then a push into the front seat.

"Denny, you drive Pancho's junk heap. It's the Packard that needs a paint job."

"I should maybe run it through Earl Scheib's," the sharp dresser said.

"How about it, Pancho? You got twenty-nine ninety-five?" Bass either coughed or laughed and jabbed Leo's arm. "Toss me the keys."

"Hand me the satchel, then."

"Tell you what. You live through the day, I'll buy you a new wardrobe."

"You want the keys, hand me the satchel," Leo commanded.

Bass offered a genuine smile. "This guy's a card, Denny. I like him just fine." He picked up the satchel, dropped it across Leo's knees. The old man dug into his trouser pocket, fished out his keys, pulled two of them off the chain, and handed them over.

As his partner turned toward the motel, Bass jammed the front seat backrest forward and climbed in behind Leo. "You got a piece in the bag, right?"

"Yeah," Leo snapped. "Any second I'm gonna unzip the satchel, dig for the gun, whirl around, and shoot you between the eyes so fast you won't see it coming."

"That won't do, will it, Jeeves?"

The driver, a sandy-haired neckless kid, turned and scowled. "Jeeves. A guy takes the wheel, you gotta smart off and call him Jeeves. Maybe you're mad at the guy. That it, Bass? On account of you can't drive?"

They pulled from the curb, swung a U-turn at the intersection, headed west on Pico.

Bass must've lost his edge, Leo thought. Twenty years ago, even the boss, Arnold Rimmer, wouldn't use his nickname. Now, he took guff from a kid. The driver had to be underage. He looked built out of stacked boxes. He had soft, beardless cheeks, blond fuzz on his chin. His hairline ran straight across the middle of his forehead.

The traffic was jumpy, every other driver hunting for a parking spot in front of the laundry or the dime store. The sun looked brownish and timid, as though sure to lose its battle with the haze. Something sharp as an ice pick jabbed Leo's neck at the base of his cranium. "Grab the dashboard, Pancho. Keep your mitts up there."

Leo obliged. The blade pricked deeper. Leaning forward, hands on the dash, he breathed rapidly through his nose and between his teeth, until his heart quit stammering. "You wanta dab the blood off my neck, Bass?"

"Mister Kitain to you, Pancho."

"Guys I call mister gotta deserve the respect."

"Hey, I'll work for the honor. What's it gonna take?"

"For a start, explain why you're shoving me into a car and poking me with a shiv."

"Got you stumped, huh? See, we're kinda like vigilantes. Somebody calls, says this old fool's spreading lies, making threats against one of the pillars of our community, we gotta take care of it. Else what kinda vigilantes would we be? Wanta know where we're going, what for?"

"What you oughta be doing is taking me to Mickey."

"Mickey who? Hey, I get it. Mickey Mouse. You wanta go to the movies. Naw, first we're gonna go to this place nobody'll hear you scream. Then we put you through all kinds of jolly fun till you spill the name of this punk says Guns for Israel was a fake. Next we go visit the punk, us and you, if you come clean early and still got all your major parts. Finally, we all reach an understanding."

"You a Jew?"

"Naw. Maybe I oughta convert. You think?"

"Yeah, after you tell Mickey he stinks worse than I figured, sending a goy out to knock off a Jew."

"Mickey again. So, after I give this message to Mickey, anything you want me to tell Donald Duck?"

"Yeah. Tell Donald to tell Mister Kitain to kiss my ass."

Bass made clucking sounds and patted Leo's shoulder.

After a minute of silence, the driver said, "Why'd you guys cut the routine, just when I was thinking you could hunt up a sponsor, take it on the radio?"

Leo glanced up at the stoplight ahead. At the far corner, around the bus stop, a dozen people stood. If the light changed in time, caught them on the red, Leo figured maybe he could throw some line of gab that'd catch Bass off guard, give him a jolt, a second of inattention. A chance for Leo to sling open the door and bail.

The light changed. The driver braked. Leo spotted the door handle, tensed his fingers in readiness. The instant he opened his mouth, hoping for something inspired to leap out, a dreadful idea froze him. These guys might've gotten to Vi. Fright weakened the muscles of his neck. His head fell forward and his mouth went dry. Phlegm began dripping out of his nose. "How'd you find me?" he rasped.

"Easy, Pancho. A pal of ours has a talk with your answering service. Susie, right? He sees her home, makes sure she gets there safe. In return, she gives him your number. He calls us, et cetera."

They swung north onto Fairfax Avenue. The beauty parlors, laundries, and service stations gave way to rows of double-floor eight-plex apartment buildings with ornamental iron-barred windows and dwarf-sized balconies, tiny lawns dotted with yellow dandelions. A few blocks south of Wilshire, Leo got his first whiff of the tar pits. In the park that surrounded them, he used to find his daughter Una sprawled on the grass in winter or under the shade of a live oak in summer, dreaming herself into prehistoric times. Back when she was whole. Before the summer she visited Austria and got beaten. Picnicking beside the Danube when some Nazi was giving a harangue and she couldn't hold her yap shut. Before the quacks declared her a schizophrenic and Leo had to question how they got away with calling schizophrenia a disease, when Una got it beat into her.

At Wilshire, the driver jumped the last instant of the yellow light, caught the red halfway through, and got awarded a symphony of horns.

Now Fairfax was lined with jacarandas, palms, elms, birds-of-paradise. Houses that Hansel and Gretel might've eaten. British cottages with mock-sod roofs. Moorish haciendas built to one-fifth scale with minaret towers where madam stored her linens. Everything that used to look silly stabbed Leo with nostalgia today. He and the girls used to live three blocks west of Fairfax in a bungalow that'd once been a duplex, with a courtyard in the middle. Out of all the stuff to remember, he wondered, what would be tops? What would blaze in his mind the last thing before he died?

As they turned right on Sixth Street he wondered what kind of prisoner he'd make. For sixty years he'd tried to imagine, ever since the first story he'd read or somebody'd told him about a firing squad and prisoners lined up against a wall. There was a swaggering colonel with a long waxed mustache, at least one prisoner down on his knees, whimpering, besides the hero who casts around his undaunted stare and, when offered a smoke, takes one puff and spits the cigaret onto the dirt. His eyes are clear and gleaming, because he sees all the way to glory.

Those sixty years had included the battle for Manila, infantry, First California Brigade, police work long enough to get him retirement pay, and private snooping ever since, yet up until now he'd never thought of death as quite so near. There'd been plenty of close calls, only none he'd had leisure to think about until they were past.

He puzzled about why it is that the older you get, when you'd figure on growing bolder since every day there's less to lose, usually the opposite befalls you. Peculiar, he thought, how at nineteen years old you could charge the battlements against Gatling guns and still feel immortal. It's later that death starts sinking in, as if something in your brain doesn't form until maturity. Like wisdom teeth.

The tires screeched, dragging both right sidewalls against the curb. Leo raised his head, snuffled, saw a yellow wooden house trimmed in white, frilled with lace curtains and fringed shades on pole lamps at each of the front windows. Suddenly his throat tickled, made him cough. Part two of the grippe he'd been fighting.

Take a puff of the cigaret and spit it out, he thought. Any way you play it, you're dead. Mickey's punks have got the numbers, the weapons, the muscle. Sure, they're not too bright, but you're no Einstein either.

The only hope, all he could list on his side, was a strangely calm feeling, as though peace was his destiny from now on. Almost as if he were already dead and looking backward.

"Bass," he said coolly. "How about I move my arms now? Else I'm gonna blow my nose on your floorboard here."

"Go on, get out."

Leo straightened up, opened the door, hoisted the satchel, and stepped onto the sidewalk. He plucked the handkerchief out of his coat pocket, blew his nose. Checked up and down the street. Nobody was out mowing, pruning, waiting for the mail. A tidy neighborhood of bungalows wedged on narrow lots between smallish Victorians and double-deck haciendas surrounded by orange trees and agave.

Leo watched his Packard pull in behind the Lincoln. Seeing the old workhorse racked him with a deep nostalgia. The first year they owned it, the summer of 1939, he and Vi and the girls had driven all the way to Oklahoma, feeling like kings of the road. He stood still a moment, hoping that dead guys didn't have to look back. Missing what you'd left behind could be hell.

Bass took his arm, like somebody leading a blind man. The driver and Denny the clotheshorse fell in behind. In the rose garden off the front porch lay a toppled FOR SALE sign. SAND DOLLAR REALTY. Leo'd seen plenty of those signs around San Diego. Charlie Schwartz's brother Al used to run the business, before a stroke knocked him out of the ring.

"Classy joint, huh, Pancho?"

"You got a nickname for everybody, Bass?"

"Fair's fair, ain't it? You know anybody calls me Gregory?"

Denny had stepped around, flung open the screen, and unlocked the door. The others followed him inside, over shellacked hardwood floors, past a green velvet wingback chair, through a dining room furnished in dusty maple, the table littered with empty beer bottles, ash trays, and a scattered deck of cards adorned with loud pink flamingos. Off the dining room, beside the archway that led to the kitchen, there was a door. Denny opened it. The stairs beyond the doorway led downward.

Denny stood aside. Bass ushered Leo in front of him. "Toss the suitcase, Pancho."

"Naw, I'll take it along."

The fist came out of nowhere, a roundhouse. It smacked Leo in the gut, dead center. As the old man gasped and heaved forward, the driver grabbed his satchel and slid it across the floor. Denny turned Leo toward the stairs. Bass gave him a shove.

"You in the market for a house, Pancho? This baby's got it all. How many basements you find in LA?"

Wheezing, staggering, Leo made his way down the staircase into clammy darkness. His head felt as if it were bouncing between the two walls.

Dripping water splashed somewhere. The only daylight entered through a screened slit near the ceiling, along what Leo figured must be the rear of the house. He tripped on the bottom stair. Tumbled to his knees on the basement's concrete floor. He stayed there until the overhead light flashed on. Denny had found the chain and pulled it.

Except for a stack of wood in the corner and an old trunk beside it, the basement was empty. Bass told the driver to run up and bring some chairs. He scrutinized the room for a minute, then directed Denny to grab one of those boards and wedge it in between the ceiling and the concrete, to cover that air hole.

"We gotta have a little air, Mister Kitain."

Bass wheeled and jabbed Denny in the chest with a finger. "You think we oughta talk this over, that right?"

"No, no, I'll just do like you say."

Leo was rising to his feet when Bass gave him a two-hand shove that knocked him stumbling across the floor and into the wall beside Denny, who stood pounding on a board with the heel of his hand. As Leo smacked the wall, his legs buckled and he dropped. The back of his head bounced down along the wall.

"Denny, long as he's got his legs like that, kick him in the nuts."

"This board ain't quite right yet."

"Shit. I gotta do it myself?"

Grumpily as a harried schoolmaster, Bass walked over and gazed down at Leo, who was trying his damnedest to squeeze his legs together. They wouldn't budge except to hop an inch or two off the ground. As Bass drew his foot back, Leo noticed the pointed toe, about a second before it hit him. It seemed to split him in two, at least chest high, and fill his belly with Ping-Pong-sized fireballs. All he did right was yell. Because Denny hadn't yet wedged the board tightly into the air slit, though Leo's head bobbed like a guy drowning in high seas, he managed a howl that could've brought a less sturdy house crashing upon them. Maybe somebody outside would hear.

"The old man's got a fine set of lungs. Denny, grab that other board and bust his ribs, will you?"

Denny gave the board in the air slit a last whack. "Sure." He stepped to the woodpile.

The driver appeared at the foot of the stairs, cussing the effort of trying to juggle two wooden captain's chairs. Denny picked up a two-by-four about five feet long and stood with it balanced on his shoulder like a rifle at shoulder arms.

"Pancho, what'd you say that fella's name was, the one works for the *Herald*? The fanatic?"

Leo managed to hold up his hand and wrestle for a minute with the question of whether he ought to confess that his story about a snitch was a lie. If he confessed, even if they believed him, they'd still finish him off. If he stuck with the lie, maybe at least he could set up the reporter Mickey had in his pocket. One less stooge.

Leo dropped his hand and mumbled the name of Mickey's reporter.

"Naw." Bass groaned. "You and me both know he ain't about to tell some lie that lands him on the rock. You a little confused, Pancho?"

"He's gonna snitch," Leo croaked, just before a fit of coughing racked him. Through the haze that whirled in front of his eyes, he glimpsed Denny lifting the two-by-four.

It caught him low in the chest, felt as if he'd swallowed a grenade. It blasted all the way to his toes, his fingers. Pounded against his skull. For a few seconds, he held still; then he started shaking like a fish trying to lose the hook.

"Look at the old guy go," Denny exclaimed.

"You really mashed him," the driver said. "Maybe we oughta put him outta his misery."

Bass gave a sigh of distress. Probably at the plight of having to work with morons. "Swell. We don't get the name, and we gotta sit here till dark with a corpse, and by the time we lug him out he stinks bad."

As the shaking eased, Leo toppled onto his right side. By now the pain centered in his chest. Like a vise coated in broken glass, cranked tight. He started breathing in short gasps. The effort filled half his mind. The other half, he focused on a tiny spot just above his solar plexus, where the pain was sharp but tolerable.

"Want me to bust him again?" Denny asked.

"Not yet. Give him a breather. We got all day."

"Lunchtime," the driver said. "We oughta leave him take a nap and us go down to that Mexican joint back on Pico. What's it called?"

"La something," Denny muttered.

Bass placed two fingers on the bridge of his nose and rubbed gently. He backstepped and dropped himself into a captain's chair, leaned forward, rested his chin on his fists, and gazed around the room like a guy who's worked in the same office a few years too long, who's counting the days until he can retire.

Chapter Eighteen

The sky had been gray-blue for an hour or so, but now the sun had topped the ridge and forest across the lake, lighted the angry black clouds as they fled south. It sparkled on the water, gleamed off the glacier-polished boulders. The shoreline fringed in ice flashed like a shattered mirror.

Wendy sat by the window. The man named Bud had let her move to the other chair. Hands resting on her belly, she felt Clifford squirming. She wondered if he'd be a terror, the kind you have to watch every second or else he'll bust stuff or disappear. She wondered if he'd have a notch in his chin like Tom did, or Tom's shiny blue eyes.

Bud sat in a rickety chair that squeaked with his every move. He used a tiny whetstone to sharpen a giant carving knife like the one Tom had saved from the restaurant he used to own, when he was married to the lady. Elizabeth's mom. Wendy called Tom's first wife "the lady" because she looked so grand in pictures. Besides, it saddened Wendy to say or even think the lady's name. Especially after she'd read Mr. Poe's story about the Usher family where another lady with the same name, Madeline, gets so sick people think she's dead. They lay her in a casket in the cellar but she scrapes and kicks at the lid, yet they don't understand the noise until finally they hear her muffled screams. The horrible thing—though Mr. Poe didn't write it, Wendy could feel the girl's horror—all Miss Usher wanted was to die or get well, either one. But God wouldn't set her free.

For days after reading the story, Wendy'd fretted about why God wouldn't spare the lady. Even if Mr. Poe made up the story out of nothing, God *did* let some people suffer that way. Twice since reading that story Wendy'd gotten a nightmare, the same both nights, about a house where she and Claire were visiting because it was for sale. It was far from the village, but Claire liked it and talked of moving there. So Wendy was already sad when they stood in the parlor and she heard scrapes, knocks, muffled screams. But she couldn't tell where they came from. Claire said maybe there was a cellar. They spotted a cellar door and ran for it, threw it open, and plunged into the darkness.

Both times she'd woken up just then, before she had to scream. So Tom didn't know about the nightmare. If she'd told him, he'd have worried awfully. She only told Claire, who didn't worry as much, though she'd taken Mr. Poe's book, traded for Willa Cather, and promised a new book every time Wendy finished the other. Claire was trying to protect her from scary authors like Mr. Poe.

But once you'd read a story, it was part of you.

Here in captivity the plight of Miss Usher gripped her heart once again. She heard the girl's frantic howling, her bloody fingers clawing the coffin lid, the coffin nails creaking as the girl thrashed harder.

Wendy riveted her eyes on the bank across the lake, where a gray fox had stood a few minutes before until something made him jump straight up on all four legs and spook off into the brush. Maybe, she wished, he saw Tom or one of his angels.

Tersh slammed through the cabin door. "Goddam jalopy won't start."

"It turn over?" Bud asked.

"Yeah, at first."

"You cranked it dead?"

"How else I'm supposed to get it started, I don't crank it?"

"Wait till the day gets warmer, that's how."

"Yeah, well, I'm sick of waiting. We been here a day and a half. The rat was supposed to show this morning, first thing."

"He found a dame, spent the night at Harry's, that's all. He's sleeping in. Maybe he'll play a couple hands of blackjack. Then he'll be here."

"*He* found a dame," Tersh growled. "Son of a bitch promised to show this morning, take the milkmaid off our hands, so we can get down to Harry's and *I* can be the one finds a dame." He stepped closer to the wood stove, peeled off his gloves, and slung them onto the floor. Rubbing his hands, he crooked his head, gave Wendy a leer. "Hey, Bud, don't she look like one of those girlies in the picture book wears the wooden shoes and the stupid hat looks like it's made out of a handkerchief? She's going out to milk the lousy cows, only she don't mind, she thinks it's peachy. You wanta know why she's happy? I'll tell you why. She's too dumb to know any better. That's why."

Bud studied Wendy awhile. "Must be. Hell, she doesn't hardly ask questions. Won't beg us for anything. Hasn't cried once. That's gotta be it, Tersh. Awful dumb."

"Whatta you suppose this guy—what's his name?"

"Jack."

"How you think he'll get rid of her?"

"Shut up, Tersh."

"Aw, you worried I'll frighten the dolly? Hey, let her sweat. This smiley-face act is getting on my nerves. Check her out, Bud, she still ain't sweating. Looks like she's waiting for the postman to bring her a Valentine."

In two strides he reached her and bowed his head, wrinkling his nose and grinning wide, lifting his brows to enlarge his eyes, which looked like prunes floating in soapy water. His hands came around from the sides and touched her cheeks.

Wendy bit her lip and pinched her eyes closed. His fingers were rough, like Tom's had been while they were building the cabin. Like her pa's and Clifford's used to get when they were farmhands. They scraped down the height of her cheek, down her neck, out across her shoulders, under the shirt until a button popped. His teeth clacked as if he'd soon bite her nose. Wendy felt her spirit compress, the way it used to: from a power that lit and flooded her body to the size of a pellet, a little petrified thing.

Tersh yelped. His head whipped backward and his hands flew back with the rest of him. His face contorted into a Halloween mask.

Bud laughed raucously. "She give you a kick, Romeo?"

"Naw—shit, ow! It's like pincers. Like they caught me right here." He pointed to both sides of his head behind the ears. "Oh, hey!" He flopped into the chair and rubbed his eyes and forehead with both hands. "Feels like I got conked with a sledge."

"Headache?"

"Yeah. Aw, yeow! I musta pulled something chopping that lousy wood. Yeah, that's it." He reached to the woodbox beside him, grabbed a stick, and hurled it at Bud, missing by several feet. "From now on, I'm the nursemaid while you do the dirty work. Hey, bring me a damp cloth or something, will you? This is a killer."

Wendy sat making herself breathe steadily, to fool Clifford so he'd feel safe, and shading her eyes from the glare that'd filled the room, as if the sun had raced down and perched just outside the window. The flash had come so bright and sudden that she'd hardly noticed Tersh back away, and the cabin had filled with dots of flame yellow and blue that gradually dimmed until she saw them like tiny birds that slowly flew away. And now that she could see Tersh and Bud leaving her be, a pretty tune filled her mind.

> *The angels so sweetly are singing,*
> *up there by the beautiful sea,*
> *the chords of their gold harps are ringing,*
> *how beautiful heaven must be."*

At first it was a single voice, maybe her own. For the chorus, a choir joined in.

> *How beautiful heaven must be,*
> *home of the happy and free.*
> *A haven of rest for the weary,*
> *how beautiful heaven must be."*

On the last notes, they'd reached a crescendo. The next moment, a stony silence fell. Suddenly, for no reason she could figure, Wendy found herself whispering, "Thank you, Zeke."

About ten times she whispered the same thing, before she stiffened and her fists slapped against her cheekbones.

"Oh, no," she groaned, and sat trembling in wait for her mind to whirl away into the starry regions beyond heaven, so distant maybe God wouldn't follow you there. To the place where she'd fled from the Nazis, from where it takes years to come home. "No!" she shrieked. "I'm staying here with Tom and Clifford!"

Tersh shot her a petulant glare, as if she'd been the one who'd conked him with the sledge, and mostly it'd hurt his tender feelings.

"What's your beef now?"

"Oh, I'm going crazy," she moaned.

Chapter Nineteen

After four bennies, Hickey'd been pacing and sucking his briar as though to interrupt either occupation would invite catastrophe. Just for the sake of moving, he would've allowed Harry to shoot pool, except while they were in the other cube, the front room might get occupied. He'd return to find a gunman crouched behind every piece of sofa, a platoon around back of the bar.

Besides, what he needed wasn't another room but to get clear out of this hideous joint before he gave over to his impulses and blasted chunks out of the Formica, heaved a chair at the snake pit, set fire to a pile of sofas.

The boss sat glowering, restlessly tapping his feet. They thumped the tile floor like jungle drums in a fierce rhythm that would settle in, then break stride, as though to annoy Hickey deliberately. Punish him for refusing to let a man shoot pool.

Outside the picture window, aside from the snow, which in sunny places was already melting, the day could've passed as summer. The noon sky was cloudless, the lake placid except where boats or currents meeting stirred up ridges and arrowheads of foam. Squaw Peak reflected so brightly it could've been a glacier rising out of the lake. Off the point at north stateline, a funnel rose. A summer squall out of season, Hickey thought, or a gambler who'd dropped his life savings and discovered a new and spectacular way to throw a fit.

Hickey stopped pacing to listen. He thrust his left hand, palm out, at Poverman and glared until he got silence. For the past half hour he'd kept hearing sticks crack, out in the woods on the south side. It might've been innocent horseback riders cutting through Harry's tamarack grove, or a gang of thugs intent on delivering their boss, maybe getting a bonus or a raise by wasting the intruder.

Tyler was still in the northeast wing with the maid. A few times every hour, Frieda would cut loose a burst of hysterical laughter, as though Tyler were tackling, and tickling her.

The phone rang. Harry slid across the couch and grabbed it. He listened a second, then bolted up straight.

"Hey, Mister Cohen, thanks for calling....Yeah, business. See, I got this neighbor, helps me out at the club. Straight arrow, ex-cop. You know, somebody's pocketing dimes, Tom's gonna snoop out the right guy....Tom Hickey....Sure it's a stupid name. ...

"See, Tom got into a jam down in San Dago. Trying to spring this old smooch of his they say put a match to Johnny Sousa. You know about that guy, right?...Sure. Well, Tom got in a hurry, smarted off at Schwartz and Paoli....Yeah, sure he's a moron, else he wouldn't of been a cop.

"But look, somebody snatched his wife. She's gonna have a baby any day now. What I'm asking is you pass the word down to Dago, say whoever nabbed her, toss her back. Tom's outta the deal, learned his lesson. He gets the girl, that's all there is. He tries to get even, I ax his lousy head off....Yeah, I'm done....Yeah, I get it....Sure, sure."

As the gambler made a sour face and replaced the phone, Hickey snapped, "What?"

"Let me think a minute," Harry growled. He stood up, spun on his heel. Kicked the sofa arm. "Okay. Mickey says he don't know from nothing about the Sousa fire or anybody's wife, or any jerk named Hickey except one used to have a partner named Leo—"

"Weiss."

"Yeah. Mickey says the next word he hears about Guns for Israel, guys are gonna start having accidents. He says the first one'll be this character Weiss."

Hickey jumped up. Revolver at his side, he edged over and grabbed the phone, carried it back to his chair. He checked the note pad and dialed the operator, gave her the Brentwood number of the Las Palmas Motor Court.

The desk clerk sounded like she had a bellyache. "Leo Weiss, you say? The stiff that ran out on his bill, same guy the cops came looking for an hour ago? That the one?"

"Yeah. He stops by, tell him to phone Tom. Got it?"

"Oh, yeah, at your service, mister."

Hickey punched down the button, swallowed the lump in his throat, and dialed O again.

As though from a phantom cloud, snowflakes had begun pelting the house. Across the lake to the north, a small black patch of sky made Hickey shiver, as if it were the eye of a tornado meant especially for him. You only have to glimpse the universe from the wrong angle, he thought, and it looks as if all the malevolent forces of nature, the cruelest angels and demons, have made a pact to liquidate you.

Leo's answering-service girl gave her name as Flora. A new one Hickey didn't know. Mr. Weiss hadn't left any number except the Brentwood one, she said. Not for Tom Hickey nor anybody. So he dictated a message.

"*Get your fool self up here, straightaway.* You writing this down?"

"Yes, go ahead," the girl muttered.

"Say: *You want to hang Mickey, wait till I get my wife and kid back. She's number one in this deal, and number two and three. Mickey's nowhere. Neither are Charlie or Cynthia. Not for now.* You got all that?"

"Oh, sure," the girl said meekly. "Shall I tell him you're upset?"

"Yeah. Upset's the perfect word."

Hickey had to lean back a minute, chew on his pipestem, force some air into his lungs. It felt as though his blood, which normally meandered like a lazy river, was approaching a waterfall. Finally he stuffed and lit his pipe, called the operator again, and gave her a number for the San Diego police.

"You oughta hire a secretary," she said.

Thrapp was out. Hickey left a message for the captain to phone him instantly. The next call he dialed himself, to Sheriff Boggs.

"Tom, I tried to ring you a couple times. Line was busy."

"What gives?"

"Zero, sorry to say. All of Harry's boys are accounted for. Still, the kidnappers might be working shifts. I guess I'll shake down the hotel. If Harry's got her, I'd give you house odds she's stashed right there."

"You think Harry's an idiot?"

"More or less."

"What'd he say?" the gambler snapped. He raised his hands, palms up, in wait for an answer. When Hickey ignored him, he muttered, "Smart enough to outwit a dozen old lizards like him."

The sheriff offered to stop by the cabin and brainstorm, in a while, after he leaned on Tom's neighbor. But Hickey told him to forget Poverman and keep badgering the snitches and tough guys. "You want to talk," he said, "call me at Poverman's. Got his number?"

"We've got his number, all right. What're you doing there?"

"Trying not to lose my head."

"Might help if you keep your eyes shut. I hear the fella that designed the eyesore is wearing a straitjacket."

As Hickey let go of the phone, the boss growled, "That sheriff's gotta call in a deputy every time he needs to find his dick."

Hickey paced to the window. The wind had kicked up. The cedars started to howl as though arguing with the wind. The wind relented. The trees fell silent. Somewhere close by, a woman sobbed. Hickey heard it clearly. He thought it must be Frieda in the kitchen. She'd looked weepy when she'd finally appeared out of the northeast wing where she and Tyler had holed up since last evening. They'd only surfaced whenever Harry yelled and one of them dashed out to empty the stockpot or bring a snack or a drink.

Turning toward the kitchen, Hickey listened more closely and resolved that the sobbing didn't come from the house. It was rising from deep in his mind. It sounded like Wendy, only back when her voice was higher and more timid, when she could hardly weep without sounding afraid that somebody was going to smack her—like a dog that's been kicked every day of its life.

The phone rang, and Hickey startled so violently his pipe slipped out of his mouth and clanged against the chrome ridge of a coffee table. Harry pounced on the phone.

"Miss Blackwood. Pleasure to hear your voice....You bet he's here. Shall I take a message?...Yes, ma'am." The boss gave Hickey a wink and the receiver.

"Claire?"

"I think I found a stooge, Tom." She almost shrieked with excitement. "He's awfully drunk, and miffed about a baby-sitting job he didn't get. But he clammed up. I think you'll need to talk to him."

Chapter Twenty

Hickey rode shotgun, pressed against the door, to keep his revolver better than arm's length from the boss, who drove one-handed while listing the foibles of Hickey's car. Its tall profile. Short wheel-base. Scratchy upholstery. Mushy brakes. The radio that sounded like a gramophone. Hickey'd decided on the Chevy because if they'd driven one of the boss's cars, a minute after the valet spotted it, every manager, bouncer, and pit boss would know the king had arrived. This way, he could try sneaking them in through the back and hustling to the cover of Harry's office, which was next to the lounge where Claire'd be waiting, keeping the stooge distracted. Unless Tyler hadn't bought his lie—that they were going to meet Claire north stateline, at the Cal-Neva. If Tyler was smarter than he looked or Harry had flashed him a sign, he'd have phoned the club. A battalion of creeps would be posted all over. Out of nowhere, a tire iron or golf club would smash Hickey's arm the same instant a blackjack thumped his noggin.

He should've put Poverman on the phone, got him to enlist a couple of his boys to deliver Claire and the stooge. But between his excitement at finding a lead and his fervor to escape the leather and Formica prison, he hadn't thought straight until five or so miles down the lakeside highway. Even then, reason only held sway for a few minutes, until Secret Harbor, when the highway turned inland and climbed into Bliss Meadows, and Hickey realized that any moment they might be passing a house, cabin, or barn where some punks had Wendy.

As they crested Spooner Summit, Tahoe reappeared, a flash of silver-blue. Hickey stared while his eyes adjusted and the western ranges appeared—the Rubicons, Tallac, Job's Peak and Job's Sister—mirrored precisely along the far shore. Last September, Wendy'd gotten so dazzled by the view from this place she'd gasped and reached for his hand, though she'd been here maybe a hundred times. Since she'd learned about the baby, the beauty of everything had multiplied. For both of them.

Poverman finished slandering the Chevy, whistled "Saint Louis Blues," then struck up a jitterbug tune. He coasted lazily down the grade.

"Step on it," Hickey commanded.

"Hey, I'm doing my damnedest to keep this rollerskate on the road."

The lower they dropped, the bigger the lake appeared, until it felt as though the earth were mostly water and beyond the rim of jagged silver-white mountains outer space began. Through Glenbrook, Harry goosed the throttle and hunched over the wheel, as though he'd remembered some urgent business at the club. They roared and skidded in and out of shady groves and meadows so brilliant they struck you blind.

Hickey pondered how to play his hand at the club. If he dropped his guard, pocketed his gun, and strolled in beside the boss like he had last week and a dozen other times when they were still the house dick and the guy who signed his paychecks—if Tyler or somebody had called an alert, Hickey'd get whacked before they passed the laundry room. But if Harry was playing straight and Tom marched him into the club with a gun to his ribs, he'd likely make a grandstand play to save face, which would probably leave Hickey with a dead neighbor and himself bleeding from a variety of holes.

They crossed the hill below Kingsbury, swerved off an ice slick near the wedding chapel, passed Lacey's Roadhouse and a field where an entrepreneur offered the tourists buggy rides, into the town of South Lake Tahoe, which could've passed for an LA traffic jam. A crowd of rubberneckers stood in the middle of the road as though, now they'd blown their inheritance, they might as well get run down.

Hickey ordered the boss to swing left onto the icy dirt road that led behind the Wagon Wheel and the Gateway Club and into Harry's casino's back parking lot. The guard was making his rounds, like Hickey'd charged him to, after a San Francisco city councilman's Lincoln Zephyr had gotten swiped and Harry'd assigned his neighbor to awaken and terrorize the security staff.

At Hickey's direction, the boss pulled into a marked space closest to the employees' entrance and loading dock, where two Chinese laborers hoisted crates out of a bobtail delivery truck. One gave Hickey a casual wave and appeared not to notice Poverman, as if you couldn't tell one white guy in an overcoat and fedora from the next.

The double doors swung open on a stiff little man in a uniform Harry's tailor had modeled after the getup of Canadian Mounties. "Say—"

"Hello, Leroy," Hickey muttered.

Noticing his boss, the guard's voice rose a step. "Mister Poverman. You're lookin' good. You—"

"Yeah, yeah." Harry chucked the guard's shoulder.

The hall was like a tunnel: thirty yards, barely wide enough to fit the two broad-shouldered men. Hickey nudged the boss a step ahead.

"Where's the popgun?"

"It's handy."

"Keep your paws in the open," Harry growled. "You make the hostage routine a spectacle, it's curtain time."

The hall was floored in asphalt tile over plywood. Their feet rapped as though on a snare drum that wanted a little tightening, until the noise got obscured—first by the rumble of washing machines, then by the pings of machine-shop hammers and the groans of several men as though one of them had told a sour joke, and finally by pots clanging in the dishwasher's nook.

As they surfaced into the gaming room, Hickey realized his pulse had been drumming his ears so loud and long, any second it might overamp and blow his lights out. He might land outside heaven and rush the guard, demanding to know had Wendy arrived yet. If the thugs cut her loose, fifty years hence he might still be loitering outside the gates.

The two pit bosses who rushed Harry looked like the finalists in a swagger-and-grin competition. They wore brown tuxedos and bolo ties noosed in silver and turquoise.

"All's well, Mister P," the winner announced so obsequiously he could've passed for a lap dog. He sported a gorgeous mop of sleek auburn hair. "A poker cheat, a couple loudmouths, is all."

The runner-up, Eduardo, a pockmarked Spaniard, asked Hickey about the family, got a nod, then turned to the boss and relayed the story that Pauline had spread, about Mr. Poverman having the croup and a touch of laryngitis.

Harry chuckled. "Pauline's got this problem. All her brains are down here." He cupped his hands at his chest. "Keep her outta my sight, would you, Eduardo? I got business. When a guy's got business, he don't need Pauline around. Know what I mean?"

"You bet I do," Eduardo quivered his head, as though the thought of Pauline had caused a spasm.

"Raymond," the boss said. "Grab a pal and follow Tom and me."

The gaming room was all redwood panels, maroon carpet, brass fixtures and spittoons. Out on the floor, change runners and cocktail girls dodged the drunks and wandering losers. Lights flashed, wheels spun, cards skittered over the felt, yelps issued from people delighted to win back the cash out of which they'd gotten swindled. A husky redhead in cowgirl duds rushed over to check the boss's and Mr. Hickey's coat and hats. Harry lifted a finger, tossed her a look, and she fled. A bartender tipped his Stetson. A croupier saluted.

Claire jumped up from the booth in which she appeared to have cornered the stooge, who sprawled as though one more sip would deposit him onto the floor. Though Claire's right hand was riding her hip, Harry grasped it in both of his while he angled toward the pit boss and his helper. "Show the lug to my office."

When Claire broke free, she started around him toward Hickey, who wagged his head sharply to back her off. But Poverman had already spun around and tossed his hands up next to her shoulders. All he needed was to grab, then Claire'd be his shield. Hickey'd be a chump. Maybe a dead one.

The boss fluttered his fingers and gave Hickey a wry smile. "Think about it, tough guy," he said, then chortled, turned and marched ahead of the pack, past the bar. He pulled a ring of keys, unlocked a carved redwood door.

The office looked like a warehouse for extra junk from Harry's home. Three black sofas, a sheepskin rug, and a miniature Formica desk that implied its keeper wasn't a sucker for paperwork. In each side wall was a door. The wall behind the desk sported an unframed canvas upon which some creature that resembled a shark labored through either murky water or rust-streaked motor oil. Claire stopped in front of the desk to gape at the canvas.

The boss pinched his nose and shrugged. "My steno, Pauline, said she learned all about painting when she used to model for some artiste. So I gave her a crack at it. She thinks it's a trout."

The stooge reeled into the office, prodded and shoved by Raymond and a Greek bouncer. The stooge stood half a head taller than either escort, with a vast, barrel-shaped torso and squat legs. His face was round, dark, and greasy. Harry motioned toward a sofa. The men dumped him there.

"Who *is* this guy?" Harry demanded.

"A sore loser," Raymond said. "Can't hold his booze. Saturday or so, we booted him out. That's all I know. Today, he shows up with a wad, drops it to craps. Plato would've gave him the heave-ho again, except the lady says you're on your way and we're supposed to sit on him."

Harry gave a nod and wave of dismissal.

"You sure, Mister Poverman? He's a big mutt."

The boss scowled. The two men hustled for the door. As it clicked shut, Hickey dug in the pocket of his overcoat and brought out his .45; the stooge's head jerked up and backward. He careened that way so hard the sofa's front legs flew up and dropped.

Hickey sat across from the man, next to Claire, feeling light-headed and slightly giddy with relief, to feel in pursuit, released from his mind. The boss sat on his desk, gazed around placidly, then wheeled on the stooge. "You looking for a job or what?"

"Yeah. You got it."

"What kind of work?"

"Aw, anything takes muscle." As though suddenly forgetting Hickey's gun, the man straightened up and stared intently at each of them, as though trying hard to focus. "You got a job for me?"

"Sure."

"What's it pay?"

"A C-note in chips."

"That ain't much," the man said cockily, then wilted under Poverman's glare. "What's the job?"

"Doing what you do best, Mutt. Running off at the mouth. See, we're looking for a gal that got snatched."

"Hey." The stooge turned to Claire and frowned, a delicate fellow betrayed. "Hey, I don't know about any snatch. I was just trying to make time with the dame."

Harry flew off the desk. "Dame! You calling Miss Blackwood a dame, moron? Tom, God's sake, don't just sit there. Punish the moron."

"My pleasure."

Hickey stood and took one long stride before the man wailed, "Naw. Naw. I already spilled the beans. I'll come clean, all I know. I was down in Reno, at the Motherlode, and some little guy—a cowpuncher, looked like—says a couple Reno boys got big dough to snatch a…lady. Up here. It ain't right, he says. Guys start poaching on the next guy's territory, what you end up with's a range war. He says."

"Who are the boys?" Hickey snapped.

"Search me. I don't even know the cowpuncher. A little guy. Brown hat. Checked shirt."

"Who they working for?"

"I don't know, pal. You got all there is to get outta me."

The stooge hung his head and stopped forward. A perfect target. In two steps, Hickey crossed the space between them. He kicked a bull's eye. Probably tenderized the man's heart. As he slumped forward, Hickey dropped beside him. Poking his .45 into the man's right eye socket, he snarled, "Where'd they take the lady?"

"Do what you gotta, buddy." The stooge caught a breath and groaned. "I'm tapped out."

"Tom," Claire said.

Hickey got up, sat beside her, and rubbed his temples. She gripped the base of his skull and pressed firmly.

The boss whistled, loud as a football coach. Before the echo died, Raymond and his sidekick came in. "Go feed the lug a steak. Give him a stack of chips. Only, if he tries to leave, lock him in the freezer."

They hoisted the man to his feet and led him staggering out the door. Hickey grabbed up the phone, walked it back to the Formica table, slammed it down. "Call Reno."

"I believe that's a town, Tom. Give me a person."

"The guy that knows who's got Wendy."

With a sneer and sigh of boredom, Poverman dialed the operator and shifted his voice a notch lower. "Yeah, cutie, give me Reno thirty-six eighteen." He shot Hickey a vicious scowl, as though suddenly he'd gotten his fill of this game. "Hey, Beau. What's cooking?…Same old stuff, huh?…Right, Friday's good. Chinese joint in Truckee. Listen, I got a problem. Pretend you're looking for a couple boys to do an odd job, grab somebody, keep her on ice, maybe buy her a one-way ticket, who do you call?

… Naw, I'm just supposing." He threw out a hand for the note pad. Hickey delivered. "Yeah, I heard of him." The boss scribbled a few names. "Who else?…This guy Rollins: he the one's been collecting for Foster?"

"Whoa!" Hickey bellowed.

"Hold on, Beau." The gambler cupped the mouthpiece and gave a queer look, one eyebrow raised, the other eye squinting.

"Frankie Foster?" Hickey demanded.

"What about him?"

"He's in Reno?"

"Sure. He used to work outta the Doubloon in Santa Monica. A few months he's been sizing up Reno, trying to muscle in on the sports book."

"Call him."

"You know the guy?" Harry switched hands on the mouthpiece, freeing his right hand.

Hickey watched sharply, expecting the boss to open a desk drawer. "He's got an in-law, Jack Meechum?"

"Beats me. Wait. Yeah, he's got a daughter goes by Meechum. Came up for a party last summer. Tits out to here." He stretched his arm far as it would go.

"Call him," Hickey commanded.

The boss glowered and uncovered the mouthpiece. "Sorry, Beau. I got a pest here. You have Foster's number handy?" He jotted it down. "See you Friday, huh?" Holding on to the receiver, he pushed the hang-up button and asked Hickey, "Where's this Meechum fit in?"

"Let's see. Make the call."

Harry tossed the receiver onto the hook and shifted himself toward Claire. "Miss Blackwood, if you don't mind, how about letting us gab on our own for a minute, Tom and me? You need a drink or a snack? How about a scarf? We got a French boutique right in the club."

"You would," Claire muttered, and strode to the door, sulking like a tomboy chased off the court.

The boss hopped off his desk, stepped around and settled into a swiveling leather armchair. He leaned back and smiled grimly. "I got more patience than the next guy. Only I used it up, being your patsy. Get straight here, Tom. You'd of been on a slab yesterday noon, if I wanted it that way. See, Harry Poverman gets what he wants. That clear?"

"Swell. You wanta get on the phone, right?"

"I wanta know who's Jack Meechum, and I want that you address me like a guy could have you put to sleep any second."

Hickey didn't see the man's foot hit a buzzer or whatever summoned the troops who suddenly burst in: Raymond and the Greek through the redwood door, a costumed security man through each of the side doors, all of them with pistols leveled at Hickey.

What surprised Hickey most was his composure, as though his nerves had gotten fried, discarded, replaced with new ones that hadn't yet learned the correct response to danger. He nodded at the security cops, greeted them by name.

Harry laughed. "Look at this guy. An iceberg, or what?" He waved his arm to the troops. "Scram."

The way Hickey measured his options, he could either call the man's bluff or play along. Call his bluff and lose, the game's over. Win, and he keeps his pride, nothing else. Wendy's still just as gone. He laid the .45 on his knee. "You wanta know about Meechum?"

"Yeah."

Hickey sat and droned the story about Jack Meechum telling the police that Cynthia'd left Eschelman's jam session to meet with the beachcomber, just before the fire.

The boss was a good listener. He didn't stir until the story was over. Then he stood, stretched his legs and arms, did a few jumping jacks, and finally stepped dangerously close to Hickey. Reached out a hand. Patted Hickey's shoulder. "I like the way the cards are falling. Yeah, I like it fine. You pin the snatch on Foster; I give you a raise for getting him outta my hair."

"Your hair? You got action in Reno?"

"Mind your business, Tom."

Poverman stepped back to the desk and reached for the phone, dialed O, and in his silkiest voice told the operator that when she next visited his club, she ought to stop by his office for some drink tokes. Finally he gave her the number and turned to Hickey. "I gotta tell you about this Meechum doll, Foster's kid. ..."

His voice slithering downward, he drawled into the mouthpiece.

"Hey, darling, remember old Harry?...Come on up then, anytime. Just call ahead....Naw, she's last year's headlines. Listen, your old man around?...Yeah, well, tell him to throw on a towel so as not to blush when he springs a big one, looking at you....Hey, sure he's your dad, but a dish like you, any man alive'd spring one....Yeah, I'm naughty, all right. Put the old man on."

Lowering the receiver, he turned to Hickey. "I gotta tell you, this one's a case. You mighta noticed her hanging around a couple days last summer—the broad can't keep her clothes on, not a swimsuit even. Out at the pool, the lake, on the boat. I hear she's got a pool in the yard down there, and don't matter who shows up, could be the Boy Scouts on a scavenger hunt, you think she's gonna throw on a robe? Right in front of her old man, she struts around in all her glory, the way I hear it. She's got this—"

The redwood door opened a crack. Claire's face appeared, and the boss waved her in. She went straight to Hickey, fed him a pretzel.

Muffling the receiver, his voice a tone deeper than any he'd managed before, Harry boasted, "I'm about to wrap up this caper, as they say, so you and I can celebrate, Miss Blackwood. Champagne dinner in the penthouse lounge."

"Where do you keep the penthouse in a two-story firetrap like this?"

"Hey, never mind the altitude. It's atmosphere does the trick. You care for gypsy violins?" He tossed up his free hand, index finger high, and lifted the receiver. "Yeah, Frankie....Sure, long time. Listen, I gotta see you....Up here, about a deal, a kinda partnership....Naw, I don't wanta come down. I got this busted foot....Aw, I was skiing, bindings jammed. So you and the kid get yourselves up here—Frieda'll have the hors d'oeuvres waiting. Whatta you drink?...Okay, four o'clock, no later, huh?"

Harry dropped the phone into its cradle, turned, and gazed at Claire, smug as a diplomat.

"He's coming?" Hickey snapped.

The gambler made an ornery face and shrugged. "He said yeah, but I don't buy it. We'll send an escort." One eye on Claire, he dialed the phone and waited. "Tyler, you think Frieda could survive you being gone a couple hours?…Hey, the horses are Mac's job. *You* go into the office, look up the address for a dame called Meechum in Reno. Take the wagon down there; pick up Frankie Foster, the gal's old man. Bring her along, she can drive for you. Foster puts up a fuss, knock him silly—only make sure he can talk when he gets here….Not the club. Bring him to the house."

Chapter Twenty-one

Leo figured it was midafternoon. Living almost seventy years can give you a handle on time, even through a less than routine day, when half of you is numb and the other half aches as though from a fever that could melt iron.

Most of the last hour the punks had left him alone. Bass paced, using a makeshift walking stick he'd found, rapping it on the floor in jazzy rhythms. Denny sat in a captain's chair, whittling a hunk of two-by-four into a cylinder. The driver sprawled on the floor leaning against the wall, his hat tipped over his eyes as though imitating the hombre in white and a sombrero who takes his siestas in the shade of a cactus.

Leo felt remote from his brain, as if it were a distant radio station with a feeble transmitter. Whenever he gave up, a signal would cut in loud and clear before long, through the static. The last time, it had sent a message he labored for minutes to understand.

"Bass," he mumbled. "I got a deal."

The man halted mid-stride. "Let me hear it."

"Give me a pen and paper."

"What for?"

"A letter. To my pal, Tom Hickey."

Bass cackled. "Hey, Denny. What do you think, ain't the old guy a character? What're you gonna say to him, Pancho? Maybe you want to give him our address, huh?"

For pride's sake, Leo wanted to throw out a wisecrack, but every word sapped him like swimming a mile in breakwater used to. "I'm gonna say, *Let it go, Tom, whatever happens. If they take me out I'm leaving Vi, Una, Magda, Elizabeth, Wendy, and the kid all in your hands. So drop it.* That's all."

Bass squinted and peered at Leo as though with X-ray eyes. "I get it Pancho. You're trying to spare his ass and save us the trouble. Yeah, why not? Denny, run upstairs, rifle the desk for a pen and paper and a book or something to write on. Pancho's doing us a favor. Helluva guy, no?"

While Denny ambled toward the stairs, Bass lifted his walking stick into both hands as though preparing to dance a soft shoe. He stepped behind Leo, hitched the walking stick under the old man's chin, and leaned backward. Instantly it cut off Leo's wind. In seconds his eyes bulged and his tongue swelled even bigger than their blows to his mouth had left it. His skull seemed to fill with tepid water.

Bass pulled harder. A large splinter pierced through the skin of Leo's neck and stabbed his Adam's apple. When Bass let go, the splinter remained.

Denny loomed overhead, offering Leo a telephone book and stationery. "This is classy stuff. Got perfume on it."

Before he accepted the stationery, Leo reached up and tried to pluck out the splinter. The tip broke off in his skin. When he swallowed, it jabbed viciously. He took the stationery, set it on the phone book in his lap, accepted the pen. The stationery had a border of morning glory vines. Leo's hands were too stiff to write. He printed in letters composed of straight lines and sharp angles.

When he'd finished, Denny gave him the envelope. He wrote Tom's name, rural route number, and town, stuffed the letter inside, licked and sealed it, and gave it to Bass. "Put your address in the return corner," he muttered. Then his head and shoulders slumped forward. His eyes shut. Both hands dropped to his sides as his brain discovered a cool, dark cavern to rest in.

"There's stamps in the desk," Denny said. "How about I go stick it in the mailbox?"

Bass tossed him the letter. "Yeah, and walk down to the grocery. Buy some gum and candy. See if they got those nonpareils."

Chapter Twenty-two

The first half hour back at the house, Hickey let the boss shoot pool while he tried to prophesy where the shots would go. He analyzed the caroms. So far, it was the best distraction he'd found. But he snapped to attention at the sound of tires on gravel. He bolted to the archway, peered into the living room; Harry sank his third straight combo.

The doorbell clanged. Frieda sauntered out of the far wing, stuck her eye to the peephole. When she opened the door, Claire hurried in, tossing her flyaway hair. Lugging her tote bag, she hustled through the maze of Formica and around the snake pit. She ran up to Hickey, gave him a kiss on the cheek, reached for his free hand, and gripped it tightly. "Tom, don't get too excited, this is a long shot. I've been calling all the lodges and hotels, describing Wendy and the car. I can't say it's them, but there's a man and a young woman, pregnant, kind of small, checked into the lodge at Carnelian Bay yesterday morning. They're still registered. The fellow I talked to hadn't seen them outside."

"When'd you talk to this guy?" Hickey rasped.

"Just now. I was on the phone to him when the food got delivered."

Hickey wheeled on the gambler, his brain pulsing so fiercely it seemed likely to dislodge his eyeballs. "Put your shoes on. We're going for a ride."

"Swell. I'll drive, huh? Miss Blackwood, you can sit up front with me."

"Claire'll drive."

The gambler shrugged and called Frieda out of the kitchen, told her to fetch him his overcoat, driving cap, a muffler, and gloves. While she was gone, he reminded Hickey that he too could shoot, and they'd do better with two guns. Hickey thanked him for the advice. He picked up the phone and dialed the sheriff's office, gave the fellow on duty his name, and asked for the sheriff and at least one deputy to meet him at the roadhouse just east of Carnelian Bay.

When Frieda returned, Harry told her to sit by the phone and spell out any messages, while Claire ran out and got her car turned around and ready to speed. It was a four-door Pontiac her dead husband had bought her for a wedding present in 1939, the year she graduated from Mills College in Oakland.

The upholstery was tattered. In back, on the passenger side behind the boss, Hickey felt a torn piece of headliner resting on his hat.

He told Claire to cut left at the end of the driveway and pull over beside his car. When she stopped, he ordered Harry to step out and stand by while he switched the .45 to his left hand, dug the keys out of his right front pocket, opened the trunk, and got his snub-nosed .38 out of the suitcase. The gambler nodded and put his hand out for the gun.

Hickey stuffed it into his own coat pocket.

While Claire sped up the hill toward the highway, Harry listed the advantages they would've gained by taking his new Ford roadster: speed, warmth, luxury, the new-car smell, and a radio that could pick up signals from Texas.

After swerving to miss a dog and fishtailing, Claire grumbled, "Aren't you going to say that in your car we wouldn't have a woman driver?"

"Hey, Miss Blackwood, I bet you could drive at Indy. I'd back you." Pretending to fool with the heater knob, Harry scooted a few inches to the left, sniffed the air, and asked, "What kinda perfume?"

"None."

He sighed. "That's beautiful. Once in a lifetime, you find a lady that smells better than all the chemists in France could dream up."

"Such a huckster. Is that and perfidy all a fellow needs to make a fortune these days?" Claire wheeled left onto the highway.

The boss crooked his neck to get a glimpse of Hickey. "Where's the justice, Tom. A guy spills his guts—excuse the lingo, Miss Blackwood—guy speaks from the heart and gets tagged with a lousy name. Huckster." He sighed again.

The few clouds over the north shore were scattered and fluffy. The dark ones had blown south over Mount Tallac. Tires had swept the highway of most of the recent snow. Sunlight flashed off the shiny asphalt, masking the windshield with glare. Claire hunched over the wheel and maneuvered as though to certify Poverman's crack about her driving. The sharp turns, she skidded around. On the straightaways, she gave the horn a toot and passed everybody. Highballing over the hill at north Stateline past the Cal Neva Lodge and the Crystal Bay Club, she sent a few pedestrians diving for cover. She had Hickey braced against the front seat. Harry gripped the dashboard, tossing her compliments and encouragement while they zoomed past the pine log and cedar shake motels of Brockway and Kings Beach.

Between the benzedrine, hope, and apprehension, Hickey felt charged enough to sling lightning out of his hands. Nerves sputtering, every muscle wound so tightly it seemed the next turn it would snap and unravel, he envisioned two men sprinting across the beach, tripping over a fallen tree, staggering and plunging into the lake. His .45 sighted between a man's shoulders, Hickey would've squeezed, cheered as the goon flung up his hands and toppled face first into the water, except Wendy stood by. She'd seen enough blood for a lifetime. He dropped his gun so he could wrap both arms around her. Her skin all over shivered against him, radiating heat. The baby squirmed. He thought he heard it coo.

The next scene, at home that night, on the couch beside the wood stove, Wendy sat on his knee, snuggling her hair against his chin. The door flew open and Leo filled the doorway. He took off his hat, flicked and sailed it across the room, onto the hook beside Hickey's black felt. The old man grinned victoriously.

Claire skidded left off the highway and gravel in front of the roadhouse, whose only sign was the neon that spelled out COCKTAILS. She finally stopped, beside the sheriff's cruiser, when she slammed into the tree trunk barrier. From inside the roadhouse, a stand-up bass, drums, steel guitar, and vocalist chanted blues. Amateur night.

Sheriff Boggs and a deputy who looked half Indian, muscle-bound and sleepy, climbed out of the cruiser. The deputy walked around and met Hickey, the sheriff, the gambler, and the lady between the two cars. Boggs stood a forehead smaller than the other men, about Claire's height, and lean. His mustache looked like the brush on a push broom. With his mouth shut, bristles hid both lips. His skin appeared diseased, raw and scaly, his eyes like bruises, as though he'd recently survived an ordeal like climbing Mount Everest.

"This here's Roy. Me and him'd like to know why you're jabbing Mister Poverman with an automatic. Not that we give a damn."

"Makes me feel tough," Hickey said. "You know Claire Blackwood?"

"Sure do." He glanced her way and touched his hat brim. "I don't care for your answer, Tom. Try again."

"It's just like it looks," Hickey said. "He's the closest I've got to finding Wendy. She turns up with somebody he doesn't know, I apologize profusely."

"Yeah, I get it. Now who's gonna tell me what we're all doing here?"

"I was calling every place around the lake," Claire said, "asking about a pregnant woman in an Olds. A boy at Pratt's Haven, up here at Carnelian, said yeah, there's a couple—just the one man and her. In cabin five."

"How long ago?"

"An hour. Maybe less."

The sheriff nodded. "We all going in the Pontiac?"

Hickey nudged the gambler into the front between himself and Claire, didn't bother with the gun, figuring Harry'd gotten plenty of better chances to throw him than with two cops in the back seat. The boss sat scowling as if the presence of cops upset his sensibilities. As they backed onto the highway, he leaned toward Hickey and whispered, "You're making me look like a chump, Tom. I'm gonna call it strike two."

It was less than a mile into Carnelian Bay. Pratt's Haven was the first lodge. Claire pulled into a turnout across the road. From there you could see small, weather-beaten, tin-roofed log cabins in two rows leading down toward the lake, a gravel driveway in between them. Hickey climbed out, put on his glasses, leaned onto the roof of the car, and squinted to see the cabin numbers. One was on the left, two on the right. That would make number five the third cabin in the left row.

Each cabin had a front porch with a door and window, and shaded windows on the east and west sides. The tail end of a dark blue Olds jutted from behind number five.

"We need three guys," Hickey said. He leaned into the Pontiac, told the boss to stay put, threw the door shut, and walked around to Claire, who'd gotten out and stood beside the sheriff and his deputy. "You wanta hold a gun on him, babe?" Hickey asked.

"I don't know if I could shoot it," she whispered.

"Neither does he. If you want it, here it is." He fished out the .38. "Just stand back away from the car. If he comes after you, scream like mad and run to us. If he tries to make a run for it, just flip off the safety here and squeeze. You won't hit him, but maybe he'll stop."

She pulled off her gloves, took the gun and measured its weight in her hands. "Okay." She sighed and gazed aimlessly around. Though she stood bundled in a cap, ear muffs, the scotch plaid coat a schoolteacher could wear—even while Hickey felt as if he were tiptoeing beside a precipice, in a gale—he noticed how splendid she looked. Elegant, like a purebred. He reached for her free hand, gave it a squeeze.

Harry learned out the car window. "Get a move on, Romeo."

As they started across the road, Hickey assigned the sheriff to the west window, the deputy the east, himself to the porch and front door. Sheriff Boggs had picked a twig and was nibbling. While Hickey gave orders, the sheriff had squinted incredulously. Roy the deputy watched him for a sign. Finally he spat out the twig, straightened his western hat, and nodded okay.

They stepped off the asphalt and onto gravel that seemed to crunch twice as loud beneath the crust of snow. They walked slowly, almost on tiptoes, but still might've wakened a drunk. Especially the Indian deputy, who probably outweighed Hickey. His footsteps sounded like the cavalry. The sheriff was quietest. Like the kind of thief who could slip in, snatch the gems, slit your throat, and disappear while your wife lay beside you telling a bedtime story. He padded in front of cabin five, ducking below window level, and wedged between the Olds and the corner of the cabin toward the west window. The Indian reached his post a few seconds later, just as Hickey took the first step to the porch.

There were three steps. Each creaked a warning, so Hickey skittered to the window beside the door and pushed his eye against the glass along the edge where the shade didn't quite reach.

A woman pranced out of the bathroom, wearing a top-knot bow and a frilly pink nightgown, leading with her massive belly, her straight dark hair cascading over breasts that would've made five of Wendy's.

After a moment during which he felt his heart liquify and bleed away, Hickey retreated to the driveway and signaled the others to follow. He glanced across the road at Claire standing still as a monument beside the front fender. His foot stubbed a pile of stones underneath a patch of snow. He reared his leg back and kicked the pile, which exploded and peppered a cabin wall.

In front of cabin number one he stopped to wait for the others, hoping the sheriff wouldn't make some wisecrack about busting him as a voyeur. Anybody made a wisecrack, Hickey doubted he could stop himself from smashing the guy.

Chapter Twenty-three

On the drive back to Incline, Hickey sat paralyzed and silent while Claire snapped one-word answers to the questions Harry tossed at her: where was she born, how'd she like growing up in Boston, did she go to college, where'd she go to college, where'd she meet Blackwood, what had she seen in the guy?

The road and the forest appeared to Hickey as ink blots of green, black, and white. If Claire or the gambler had questioned him, he probably wouldn't have realized. As they crossed the state line, he noticed people swirling by, buildings upside down, neon flashing so brutally it seemed a threat to his brain. He thought, so this is what the earth without Wendy looks like.

When Claire's Pontiac bounded into the driveway, Hickey broke out of the spell. He scanned the woods and corrals, looking for shooters. He peered at the roof of the stable and garage and at their corners. Nothing peculiar. Still, en route to the house, he cozied up to Poverman as if they were Siamese twins, his gun barrel fondling Harry's neck.

Frieda met them at the door. "Mr. Hickey, there's a guy wants you to call him bad. I wrote the number down. A police captain, he says."

Hickey gazed around the main room, then roamed, inspecting behind the bar and a few sofas. Finally he ushered the gambler back to his couch by the fireplace and picked the phone off the Formica table. He sat down and called the operator, reached the captain in his office.

"Tom? You got her back?"

After three long breaths, Hickey summoned the power to admit it. "No." Wearily, as if the heart, the hope, and the benzedrine had forsaken him.

"Nothing's turned up?"

"Nothing except Frankie Foster," he mumbled.

"Foster, you say? What about him?"

"He's living in Reno, is all, and he's got an ex-son-in-law named Jack Meechum."

"Meechum. The guy that saw Cynthia with the beachcomber?"

"Yeah."

"And?"

"And nothing."

"Pretty flimsy, Tom."

"Uh-huh."

"Say, I've been calling you since ten this morning, when I started getting worried about Leo."

Hickey jolted to life. "What's with Leo?"

"Well, last night, about midnight, some goon—could be one of Schwartz's redhead boys, the fat one—he shows up at Ada's Answering Service and slaps around this girl, Susie, till she gives him the number where Leo's staying—I traced it to the Las Palmas Motor Hotel, in LA. Downtown on Pico. So I call the place. Leo slipped away before nine this morning, ran out on the bill."

"Not a chance," Hickey said.

"Sure. Something's gone rotten. I called the LAPD. They're supposed to nose around, get back to me."

"Nobody's heard from him?"

"Not a peep."

"How about Vi?"

"Where the hell is she?"

"Beats me." Hickey set the .45 on his knee, plucked his hat off, and sent it skating across the floor. He gripped his forehead, kneaded it hard. "Call the FBI, a fellow named Gomez. Something Gomez—I forget. He's the kid of Leo's old partner,

Arturo. Leo was supposed to meet him this morning, only I told him to skip it and race up here, give me a hand."

"What's the deal with Gomez?"

"Leo's got some half-baked idea he can shove Mickey Cohen into a corner about Guns for Israel. When Mickey comes out fighting, Leo figures he might pull something stupid, get hung for it."

"Leo's taking on Cohen?"

"Yeah, except he promised to drop it for now and throw in with me. After Wendy's home, after the baby, I'll tie him to a tree, make him promise to be good, and send Mickey an apology and a box of chocolates."

"All that'll do is get Mickey constipated, give him an excuse not to show for Leo's funeral."

"We'll hide him out, then. Nobody's gonna touch the old man if I can help it."

"Sure, Tom, I know you guys, remember. Anyway, you got it right—let's don't worry about Leo right yet, except I'll phone this Gomez. There's something else you oughta know, came up after I started calling you. About noon. A lifeguard at OB found the beachcomber."

"Teddy."

"Yeah. He washed in this morning at high tide."

Hickey started restlessly pounding the heel of his fist and the gun butt on his knee, losing even the tattered remains of his patience, having to check himself from snapping at his pal that none of this mattered a damn until Wendy was back at his side. "It figures," he muttered.

"What figures? Somebody hired Teddy to torch the Sousa place, then dunked him?"

"Yeah."

"We're thinking the same. Yesterday I talked to Robeson, the DA assigned to burn your pal Cynthia. I laid the whole deal out for him—Angelo's boys shooting at you and staking out Elizabeth's place, Wendy getting snatched—so this morning when he hears the beachcomber's dead, he gives up. Cynthia's off the hook, for now anyway."

"Swell. Just keep it under your hat till Wendy gets home, that's all."

"Yeah, well …"

"You can't spring Cynthia, Rusty, not while they've got my girl. Cynthia hits the street, the punks look at Wendy, all they see's an accuser."

"Tom…Robeson already cut Cynthia loose."

"Aw," Hickey groaned. Dropping the receiver on his lap, he doubled over. His gut felt imbedded with a pickax. Surely an organ had burst. Any second he expected to reel away, unconscious. But the pain kept throbbing, and the tyrant that ruled his brain ordered it onto alert. His skin flushed, then chilled. His teeth began to chatter.

"Tom, you there?"

"Didn't Leo call? Tell you no matter what, don't let her go till Wendy's back?" Hickey clamped his jaw and listened to the crackle of the line.

"You're not all there, are you, pal? I'm saying Leo's missing. Wouldn't I have told you if he'd called?"

"I'm all here," he snapped. "Last night, I told him to pass along the message."

"Well, he didn't. But it wouldn't of mattered. I'd figured the same thing. I had Robeson convinced we should drag our feet, keep her around at least till the couch doctor gets a shot at her. Take another couple statements, maybe she'd spill a lead. Robeson was with me, until Mrs. Sousa showed."

"Laurel?"

"Yeah, Laurel. She came, wearing a ton of gems, brought *two* shysters along, got her sister out before anybody said boo to me."

"They turned her over to the Bitch?" Hickey yowled.

"That's the one, all right."

"They released her to the one whose house she might've burnt down and whose husband she killed, maybe? What, you guys got a murder quota nowadays and didn't fill it this week?"

"Whoa, Tom. You're the guy's been saying all along Cynthia didn't torch the place."

"What I said was you didn't have enough to hold her. Meaning if she torched the place or she didn't, there's no use locking her up. You know damn well, Rusty, that family's gonna kill each other off till they're extinct."

"Look, I know things don't look rosy, but Wendy got outta hell before." Thrapp's voice had acquired an indignant rasp. "She's probably okay."

"Probably," Hickey snarled.

As if they'd squared off against each other, a minute of silence held before the captain gently offered, "How about I fly up there, give you a hand?"

Hickey slumped forward, squeezing his head between fists that gripped a .45 and a phone receiver. "Leo's gonna be here soon. I've got Claire, and the sheriff's working on it. You can do better down there."

"Anything special you want me to do?"

"Yeah. Go talk to Laurel. Let on you figure this whole deal— the fire, the kidnapping—belongs to her. See what slips out."

"Good enough. I'll try that angle."

"And you could look around for Vi. Leo's got her hiding out."

"Sure, that's what he'd do. With him on a crusade, after Angelo's boys shot holes in his welcome mat."

"Yeah, where are they now? Angelo's boys."

"On bail. Keep your chin up, pal."

As Hickey pushed the button, Claire grabbed his wrist and squeezed. "What'd he say?"

If the boss had jumped him that moment, Hickey wouldn't have noticed until he was already on the floor, he'd submerged so deeply into his mind. To a place from where he beheld distinctly the chain of errors that led to the swamp where he wallowed, appalled by the magnitude of his stupidity. From here, the Tom Hickey who'd left his wife alone, bullied Schwartz and Paoli, got Leo into a fix because the old man pounced on Charlie Schwartz trying to clean up the mess his partner had made—that Tom Hickey looked like the foulest culprit.

About the fifth time Claire shook his arm he ventured back into the world. He told her about Leo's beef against Mickey Cohen. That somebody's muscled the answering service girl. That Leo was missing but probably on his way up here.

Claire sat beside him, nodding encouragement. "Then you can catch a nap," she offered.

Hickey socked his knee. "The hell he's on his way. The old man wouldn't run out on a motel bill."

"Neither would you," Claire said. "But you did."

"I paid the damn thing."

While Hickey passed the news about the beachcomber washing in with the tide, his voice began to slip like a boy's, jumping a whole octave. By the time he'd gotten to the part about Cynthia going free, he couldn't speak a whole phrase at once. He had to stop and let his heart settle between words. He felt like a drunk who's one shot from the blackout. Yet during each pause, he gained a morsel of strength. As his story concluded, he recalled how Wendy used to sit whole days in perfect silence, as if a whisper could waste her final breath.

"I've got a hunch about this Foster," Claire said. "Him being related to the fellow who sent the girl to jail—that seems a darn good clue to me."

Trying to see it her way, Hickey reflected how Foster was related to Meechum, who might've been a sidekick of Teddy the beachcomber's at Agua Caliente—where they probably both knew Elizabeth's no-good husband. Hickey decided to give Stuart a call, as soon as he fixed another matter. He turned to the boss, who sat pouting like a rookie on the sidelines.

"Your boy Mac's been keeping my phone tied up."

"Sure," Harry said. "Mac's a phone hound. You don't put a leash on him, he won't eat or sleep till there's nobody left to call. By now, he's probably working on China and points east, gabbing with dames. He's got 'em all over the globe, from his navy days."

"How about Tyler?"

"Tyler doesn't gab much. He's the silent, touchy kind."

"Soon as Tyler gets back," Hickey said, "Switch him with the cowboy."

"I don't know. It'd be a dirty trick, interrupting the lovebirds again. See, Tyler's a big fan of this having some cluck hold a gun on the boss. I mean, how's the boss gonna keep him and Miss Dustmop from making like bunny rabbits? Aw, nuts, there I go." He turned to Claire. His voice got lower and syrupy. "Pardon the innuendo, Miss Blackwood."

"Never mind that," Claire snapped. "I'll go over there."

"Hey, I'd much rather knock Tyler outta the saddle than lose your company, Miss Blackwood."

"I don't like the way you say Blackwood."

"I pronounce it wrong?"

"Yes, like a cuss word."

The gambler managed a sheepish nod. "Habit, I guess. You hear somebody thinks you're trash, makes you wanta return the compliment. How about I call you Claire?"

"Fine, and let's get this straight. The Blackwoods and I don't agree on everything, but they've been good to me. You want to cuss them, swell. Only wait till I'm gone."

"Hey, I'm convinced. They're good to you, that's enough for Harry. I'm starting a Blackwood fan club."

Rolling her eyes, Claire stood up. "I'll get over to your place, Tom. You ought to be set for food and all till Leo shows up, but I'll check in frequently." She gave him a lingering kiss on the forehead, muttered goodbye to Harry.

As she left, so did Harry's cordiality. His arm that'd been draped across the couch fell off, dropped the hand into his lap. He began rapping the knuckles on the back of his left hand. For a minute he sat glowering at Hickey and finally wagged his head severely. "Tom, any minute I'm liable to give the nod and watch you do the last tango."

"Guys drawing a bead on me through the peepholes, that it?"

"Something like that."

"I oughta call Sheriff Boggs, tell him to sweep the woods and go through the place?"

"Yeah, and remind him to bring a lotta handcuffs and be sure to dream up some charge he can lay on *my* employees for trespassing on *my* property, watching out for *me*. Disturbing the peace, maybe?" He shouted for the maid, ordered a snack and a beer.

Boots tromped the north deck, and Mac walked in. Head down, he crossed the room and stood before Harry. "You wanta see me, boss?"

"You get any rest over there, Mac, what with having your own phone line?"

The cowboy folded his hands in front of himself, drooped his shoulders. "Sure, I spent lots of time snoozing. Not much else to do."

"Who'd you call?"

"My mom," he mumbled. "Uncle Phil. Couple others."

"Where they live?"

"Mom's in Cleveland. Roy's staying up in Idaho—Pocatello. There's this French girl, Gigi—"

"France?" Hickey said.

"Naw, don't worry. She lives outside New Orleans. And I rang up—"

The gambler waved his hand for silence. "Around the lake, Mac. Who'd you call around here?"

"Um …"

"You remember Barney?"

"Yeah."

"Seen him around?"

"After you busted him cheating?" Mac asked sheepishly.

"Cheating I can live with, the first time, long as it's penny ante. Cheating's what makes this country great. It's lying that steams me worst. A guy lies to me, I see red. You run into Barney lately?"

"Nope, but I heard he looks bad. Is that what you're getting at?"

Harry shut his eyes, nodded, and grinned like an addle-brained fighter with his glove lifted high.

"Boss, I called Goldie. Once at her place. Other time down at the club."

"Yeah. What'd you tell Goldie?"

"Just I was working, couldn't get over there."

"Nothing about why, what you were doing, what me and Tom were up to?"

"Well…boss, I made her swear she wouldn't shoot her mouth. See, if I didn't come clean, she woulda figured I had another dame around."

"You did," Harry growled. "Gloria? Remember her? The one that's got my Jaguar?" The phone rang. Murmuring curses, Harry leaned to answer it. "Yeah….Yeah, he's here." He looked up at Hickey, motioned with his head.

Hickey got up and took the phone. "Who's this?"

"Tom, it's Vi. A person at your number gave me this one. If you're visiting, you must've found Wendy?"

"Not yet. What gives with Leo?"

"Not a word. Tom, I'm scared."

Chapter Twenty-four

The physical suffering, Leo could bear. Pain had limits. At its zenith, a piece of his brain seemed to explode, and when the smoke cleared there remained a dead zone between the pain and his feelings.

Anguish was harder because it flogged him with blame. It insisted that nothing happened without reason. Every joy was a reward, every torment a punishment for something he'd done or failed to do. So when the punks clobbered him or sliced a line across his eyelid, even though after the shock, when the body part numbed, he could curse Bass, the driver, Denny, Mickey Cohen, or Tom for diverting him from the chores Southland Insurance threw his way—such as littering a sidewalk with dimes and quarters, then lounging in his Packard, camera at the ready, until Lester Fortenoy came out for his newspaper, walking stiffly in the back brace, then gingerly bent to scoop up some change—he could blame lots of guys, but Leo Weiss got the darkest curses. It was Leo who'd risked the grief of Violet, Magda, and Una for the sake of revenge. He'd plunged into the water with the sharks, like Tom, only twice as stupid. Tom had leaned on some hammerheads. Leo had taken on the great white.

The blame was doubly tough to endure when you couldn't make a vow to right things, because your time was up. And memories besieged you. Maybe if death gave some warning, the memories would treat you gently—if you could count on a month or so to savor them, rein them out a little farther every day, and finally release them from a distance. Leo would've preferred meeting death step by step, the same way he tiptoed into the cold ocean on his daily constitutional. But when, over lunch, the punks talked of carrying him out in a sack at first dark, so Denny could meet a skirt of his at Ciro's by nine, the memories walloped him. Exquisite memories. Seldom of victories or occasions when anybody sang his praises. Instead they recalled when some person, or some glimpse of beauty, had touched him and his heart swelled. There was a runny-nosed Filipino kid in Manila who begged him for a coin, whose toothy grin still shone after fifty years. And one foggy morning when the gray whales were migrating past his beach, and the dolphin fins, a dozen or more, spiked out of the water just beyond the breakers. Pelicans, gulls, and cormorants hovered. Back in paradise.

The driver tugged and Denny kicked him to his feet and Bass placed the hat on Leo's head and they dragged him upright, out of the cellar. When he saw dark had fallen and knew he was still alive, a small dose of hope invaded him. If he could get to Cohen, maybe he'd find a word that'd sting the bastard. One final satisfaction. Or convince him to lay off Tom. One last good deed.

Through the living room and off the porch he struggled to move his legs. He didn't want the punks carrying him. He tried to shake their hands off. They gripped like crabs.

"Shove him into the junk heap," Bass commanded.

The punks cut across the lawn and through the row of pansies. Denny opened the Packard's passenger door. The driver pushed Leo in. Bass hustled around and got into the back from the driver's side. As Denny stooped to climb in, Leo mustered the breath to stammer, "Where's my satchel?"

"Aw, shit. Go get it, Denny. In the dining room, I guess."

"What's he gonna need the suitcase for?"

"Think a minute, genius."

"What?"

"We leave the satchel, you wanta leave a note too, all about how we treated the old man?"

Nodding glumly, muttering, "Oh, yeah," Denny skulked out and ran across the lawn.

"Where we going?" Leo's tongue was like chopped meat, his lips swollen and bonded together with blood and the ooze that wouldn't scab.

"Hey, I'm tired of your voice, Pancho. All I wanta hear's the name of this fanatic."

"I'm gonna tell Mickey his name."

Bass groaned. "What'd I do made you think I'm a moron? We knock you around all day, you say there ain't no such fanatic. Now, when time's up, you wanta talk to Mickey, buy a couple hours more. You weren't such a tough old guy, I didn't like you, I'd of iced you a long time back." He plucked a case out of his coat pocket, inserted a stubby French cigarette into his mouth, and flipped open his shiny lighter. "Tell you what. Feed me the name, maybe we can work something out. Could be I'll save your old ass, just for the hell of it. You give me the name, we check into a hotel. Tomorrow, who knows? How about it?" He sparked the lighter, made a three-inch flame.

"Naw."

Denny tossed the satchel into the back seat, climbed in, and started the motor. Without letting it warm up, he pulled out and lugged down the street, while Bass unzipped Leo's satchel, searched it with his hand. "Nothing but underwear and this old Luger." He laid the gun on the seat beside him and lifted the satchel over the backrest, dropped it onto Leo's lap.

The old man leaned onto it, used it for his pillow. For a while he let his brain scan his body, separate the pains from each other. There was his big toe with the nail plucked out, the kneecap they'd cracked, the ribs that felt like a bundle of splinters, a couple of them jabbing his lungs. The eyelid they'd slashed. A sliver of light glared through.

Denny made a fast right turn, slinging Leo against the car door. As he bounced off, his mind spun away as if it'd gotten seized by a whirlwind. After a second, when he landed, he was a young cop. His third year: 1906. Vi was a sophomore at Pasadena

College. A creep had been stalking the girls from her boarding-house. On patrol, Leo spotted a character in some bushes down the street. Tall, pale, curly-haired. Leo snuck up, grabbed and cuffed him, and marched him straight to the boardinghouse, where the girls sat around their supper table.

The house mother jumped up and railed at Leo. Said she'd given the description a dozen times, and this guy was twice as tall as the culprit. While the old buffalo read him off, all the girls snickered except the small brunette, who followed him outside to say thanks for his zeal. On the sidewalk, hallowed by the moon, she told him her name was Violet, then raised onto her toes, pecked his chin, and ran off.

The suspect had hung around to watch the encounter. "Ain't that sweet," he said. "She's gotta hurry and wring out her panties. That's the way those Mex gals are."

Leo busted him for trespassing, cuffed him so tight he yelped and squealed all the way.

Every small hump sent the Packard bounding, and the pains seemed to jolt him awake as though out of a snooze. The satchel helped absorb the jolts. Leo only heaved himself up to look a few times. Once as they made the turn off Fairfax onto Sunset Boulevard. Once when Denny tapped the horn and waved at somebody stepping out of a Rolls in front of the Dancers, a supper club where Leo could've bought a cup of soup for about the value of his Packard. Cold soup, garnished with one sprig of parsley. And he noticed the violet buds and lacy finger-sized leaves on a jacaranda, along the foresty drive beneath Bel Air.

For a while he got lost, dreamed he was catching a lift up to the mountains, to Tom's place. He got a whiff of redwood scent on thin air. Then Denny jumped on the brakes and pounded the horn, pitching him back to real life.

His eyes dripped, his throat blistered while he thought how he could've been with Tom by now, easily. He should've started out last night, the second he got off the phone knowing Tom wanted him up there. If he'd been a decent pal.

He tried to remember a single incident when Tom had let him down. There must've been one or two, but the memories got displaced by dozens of times when Tom had risked his neck, his marriage, or his savings. Every chance to strike it rich, Tom had invited him in. In a scrape, all he'd needed was to hint and Tom had come on the double. To imagine his pal thinking bitterly of him, when the chance to redeem himself was gone, felt insufferably wretched. He'd think about Tom no more, ever.

On some mountain road that he placed around the junction of Beverly Glen and Mulholland, he reached for the dashboard and boosted himself up. To the left, what at first looked like city lights he recognized as moonlight glinting off the mica embedded in the face of a boulder. Either there were hitchhiking midgets, a few yards off the road, or barrel cactus. The road turned to washboard. The punks were gabbing about movies.

"Roy Rogers is queer," Bass said. "Gene Autry...let me tell you what my cousin Andrew says. Andrew, he's a rancher."

"For real?"

"Hey, I say he's a rancher, it's a fact. He says you're risking your neck if you as much as light a smoke while you're riding, and no damn fool gets away with sitting on a horse's ass strumming a guitar."

"You watch *Stagecoach*?" Denny asked. "Wouldn't catch John Wayne picking anybody's guitar."

Bass proclaimed, "The only Western worth the quarter's *Ride 'Em Cowboy*. Abbott and Costello."

When Leo peeled his lips apart and tried to use the fat, raw tongue that lay throbbing on the floor of his mouth. The first phrase sounded like one long word in Arabic. The second try, he took more care.

"Suppose I'm telling you straight...the informer's for real. He snitches, Mickey loses...his head....Yeah? Asks why didn't you bring Weiss to him?"

"Turn on the radio, would you, Denny?" The radio clicked on to Perry Como. "Not that bum," Bass said. "Find something loud, with horns."

Denny spun the dial while Leo dug through the rubble of his brain for a scheme, a way he could talk the punk into carrying him to Mickey, though he'd forgotten why he wanted to see the man, except it felt like you ought to meet the guy who was killing you. Maybe give him something lousy to remember.

Denny had found a jazz station. To the blats and wails of Charlie Parker, they started up a grade on a skinny road lined and sometimes overhung with pepper trees. They passed a field around which boulders were scattered like ancient headstones. Beyond it lay the ocean. Leo could spot the Pacific even in the dark, from the shade lines of its horizon. He placed them a few miles east of Malibu or the Palisades.

A strange lightness possessed him until, after one long free-for-all solo, they drove into a soupy mist. Leo stared into the gray dark. After all the rest, he'd lost sight of the ocean. There must be a God, he thought. How could blind fate treat a guy so wickedly?

But if God was actual, he argued for the thousandth time in the past dozen years since the Anschluss, why the hell would he choose a race of people, call them his own, then pitch them the nastiest curve balls ever thrown? No matter what their iniquities, Leo couldn't imagine a father shooing his favorites into the wilds and loosing the wolves and jackals. If they were rotten kids, who was it made them so?

"Turn in," Bass said. To Leo, it sounded like the command to fire.

The brakes screeched and tires slid across the gravel. Leo'd raised his head an inch or so when the blackjack whopped him just above and behind his right ear. It felt like somebody jabbed a trowel deep into his head. For an instant, as though wires crossed and sent a freakish signal, he didn't hurt—rather he *heard* the pain. It bellowed like a great sea creature.

Maybe he died for a moment and returned just as fast. Anyway, he sensed himself rolling and tumbling like a skinny kid walloped and shanghaied by the surf. Inside a cloud of light, the Packard materialized around him. Two car doors slammed.

Somebody grunted. "You call that pushing?" a different man yelped.

"Damn! Ouch!"

"What?"

"The junk heap ran over my foot. Piece of crap!"

Every time Leo blinked, he got blinded by the light. As the last voice faded, Leo heard the Packard's springs giving a mighty shriek just before the old workhorse seemed to vault upward, then topple and flip. It dumped him off the seat and under the dashboard, where he curled around the satchel and squeezed hard as if it'd been Vi or one of his girls suddenly come to his rescue.

Chapter Twenty-five

Wendy saw the headlights first. They jittered and bounced through the forest across the lake. Sure it was Tom, she wanted to holler for joy. Instead, she covered her mouth with both hands and only glanced sideways at the window.

The men sat hunched over the little table beside the kitchen, playing poker. Tersh scooped in a pot, added it to the pile of bills and mound of coins on his side. He gave a malicious chuckle. Bud stacked the few coins he had left, caught a deep breath, let it out in a sigh, and gazed around the room with eyes that seemed accustomed to witnessing their proprietor lose.

While she'd watched the game, Wendy'd pulled for Bud, silently, or else Tersh would've socked her again like he did when she couldn't stop crying. Before dark, when she feared going crazy.

His fist had been good medicine. A minute of anger had ousted her fear, and during the break she'd gotten busy praying.

The men were too busy winning and losing to notice the headlights or hear the faint motor noise. The car crept along the road behind the tallest stand of yellow pine across the lake, halfway up the grade. It wasn't Tom's Chevy. Though she could only make out the slightest drone over the trees' rustle and creaking, she recognized the difference because so many times she'd sat listening for Tom to come home. This one sounded like a bigger car. Maybe Claire's. Or the police.

As the car drew closer, Wendy got nervous that the men would hear. To cover the noise, she prayed out loud. Excited, anxiously following the headlights, she couldn't think up words of her own, so she recited from psalms she'd memorized. "Oh, Lord my God," she mumbled, "if there be iniquity in my hands; if I have rewarded evil unto him who was at peace with me, let the enemy persecute my soul. But...I trust in your mercy. My heart will rejoice in your salvation. Pretty soon, I'll sing to the Lord because he has dealt bountifully with me."

"She's at it again," Bud said. "If she's a nitwit, how do you suppose she remembers all that rigmarole?"

"She's making it up." Tersh sat upright, raised a hand for silence. "That a damned motorboat?" He turned slowly and peered out the window, then jumped from his chair and strode across the room, pushed his face against the glass. "A car."

"Probably the snowplow guy," Bud offered.

"It was a snowplow, I'd call it a snowplow. It's a car."

"Maybe the snowplow guy's got a car."

"We'll see."

Bud joined his partner at the window. They, and Wendy, silently watched the lights jittering up the last stretch of road before the fork, where the car swung right. A few feet ahead, it stopped alongside the Olds that had glinted for a moment in its lights.

"Lash her up," Tersh growled.

He dashed to the chair by the door where two weapons perched. A sawed-off shotgun, twelve-gauge pump, and a Thompson submachine gun. Grabbing the twelve-gauge in one hand, he reached with the other hand for the pistol he'd left atop the kitchen hutch. He stuck the pistol under his belt. "Get a move on, Bud." He pushed the door open slowly to minimize its squeak, stepped out, and closed it the same way.

Bud ordered Wendy to put her hands in her lap; then he wrapped the heavy cord around her, waist to shoulders, and around the back of the chair. He gave her a wink, blew her a kiss, and hustled outside, grabbing the tommy gun on the way.

◇◇◇

The footsteps stopped crunching. Tersh was leaning against a tall blackened stump on the hill side of the road. Bud knelt behind a clump of saplings on the lake side. They'd come a hundred yards or so, to halfway between the cabin and the car that had parked next to Tersh's Olds, just beyond the gorge a stream had carved across the road.

The man had gotten out of his car. From here it looked like a Plymouth. He'd walked about fifty yards and stopped. He stood still for a minute before he said, "Hey, hey, somebody there? I'm Frankie Foster's pal. The guy you're working for." He braved a few more steps and hollered a little louder. "You hear me?"

Bud lifted a hand to keep his partner quiet. They watched the man near them a few steps at a time, punctuated by his greetings. "You there? Cut the ghost routine, will you?"

The voice got more quavery every time. Bud had to cup a hand over his mouth to mute his sniggering. Even Tersh's sour mug brightened. When the man crossed the invisible line between them, Tersh and Bud sprang out and froze him with a Thompson aimed at his nose, a shotgun at his middle.

"Don't believe we've met," Bud said.

The man's knees and shoulders quaked. He nodded frantically. "Yeah, well…Meechum."

Even in the woolen, padded lumberjack coat, he appeared lanky. Big ears jutted out, like handles, through his wild yellow hair. Beneath a growth of blond stubble, his face looked raw, as though he'd walked miles through a blizzard. The upper lip appeared caked with greenish frost.

Bud let the tommy gun fall to his side. "Must be the guy. He's ugly as Frankie said."

"I'm the guy, all right. How else do I know you're here, chrissake?" The man's left arm remained tense against his side, while the right hand began jumping incessantly, from his hair to his nose to his thigh.

"Maybe you're one of these spacemen from Krypton." Bud snorted and grinned.

Tersh finally loosened his grip on the twelve-gauge, stepped back, and looked the man over. He hacked a cough and spat copiously. "What kept you?"

"I got delayed."

"Me and Bud figure you been chasing dames, shooting craps. It's gonna cost you."

Jumpy as his right hand, Jack Meechum's eyes darted between the men, to both sides, and over his shoulder as though watching for pursuers. "The hell," he said meekly. "Put down the artillery, would you?"

"Not a chance."

He tried bluster. Cranked up the volume, lowered the tone, and growled, "I had a breakdown in the desert fifty miles out of Vegas. Had to drive all night long with a heater that thinks it's an ice machine. The girl still alive?"

"What, you figure we're going to waste her gratis?" Tersh said. "We only got paid for the snatch, chum."

"Take a look." Bud motioned up the road toward the cabin.

Meechum followed, stumbling every time he glanced back at Tersh and the shotgun. He tripped over the threshold. Once inside, he dodged around Bud and reached the girl in two long bounds, as if she were a trophy that'd evaded him for years.

All the time they'd been gone, Wendy'd fought against her imagination, which listened for gunshots, screams, and blood. She wanted to picture Tom running in to grab her up and squeeze her, tickle her neck with hot kisses. Anything else, she refused to imagine.

To distract from her wicked imagination, she'd been trying to recite an especially pretty psalm. But several lines of one verse wouldn't come. She remembered, "In wisdom have you made them all." She knew another was, "Yonder is the sea, great and wide, which teems with things innumerable." The verse ended with, "There go the ships, and leviathan which you did form to sport in it." Now she sat pensively chewing on her bottom lip.

The door slamming open had jolted her so fiercely, her eyes bugged at the new, clumsy man and she bit a small nick inside her lip. The man looked furious and hateful, crazy as the devil, with something reddish that flickered out of his slits of eyes. He had his hands clasped together in front of him, as though he were strangling the life out of something. He unclasped them, reached out, and pinched her chin cruelly. The tips of his thumb and finger were calloused hard as wood.

"Your old man's a nosy bastard," he whispered. "A lousy snoop," he yelled. "He would've kept his ass at home with you, stupid little bitch, I wouldn't be…goddam him. What's the deal, honey, you couldn't keep your man home?" By now he was wrenching her chin so it bent her head sideways and made her eyes bubble with tears.

On the window side of them, Tersh grinned and nodded slightly as though at a cockfight, waiting for blood.

Suddenly Meechum let go her chin, cuffed it, turned, and staggered across the floor to collapse into a chair beside the table. His arm knocked over Tersh's money pile. He sat glaring at the floor, gasping long breaths through his flared nostrils. The exhales came so hard they were like snores. Finally he reached into his coat pocket for an envelope. He pressed the ends to open it, peered inside, shook the contents into one corner, and poured a few dashes into the wedge he made between his left thumb and forefinger. He snuffed most of it through one nostril and finished it through the other.

"Ain't you going to share?" Tersh asked.

"Hell, no," Meechum snapped. Then, as if remembering the Thompson and the shotgun, he said more diplomatically, "I got a habit and I'm damn near dry."

"Yeah, yeah. What you think, Bud? The junkie shows up half a day late, and he shows up damn near dry."

"He's got problems," Bud drawled. "Matter of fact, they're breaking my heart. Mind if I step outside and blubber awhile?"

"Go ahead and blubber in here. I get a kick outta watching that stuff."

"First we gotta settle up. I figure, we put in a fair day's work. We turn the doll over to Jacky here, collect our dough, and get a jump start off his jalopy. Then let's you and me cruise on down the mountain. Drink a few rounds, lose a buck or two, take our turn with the dames."

"Not till he knocks off the girl. She gets loose, we're in the big house waiting for our turn at the hot seat."

"You're telling me we can't trust ol' Jack?"

"Why should we? He don't show up on time or remember to bring us a snort. It's like he gets invited to dinner, walks in late, and don't even bring any wine."

"Somebody oughta send him to finishing school," Bud said.

They both stood watching Meechum, while his hand kept flying around to rub his ear, his ribs, his eyes. Finally Tersh stepped to the woodbox beside the stove, picked up the ax. He carried it to Meechum and held it out, the blunt end up.

"Whop her with this side, won't be so much blood."

Meechum looked up dreamily, his eyes wandering toward the window and back. "How about I shoot her?"

"You got a piece?"

"I could borrow yours."

"Like hell you could. Anyhow, it's no sense making noise. You knock her with this, tie some rocks on her—there's plenty along the shore. I'll help you dump her in the lake for a C-note. You want me to knock her *and* dump her, it'll cost you a grand."

"You know," Bud mused, "I mean, look at her. Now, that's a pretty thing to waste. Suppose we blind her. How'd that be? She couldn't pick us out of the scrapbook."

Tersh squinted at his partner, then at Wendy. After a sullen minute, he took the chair beside Meechum and sat, his face wrinkled pensively. "How do you blind somebody? I never done it."

"Throw some stuff in her eyes, if you got the right stuff. Fire'll do the job. Coals'd do it, huh? We got plenty coals."

"That'd wipe the smile off her."

Meechum's wild stare kept shifting between the two men, following their talk, while his hand bolted from one destination to the next as though searching for the right button. At last, he said, "You guys are nuts."

Tersh formed his eyes and mouth into near-perfect O's. "Nuts, are we?"

"How about her tongue, you gonna cut it out too? And her hands so she can't write?"

His malicious grin warping into a frown, Tersh gazed at his partner. "You wanta blind her, how come the whole time we been gabbing like there's nobody here? How come yesterday you talk like she's good as dead, tonight you say give her a break? Like she won't remember our names, or what? I mean, sure there's a million Bud's around. How many other guys you know named Tersh?"

"I was just saying she's some doll. It's a damn shame to waste her."

"Maybe you'd like to stuff her, take her home," Meechum snarled.

"You implying I'm a pervert?" Bud asked coolly.

"What if I am?"

"Look," Bud mused. "If her old man gets her back, maybe he's too busy taking care of her to try and hunt us down. See, the way I figure, we snuff the girl, we gotta knock him off too. This is one tough guy, the way I hear it. Busts heads for Harry Poverman." He glanced at Meechum and nodded slowly, ominously.

"Yeah," Tersh said. "Barney claims he ain't exactly mean like some of your bulls that just like to beat on guys. I mean, he catches a cheat, somebody pilfering, he won't rough 'em up or nothing. It's just he goes wacko about dames. There was a creep played this game. He'd buy drinks for some tourist doll, drop a little powder in it. She gets woozy, he hikes her to the room, next thing she's out and he's all over her. She wakes up in this room that's registered to some corny name—Johnny Appleseed was one. Anyway, this Hickey corners the guy—they damn near had to use a cable and winch to pull him off. The creep was seeing nothing but stars for three days."

"Yeah, I heard," Bud said. "Another time, there was a slot mechanic dropping sexy notes to a cocktail gal, scaring the pants off her. Looked like the cops couldn't pin the notes on the punk, but everybody knew it was him. Hickey chased that boy off the mountain so good, I hear he's in Brazil, still running, and he ain't gonna stop till the Arctic."

"We gotta take him out," Tersh muttered. "Only question, how much do you pay us to hit the big fella, Jack?"

"Shit. If that's gotta be done, it's part of the deal. You guys knew about the doll's old man before you grabbed her, didn't you?"

Bud plucked off his hat, scratched his crown. "Me and Tersh aren't known for our foresight."

Meechum heaved himself out of the chair, made a pass by the window, and stared out. Then he turned back and glowered at Wendy.

Though she'd tried to keep attentive, she'd only heard clips of the men's talk. Just enough. Fright or something had confused her body, made it go fiery hot on the surface but icy inside, so cold she imagined Clifford freezing solid. Meantime, an idea was possessing her. Maybe, she thought, if she pleaded, they'd save the baby. As soon as the man lifts his ax, when it's sure Tom hasn't rescued her in time, she could beg and argue. Explain how, if they killed her but spared the baby, and if she wrote a note asking for Tom's promise to leave the men alone on account of he might get killed or tossed into prison where he couldn't take care of Clifford, he'd be sure to abide by her wish. She could even write how she was thankful to the men for saving Clifford when they didn't have to.

Anyhow, the baby couldn't do them any harm. Wendy prayed silently that one of the men, at least, would prove a little kinder than a monster. She was repeating the prayer when Meechum's hard fingers touched her cheeks.

While Meechum stood petting her, he glared furiously as though she'd rigged his every trouble and woe. He made a hiss and slapped her hard across the cheekbone, then squared his shoulders back.

"Let's get it over with," he snarled. "Give me the damn ax."

"What about her old man? Soon as we get rid of her, we go down and pop him, right. And for that one, you're paying us two grand each, up front."

"Who's got two grand?"

"Foster."

Meechum rapped his ears with his knuckles. Noticing a mousetrap on the floor, he reared back and kicked it hard. "Forget the husband."

"How are we gonna do that, when he's dogging us?" Bud asked.

"He won't be dogging anybody. Hickey's a goner."

"Right," Bud said. "You're gonna tell us you whacked him all by your lonesome."

"I'm telling you Harry Poverman's gonna take him out."

"Get lost. Harry likes the guy."

"Not after he lost his head, made the dumbest bonehead move I ever heard, pointing a gun at Harry. By now, a dozen sharpshooters are waiting outside Poverman's place. He steps out, they fix him. Hickey's a dead man."

"Who says?" Tersh grumbled.

"Foster told me, a couple hours ago in Reno. And I stopped at Harry's club for a minute, heard the same story. Everybody knows it."

"Stopped by the club, did you?" Tersh lifted the ax to his shoulder as though contemplating decapitation. But Meechum ignored the gesture. It must've been single-mindedness that turned him so cocky and bold. He reached for the ax, grabbed it out of Tersh's hands.

He was checking its weight when a noise from outside interrupted. A rumble, then a whoosh, and finally a boom that made the cabin tremble.

Chapter Twenty-six

A cluster of stars appeared and beamed on the lake for a moment before the lacy fringe of a cloud mass blotted them over. It blew from the northeast, toward the Rubicons. The willowy lodge pole pines bowed, rose and fluttered, like a chorus line.

Beside the picture window, Hickey stood condemning himself. The more fatigue, the more benzedrine, the more viciously he lamented his stupid mistakes. Leaving Wendy alone. Throwing up the gauntlet to Paoli and Schwartz. Involving Leo.

For years, Hickey'd posed as a fatalist. Never in that time had fear gouged him so deeply. With Cynthia on the loose, Wendy wouldn't mean a damn to the freaks. If they hadn't killed her already, not a chance she'd survive the night.

An hour ago, at twilight, he'd tried exorcising his remorse by confiding in Poverman and Frieda, because they were the only available humans except the cowboy, who'd gone to check on some whinnying they'd heard from the stable. Frieda, while delivering an ale, had asked if somebody might tell her why Mr. Hickey was mad at the boss.

Harry suggested that her muscle-bound pal must've told her, but she claimed that if Tyler knew the scoop, he wasn't talking. So the gambler deferred to Hickey, who explained he'd gone off on a case and rubbed the wrong guys the wrong way.

But why, Frieda asked, did he leave his pregnant wife alone?

To contend that Wendy had wanted him to go, because somebody needed help, seemed a miserable excuse. So he confessed to being one of those jerks who had to become a soldier, fireman, cop: a dope compelled to risk everything for somebody else every chance he got. Trying to earn his way out of purgatory.

Now he watched the stars tease. They seemed to duck behind clouds, peek, then spring out and flash their brightest. Even distracted by the view and his remorse, Hickey didn't worry about the boss jumping him. If Poverman rubbed his nose or scratched his ear, Hickey'd hear or feel the movement in the air, electrified as his senses were. He could hear cars from the village a half mile up, through the woods. Every one, he fervently hoped, was the station wagon delivering Frankie Foster.

A sleek cabin cruiser ran circles a hundred yards out from the shore, bounding and leaping over its own swells. Probably a drunken playboy impressing his gal.

Out in the woods, somebody coughed. Hickey'd caught the noise of sticks cracking underfoot and a whistle, probably of a goon who thought he could imitate a bird and didn't know the difference between summer and February. About twenty minutes ago, just after dark, a man had sauntered along the beach, making like he was out for a stroll, bareheaded, in a tailored overcoat. Every few feet he'd sneak a glance at the picture window. Finally Hickey'd recognized him as a pit boss from the casino.

Four months ago, when the baby'd started kicking, Wendy had developed a new tone of voice in which she called Tom's name. She gave it two syllables, the second a fluttery sound that tickled his heart. She only called him that way when she wanted him to feel her belly. Just as the cruiser finally bounded out of sight, he heard her beckon him like that. The voice was so real and close, he wheeled, truly expecting to see her at the front door. Only it was a phantom. He turned away from the window, flopped into his chair. The gambler was staring menacingly.

"You got a problem?" Hickey muttered.

"You bet. I gotta decide how long to keep playing this game and when to call it a night and put you outta your misery."

"Tell Frieda to bring me a scotch."

"On top of the bennies, you're liable to get crazy." He yelled for the maid. "You're not worried she's gonna spike the drink with a goofball?"

"Oh, yeah. Never mind the drink."

"You're losing contact, Tom. Another hour, I breathe hard, it'll knock you over.... Okay, what I'm thinking—you give your word you'll tell darling Claire nothing but my virtues, I'll give you to midnight."

Hickey answered him with a scowl, and Frieda came scurrying out of the far cube, hair in rollers and face blotched with vanishing cream that hadn't vanished.

"Coffee," the boss said. "And how about, we got any of those Italian cookies?"

Before she could answer, tires squealed off the road and clattered on the driveway. Hickey motioned the boss to his feet and followed him to the door, while Frieda hustled back into the bedroom cube as though she feared the car might be full of movie scouts whom she'd get only this one chance to dazzle.

The gambler stood at the window beside the door, with Hickey an arm's length behind him. They watched the Chrysler station wagon roll to a stop. First out was Tyler, who ran around and let a woman out the rear passenger door: a little blonde, her hair stacked and sprayed into a cone. She wore a long silver-fox coat.

Frankie Foster climbed out of the shotgun seat. He had big flapjack ears and slicked dark hair, sloping shoulders that made his neck appear stretched.

As Tyler started following the others around the car, he suddenly turned and looked off into the woods toward Hickey's place, then backstepped that way, keeping an eye on Foster. He stopped beside a tamarack, its trunk the width of an oil drum, and leaned against it. No doubt talking to one of Poverman's boys hidden behind the tree. Hickey made a note that if ever the world got right again, he'd ask Tyler who he'd thought he was fooling.

Foster and the blonde stood beside the porch rail, waiting for Tyler, who finally returned and led them up the steps, across the deck to the front door. The woman pranced in front, on her high spiked heels.

Harry swung the door open. "Hey, Laura.

The woman offered him a kiss and Harry graciously accepted, wrapping her and the silver fox in his arms. Eventually he let her go and stepped back out of the doorway. Foster walked at the woman's heels. He was short, level with the tiny woman on her stilts. Though his skin was smooth and taut, he looked about sixty. He had a generous mouth and lips that curled down on the right side. His eyebrows were high and curved like a beauty queen's. He shook Poverman's hand but declined to return the smile.

"What'd I do, Harry? Why don't you trust me? I got a car. My kid's a good driver. We'd of been here on our own in a hour or so."

"Trust," Harry said ponderously. "Trust you, huh? I gotta look that word up in my dictionary one of these days." He turned and called, "Frieda, there's a bunch of thirsty guests out here."

Hickey'd stepped far enough back to watch all of them. The woman gave him a sidewise glance, then turned to scrutinize him while she peeled off her fur. Her lipstick was scarlet outlined in black. Her eyelids were plastered blue. She wore a tight golden sleeveless and shoulderless dress, with necklace and earrings to match, over a startling body: breasts and rear end enough for a goddess eight feet tall, and a waist so slight a guy might've encircled it with his thumbs and forefingers. Spotting the pistol at Hickey's side, she leaned toward Poverman. "Who's the bruiser?"

Harry didn't answer. He stood listening to Tyler, who'd stepped up close and was talking low. When Tyler finished, the gambler put a fatherly hand on his shoulder and boomed, "Get the creeps outta Tom's house. Tell 'em, anybody so much as cussed in front of Miss Blackwood, they'll be working graveyard as a slot runner. Matter of fact, bring Miss Blackwood over here. Tyler, you take phone duty at Tom's place. All you gotta do is stay off the line and pass messages. You got my number. We go anyplace, we let you know. Come on, move it." He gave Tyler a shove. "On your way, make a spin around the house and tell the boys out there anybody messes with Tom before I say so gets sautéed and dumped in the spaghetti sauce."

Hickey stepped closer. "Nice act."

"Act, huh? What was that word Frankie used, the big one? Trust. Now I remember what it means. How about this—Tom, you trust me; me, I'll trust Frankie. Frieda!" he yelled. "Last call, honey. We got a toast to make."

Frieda came running, in her maid costume, her hair fluffed except in front where one roller dangled. She took orders for Harry's martini, Foster's scotch mist, and the woman's double vodka with a lemon wedge and a single ice cube. Poverman led the way through the leather and Formica maze.

Laura sat on the couch beside him, shimmied her behind into the cushion, while her father perched on the window seat, gripping the edge, his toes on the floor as though making ready in case he needed to bolt. He looked at the stockpot beside him, took a whiff. "What's this thing?"

"I was peeling potatoes. Frieda'll get it outta here." The boss motioned toward Hickey, who'd flopped into his chair. "My neighbor, Tom Hickey. You heard the name?"

Foster appeared to sift through his memory before he shook his head. "I should know him?"

"Sure. He gets around, same as you. Tom's an old cop, works for me now. Few days ago, he goes to help out a doll he used to know, sticks his nose in the wrong hole, and gets bit. A couple guys snatched his wife, who's gonna present him with a baby real soon. You see what I'm talking about? These guys come right into my neighborhood, grab a friend of mine. You think I'm gonna sit still for that?"

"Hey, I sympathize," Foster said. "Now, how about you tell me what I'm doing here?"

The boss flashed a grin, patted Laura's knee, then fixed his gaze on Foster. "You're gonna rat on the guys I was talking about. You're smart, you'll tell us where to find them. Get this: We're not gonna ask you to say who these guys are working for, on account of we got no beef against you, Frankie. All we're doing is, things went wrong, we're setting them straight. Soon as the girl's back, healthy and all, the whole deal's forgiven. That right, Tom?"

"Good enough," Hickey mumbled.

Laura had cocked her right arm, hand beside her ear like Yogi Berra setting to throw. Her lips had curled. Noticing she was going to belt him, Harry slid to the end of the couch.

"Why're you putting this on Frankie?"

"Shut up, honey," Foster said. He folded his hands, rested his chin on his thumbs. "Like she says, why you putting this on me?"

"You're telling me you don't know about these guys?"

"Yeah, that's what I'm telling you. I heard nothing about any snatch. Somebody say I did?"

"We pieced it together. Tom's a dick, remember. You wanta hear the pieces?"

Foster gazed wearily at the two other men while Frieda swiveled between couches and coffee tables and around the snake tank, carrying drinks on a wooden tray. After Foster took a sip of his scotch mist, he held it on his knee. Frieda disappeared, leaving the place quiet enough so Hickey could hear the shaved ice rattle.

"See, Frankie, there's a guy in Dago…I forget his name, but he was the one that blew the alibi for Tom's old girlfriend that got popped for torching Johnny Sousa's place. This guy, what's his name?" Harry slid across the couch, leading with his chin as though offering it to Laura so she could sock it, and patted her knee. "Come on, what's his name, the guy you were married to?"

"Jack?" Her eyes looked demonic, all painted and squinting fiercely. "Jack can go to hell."

"What about Meechum?" Foster snapped.

The boss had slid away from the girl and leaned back into the hands folded behind his neck. "Tom, give it to 'em, will you? You got all the names straight."

Hickey sat quietly, staring at Foster until the man blinked. "Charlie Schwartz had the hots for two sisters, Cynthia and

Laurel. He got burned by both of them. Then Johnny Sousa, who was Laurel's husband before he got toasted, started making pals with the Italians. Maybe Charlie figured he was grazing on both sides of the fence."

Hickey noticed his voice had gone thin, as though he needed to ration the air in his lungs. He felt his skin tighten and chill in expectation. Any second he might learn if he still had a wife and baby.

"The way it fits," he said, "Charlie saw a way to fix all of them at once. He gets somebody to torch Sousa's house and plants Meechum to hang it on Cynthia. Now Laurel's a widow, Johnny's ashes, and Cynthia's in the joint, which makes Schwartz one happy fellow."

Foster unfolded his hands, leaned forward, and gripped them around his knee. He made a sneer, offered it first to Poverman, then Hickey. "Yeah, well, I don't talk to Jack. The rat was stepping out on my daughter. That's why she dumped him."

"Shut up, Frankie. Let Tom finish."

Hickey'd gotten out his Walter Raleigh. He stuffed the pipe, lit up. Thinking he glimpsed a light flash outside the picture window, he shot a glance over his shoulder. While he scanned the dark woods, confusion knocked him silly. Lost as though he'd just awakened in a foreign place, he felt the men staring at him and turned, his .45 lifted and ready to clobber somebody.

"Whoa, pal," the boss whispered soothingly. "You wanta thump him, okay, but finish the story first."

Hickey rubbed his sore eyes, sat back, and hung his head. "Cynthia wants me to spring her, so I go down and make a mess of things, including I spook Charlie Schwartz." His voice had dropped to a gruff monotone. "See, Laurel's probably got more pals at city hall than Charlie does. Could be he doesn't walk this time. If Charlie goes down, Meechum gets hit with perjury, conspiracy, aiding and abetting; he loses his union cabaret card, where's he gonna blow, street corners? You following me?"

"Keep talking."

"Another thing is, Charlie hates my guts from way back. And Meechum's starting to. So they're gonna mess with me, and get me outta town till Charlie can fix things, make the right donations and all."

There was clomping on the front deck. The door flew open. Claire Blackwood entered, with Tyler close on her tail. Harry stood up. As Claire approached, he swept his hand, offering her his seat on the couch beside Laura, who sat smoothing the golden dress over her thighs and scowling at the new competition.

"Miss Blackwood." The boss nodded toward her. "Frankie Foster and Laura Meechum."

"Laura Foster," the woman hissed.

"Oh, yeah." Harry remained standing, admiring Claire's features even while he questioned the old man. "How about it, Frankie? Where do we find these guys?"

"Beats me. I got nothing to do with Schwartz or Meechum."

Harry shook his head glumly. After a long, heartful gaze at Claire, he gulped a breath and blew it out slowly, his lips pursed as though for a whistle. His eyes had swollen and sunk deeper, as if he were an innocent who'd just witnessed mayhem. He gave Hickey a grimace, then looked around the room and shouted for the cowboy, who appeared in the doorway to the kitchen, a large sandwich in his paw.

"Mac, go warm up *Prudence*."

"Warm up what?" Hickey growled.

"A speedboat."

Chapter Twenty-seven

What the hell?" Laura snapped. "A boat ride? You ain't getting me out there this time of year."

"Just the boys. Mac, Frankie, me, and Tom."

"No Mac," Hickey said. "Just you, me, and Frankie'll be plenty."

The boss dramatically rolled his eyes. "Miss Blackwood, what've I gotta do to make this character trust me?"

"Three or four years in a monastery might do the trick."

"You got a wit."

Claire walked over and sat on the arm of Hickey's chair. "Nobody called."

"I figured you would've said."

"You okay, Tom?" Between the frown and her quivering chin, it looked as if the wrong answer could've launched her into hysterics.

"Swell," Hickey muttered.

She petted his hair, stood, moved behind the chair, and began kneading his shoulders. Every minute or so, she'd bend and tell him something hopeful. Wendy was strong. Maybe she'd gotten away. Any second the phone could ring. She had to lean close to Hickey's ear, to make herself heard over the noise of Laura spitting curses at Harry for accusing her father of teaming up with a bug like Jack Meechum and for letting some damned cop hold a gun on his guests. Harry stood grimacing, hands folded behind his back. Every time he glanced at Claire, Laura's nostrils flared wider.

When Mac returned and said the boat was ready, warmed up and tied at the end of the pier, Harry made a signal to Claire, called her aside, and started toward the southwest cube. Hickey caught up. Handling the gun in his coat pocket, he followed Claire into the poolroom.

Claire gazed sourly around at the decor. A Picasso still life beside a Remington noble savage. The corner above the refrigerator twinkled with green and mauve neon stars. Shaking her head, she turned to the gambler. "Are you going to hurt the old man?"

Harry picked out a cue and screwed the two halves together. "Let me ask you something. Suppose the old boy don't make it back—are you gonna think I'm a louse?"

"Sure.…But I won't turn you in for it."

He rapped the butt end of the cue on the plush carpet like a ballplayer checking for cracks in his bat. "Keep in mind, if Frankie disappears, I'm not the dealer here. It's Tom calls the game. Whoever makes it back and who doesn't, that's on Tom's say-so. Agreed, neighbor?"

"That's how it is," Hickey muttered.

Claire removed her snow cap and wrapped it around her hands. "If Foster doesn't make it back, what do you do about his daughter?"

"We let her try and prove it wasn't an accident. Say, you're gonna stick around, aren't you?"

"I can."

"You know what it means, *mi casa su casa*, right?"

"Let's go," Hickey commanded.

Out in the living room, a gesture of the .45 got Foster to his feet and started toward the door. But Hickey had to shout twice to pry Poverman away from Claire.

Harry made a little bow to her, then called Mac to walk beside him. "Keep the ladies happy. You find yourself reaching for the phone, or the Foster broad starts to go for it, think how displeased Harry's gonna be. Can you handle that, Mac?"

"Oh, yeah. I would've stayed off the line before, boss, except you didn't say to."

"I'm saying it now, Hopalong. Stay off the phone, don't let the Foster broad outta your sight. If she starts peeling off her clothes, get her a robe. Her mouth gets too dirty, stuff a sock in it. What I don't want is you or her or anybody offending Miss Blackwood. Get it?"

Foster, Poverman, and Hickey grabbed coats and hats off the rack in the entryway. The cowboy opened the door, and the others walked out and across the deck single file. From the bottom of the steps, a trail led past the row of tamarack and through the grove of lodge pole pine toward the lake. The trail was marked every few feet by the corner of a stepping stone jutting out through the snow.

Foster halted and spun around. "Hey, I'm not getting on any boat. You wanta rough me up, do it here."

"Okay," Harry said. "Clip him, Tom. We'll dump him in the lake, then go back and knock his little girl around. She probably knows as much as he does."

Hickey raised his Colt, zeroed it between Foster's eyes. The old man's arms flapped like a pair of crippled wings. He muttered curses and turned back down the path.

Because every step he expected a bullet to zing from behind a tree, Hickey walked in zigzags and bobbed slightly. From inside his head came volleys of croaks and chirrups, like monstrous bullfrogs and crickets at war. They faded and ceased as he reached the dock.

Prudence, a twenty-foot Chris Craft mahogany speedboat, bobbed on choppy water at the end of the pier, beyond the aluminum boathouse, trembling like a Thoroughbred at the starting gate. The Chrysler power plant grumbled as though chomping at the bit. The pier was icy. Foster slipped twice, fell to his knees.

The boat featured custom swivel bucket seats at the wheel, at shotgun, and in the middle. A padded plank in the rear. Harry ushered Foster into the left middle seat and got behind the wheel. He loosed the mooring rope as Hickey settled onto the rear plank.

The boat took off like a dragster, the front end lifting, whopping, lifting over the choppy water. Surrounded by a tent of dark spray, they couldn't see the shore or the mountains until Harry cut the throttle and they drifted to rest about a mile off the point at north Stateline, on a dead line between Incline and Hurricane Bay.

The only clouds looked like a blanket made of charcoal topping the South Carson range and feathery wisps over Mt. Rose. The stars were hot and greenish seen through Hickey's eyes, which felt coated with rust. Close around, the water was the royal blue that meant if you dropped a stone into it and chucked another stone at the moon, no telling which would hit its target first. The quivering sickle moon seemed to teeter above the Desolation wilderness.

Nobody else was out on the lake except an antique steamer that chugged southward along the western bank, and a small fleet of lighted fishing boats a few miles south. Alongshore there'd been breeze and swells. Out here the air and water were mostly still. Yet, as though to help strike terror into Frankie Foster, an eerie moan like wind through a tunnel issued from someplace invisible.

The boss swung his seat around. "Okay, Frankie. You get the rules? See, we're gonna finish this, one way or the other, before our nuts freeze. So don't jerk us around. How about it?"

"I been telling you straight," Foster muttered.

"That right? I must've missed it, maybe when I was rubbernecking your daughter. Say it again, Frankie, would you? Where do we find these boys and Tom's wife?"

Foster sat crouched over, head nearly on his knees, blowing into his hands. "It's like I told you. I got nothing to do with Meechum or Schwartz."

"Dunk him," Hickey said.

"Yeah. On your feet, Frankie."

He didn't budge. The boss stood up, caught his balance. He plucked Foster's hat off and grabbed the man by the collar, heaved him off the seat as if he were weightless. Jammed him against the rail.

"What do I gotta do?" the old man yelped, clutching at the rail.

Harry shoved him, head and shoulders, over the side. Dunked his head and neck and held on. Foster's legs kicked out behind him. His belly across the rail, he squirmed and thrashed with his right arm like a skin diver who's run out of breath and has to dash for the surface. When the boss yanked him up, he gasped and made toots like a toy choochoo. "Swear to God," he wailed. "I don't know nothing!"

Harry threw him into his seat. Retrieving a hat from the deck, he smashed it onto the old man's head. "Yeah, you do. Think about it a minute. Warm yourself up, Frankie. Next time you're going in all the way."

"Look," Foster gasped, "maybe I can find out. Back at your place I'll make some calls."

"You think he's on the level, Tom?"

"Maybe."

"Yeah. That shows what a smart guy you are. What, you think you're talking to a Boy Scout leader? This guy's the only one of Bugs Moran's boys Capone didn't knock off on Valentine's Day. On account of Frankie overslept. They're all invited for tea and crumpets in this warehouse. Everybody else Bugs invited shows. Nine or eleven of them, I forget, but no Frankie. He's home snoozing when Capone's boys crash the party. Nine or eleven guys get stuck with a one-way ticket, but not ol' sleepyhead."

The boss chucked Foster's chin.

"Overslept, did you, Frankie? Or set your pals up, like they say? Capone see to it you got outta Chicago safe?"

"What the fuck's Valentine's Day got to do with this cop's wife?" Foster yowled like an indignant tomcat. "You got it in for me, Harry? You trying to muscle some of my action in Reno? That it?"

Poverman chuckled. "Hey, I got a whole casino. Better than half the take goes to me. So I'm gonna try and squeeze your puny book?"

"Yeah, maybe. Some guys want in on all the action. Look, you can't get rid of me. It don't work. Beau knows I'm up here.

Laura, Beau, all they gotta do is call Graham or Lansky; a half hour later, you guys are on ice. Unless you figure on drowning Laura and Beau."

"Aw, you're all wet." Harry reared back and laughed. "Get it, Tom?"

Hickey nodded anxiously. In some cranny of his mind lurked the thought that someday he'd look back in astonishment at the bloody stupor he'd fallen into, where it seemed he could've witnessed a dozen murders, or the massacre of a city, without a twitch. The way he felt now, he would've swapped every soul on earth for Wendy. He could hardly make sense out of Harry or Foster's talk, while listening so hard for the moment the old bookie would come clean.

"Hey, nobody cares about you, Frankie. Graham, Lansky— it'd be like somebody called them to snitch that Harry Poverman just stepped on a sow bug. Beau's a hired hand, pal. He goes to the highest bidder."

"Laura," Foster moaned. "You gonna clip her too?"

Harry snorted. "Suppose we go back, tell her you're sunk; the broad'll propose a toast. She hates your guts, Frankie. Told me that three, four times last summer. Why do you think she struts around nude in front of Daddy? She laughed like hell, telling me about it. Gives her a kick, to watch her old man limp around with a boner. She's a real gem, Frankie."

With a chirp like Hickey'd heard out of penguins, Foster curled back up, hands between his thighs and forehead on his knees.

"You gonna talk, Frankie?"

"I said it all."

"Okay. I wonder how far you're gonna sink. You know, nobody's ever found the bottom of this damned lake. Maybe you'll wash up in—what's on the other side of the world from here, Tom?"

"Must be Siberia."

"I wonder why it is, everyplace else, some guy drowns or gets dumped in a lake, mostly he'll float to the surface—but Tahoe, nobody does. Every body sinks. Could be there's a dragon-fish, like in Scotland."

"Let's get it done," Hickey snapped. He laid his gun on the plank beside him, got up, and teetered to Foster's right side, because Harry was already on his left, prying the man's arm out from between his legs. When they'd gotten the arms gripped tightly, each of them grabbed an ankle. They lifted the bookie straight up. As they stepped to the rail, Hickey swinging around the seat toward the front, the boat listed. It might've capsized, except they tossed Frankie into the water.

His head knocked against the rail and bounced down into the dark, below the surface. His shoulders and carcass followed. All they held onto were his ankles.

And Hickey thought, Oh, Lord! Harry was on the wrong side, about three feet from where Hickey'd left his .45. If he let go and lunged for the gun, in the second it'd take him to drop Foster and squeeze between the middle seats, Harry could easily beat him to the gun and waste him.

"Pull him out," Hickey yelped.

"Naw, give him another few seconds. I don't wanta have to do it again. I'm getting cold and thirsty."

Hickey couldn't pull him in alone. If he wanted the gun, he'd have to give Foster up to the lake, and Wendy along with him. So he waited until the gambler called out, "Heave ho!"

They gave a yank and Foster came flying up like a huge trout wearing an overcoat, hooting in soprano. Poverman slammed him into the seat. Hickey jumped back to his automatic.

"See the dragon?" Harry asked.

"Yeah," the old gangster whimpered. "Don't put me down there no more."

"Suits me. You're gonna talk, right?"

"Yeah. This is Meechum's deal, all right. It's none of mine."

From the way everything brightened, Hickey could've sworn the moon had miraculously become full. He checked and saw it remained a sickle. He looked around for a Coast Guard boat or a yacht throwing a rescue beam. Nothing. The new light must've been his eyes dilating and swelling in accord with his heart.

"Go on."

Between the chattering of his teeth and the pauses when all he could manage to do was tremble, Foster stammered, "Look, all I did was call a couple guys. Laura begged me, to save Meechum's neck. She's still got the hots for the rat, thinks they can work things out. Meechum gave her a line of crap, I don't know exactly, but I got the truth out of him."

The old man shuddered so wildly, Hickey grabbed him by the shoulders as though holding him still could keep him alive. "Talk!" Hickey roared.

"Yeah, I'm talking. This Cynthia dame, she made a deal with Jack, got him to connect her with an arsonist, let on she'd put out for him, then reneged because the arsonist wanted too much loot. Meechum's nuts about this Cynthia; besides that, he needed lots of dough to pay off a Mex bookie. So he torched Sousa's place himself, took what money the gal could raise."

Foster gritted his teeth and appeared to intercept and hold a shudder before it cut loose.

"He didn't know Sousa was in there. When Sousa burned, Jack got spooked. He's a sissy. I don't know what she sees in the punk except she's always mooning over some fruit that blows a horn."

"Leave out the gossip, would you?" Harry grumbled.

"There was some beachcomber that saw him in the act. So Jack got the guy tanked, whopped him with a hammer. A couple days later, Jack's in Vegas and gets a phone call says this old pal of Cynthia's is snooping around. Putting heat on Charlie Schwartz and the wops. So he gets crazy from thinking pretty soon one of these guys—Charlie, Angelo, the snoop, maybe the cops—are gonna nail him."

Hickey couldn't stop his hands from lunging, grabbing the man's neck, pressing his thumb against the windpipe. "Where do you come in?"

"Somebody tells Jack the snoop that's cooking his goose lives in Tahoe. He phones me. I put him in touch with a couple of guys, is all."

Hickey loosed the windpipe, turned his palm up against Foster's chin, and shoved the man's head back so hard it lifted him over the seat, landed him on the deck. "Where'd they take her?"

The old gangster curled his knees up, turned his face to the deck, and muttered something. Hickey stepped on his neck.

"Easy!" Foster wailed. "There's a guy named Bishop, a banker likes to bet on the ponies. He's got a cabin up here. I never been to it. Some lake. Petunia, Daisy, I don't know."

"Flower," Hickey said.

"Yeah. Flower."

"Thanks, Frankie." The boss gunned the motor and hollered, "Tom and me each owe you one."

Chapter Twenty-eight

Hickey got to the house first, by a hundred yards. He leaped to the deck, slammed the front door open, rushed in. Dodging furniture like a halfback, he dashed to the phone on the Formica table beside the couch where Claire lay napping.

As the two gamblers entered, Laura Foster was standing behind Mac a few yards back from the door. She wore her fur coat with the collar flipped up around her neck and her chin tucked against her chest, so her face was largely in shadow.

"Oh, God, Frankie!" she screeched. Her father looked as if he'd trudged miles through a hurricane. "What'd the rats do to you?"

"Don't fuss about it. Let's get outta here." He leaned toward the door, then did a double take, stepped closer, and lifted her chin. "What happened to you?"

She had a dark shiner and a line of scratches down her cheek. Her hair had fallen out of the cone into spikes and tangles. "The bitch wouldn't let up. Kept grilling me, like I was supposed to know something. I called her a couple names. She started clobbering me. Everybody around here's got a screw loose."

Harry looked at Mac. The cowboy nodded. "Miss Blackwood kinda flipped, boss. She's a tiger."

With a chuckle and a grin, Harry stared across the room to the corner near the fireplace. Claire had gotten up and knelt beside Hickey, who sat hunched with the phone receiver at his ear.

"Some dame." Harry sighed.

Laura Foster clutched his sleeve. "What about it? You done playing games with us, so we can scram?"

"Oh, yeah. Sure. Run 'em home, Mac. First, though, on the way to the car, take Frankie around and introduce him to the boys. Then he can wonder which one's going to plug him if he fed us a line."

"Huh?" Laura squealed. "You snitched on Jack?"

"Shut up, honey." Foster grasped her arm and tugged her toward the doorway while she lashed him with curses. The cowboy followed and shut the door.

Combing his hair with his fingers, Harry strolled across the room. He found the maid in the kitchen and told her to brew a pot of coffee and lace it hard. He walked past the fireplace, threw on a log, then tiptoed up behind Claire and rested a hand on her shoulder. "I wouldn't of made you for a scrapper."

"Sshh!" she commanded.

Hickey was barking into the phone. "Not a chance, sheriff. You wanta wait till dawn, that's your business, only if she dies tonight, you and I are gonna be on the outs till eternity. Look, I'm going up there in about two seconds, and I'll be driving like Mauri Rose....Yeah, all right. I'll meet you at the turnout by Watson Creek in a half hour....Okay, forty minutes."

Hickey dropped the receiver, leaned back, and exhaled deeply. He stood up and put his arms around Claire. "You can go home now, babe. It's all over but the fireworks."

"Don't you want me to drive or something?"

"No," Hickey said firmly. He gave her a kiss on the forehead and started for the door.

Beside the snake tank, Harry caught up. "Tom, I'd go with you or send some of the boys, only it'd be my neck if these guys that snatched her were connected with certain people. Know what I mean? You sticking me up, that's one thing. Me going on a posse, that's something different."

"Sure. You got a business to run."

"Yeah. You know the score. Now, how about you think of an excuse I can feed Miss Blackwood?"

"Excuse for what?"

"Why I'm jumping off here."

"Tell her you offered to go along and I said get lost. Act like I broke your heart. That'll melt her."

The boss clapped Hickey on the shoulder blade. "You're okay, Tom. Trigger-happy, but okay."

Chapter Tweny-nine

Bud stood glowering at the cedar that had fallen across the road. In two hours of chopping, they'd cut a wedge about halfway through.

"Bastard's petrified."

If the tree hadn't toppled, or if it'd waited an hour or been fifty feet up the road, beyond the cars, by now he and Tersh could be warm, dry, buzzed and smelling perfume.

He lifted the ax so ferociously it nearly tossed him over backward. He groaned. Snorted as he slammed the thing down. A few chips popped out of the wedge. He flung the ax and cussed while he peeled off his gloves, turned toward the firelight, and stared at his palms. Scowling viciously, he pointed to the left hand. "Look at this blister—like half a golf ball." He kicked the ax handle and stomped past his partners. Flopped down on the log beside Tersh. "Your turn, Jackie."

Meechum stayed crouched over the fire, resting his chin on his hands, until Tersh flung an elbow into his ribs. "Get with it, Jack. I'm not sitting on a bar stool by midnight, I turn into a werewolf."

Meechum dragged himself up, staggered to the ax, and picked it up. He made a few weary chops, then rested, leaning on the ax handle.

"Say, Jack," Tersh snapped. "You want a grave of your own, or should we dispose of you along with the girl?"

"Lay off. I'm getting blisters, same as you guys, and I gotta blow in Reno Tuesday. What's with this damn tree? We've been bashing on it for a couple hours at least."

"Keep bashing."

"Maybe we oughta take a break and finish up with the girl. That way, anybody shows up, we got nothing to hide. Hell, after we ditch her and clean up the mess, we could snooze till morning, go up after that snowplow guy. He's gotta have a chain saw, right?"

"Didn't I just tell you, chump, we're long gone by midnight or you're doing time with the worms?"

"Yeah, I heard you. Anyway, I think we oughta take care of the girl. Her bein' still up there gives me the creeps."

Staring into the fire, Bud offered, "How about we burn her up? You ever see anybody get burned? I wonder what color the smoke is."

"It'd stink up the whole basin," Tersh said. "All we gotta do is stomp her a little, get all the air out, tie a couple rocks to her, and heave her in the lake."

"Tie her with what?"

"With what? Rope, stupid."

"Yeah, and some damned fish'll make a meal outta the rope. A day or two, up she floats."

"So what? By that time she'll be a skeleton. It'd take Einstein to tell whether she's the doll or some prehistoric squaw."

"I don't know. Maybe the freezing water'll preserve her."

"Aw, think about it, pal," Meechum groaned. "If the water was freezing, the damned lake'd be frozen."

"You better get chopping," Tersh snarled, then turned to his partner. "What's the big deal if they find her? What's the difference? Either way, they ain't about to catch up with me. Not unless they got agents in the French Foreign Legion."

"Going to Africa, are you? You that scared of Tom Hickey?"

"North Africa's the promised land, is why. Behind every other door's an opium den. Maybe I'll round up a harem. I got a few grand stashed away."

"I don't want her in the lake," Meechum said. "We gotta dig a grave, deep where the wolves can't smell her."

Bud jumped up, made a turn around the fire, and grabbed Meechum by the collar. "You blow your brains out through the trombone, or what? A grave? By the time we move this damned log, we got hands like sausages. What do we dig with, smart guy?"

Chapter Thirty

At 9:53 P.M., Hickey pulled into the turnout beside Watson Creek. Both tires on the right side sank into mud. He left them embedded and sat stiffly behind the wheel, trying to breathe evenly, silence the fears that assaulted him, blot out the hideous vision that besieged him, of Wendy in death. She lay on her side with her head turned straight upward. She looked astounded. Her chest and her hair were soaked in blood. Her arms clutched her belly.

Hickey rolled down the window to let the heat out and the frost in. Sweat kept beading on his forehead. When he wiped his brow, his hand felt like a frozen block. He sat listening for tires and motors. Bounced his forehead off the steering wheel, cussing the miserable part of his brain that sought to prepare for the worst, that kept reminding him how often he'd suspected that Wendy couldn't live much longer. How she belonged in heaven, if heaven existed; no matter, she wasn't suited for the world. A hundred times in the past eight years he'd wondered if his calling wasn't only to protect her for the little while until she finished her tour on earth. One hell of a job he was doing.

Several times he reached for the door handle or the starter button and had to suppress the urge to rush the cabin alone. It seemed he couldn't wait another moment. His fingers burned. His feet threatened to leap out of his shoes.

Six minutes after ten, the sheriff's cruiser rattled into the turnout and stopped beside him. The four doors of the cruiser sprang open at once. The muscle-bound Indian named Roy had been driving. Two more deputies climbed out of the rear. The three deputies and Sheriff Boggs gathered around Hickey. Roy carried a 30.06 with a telescopic sight. The others held lever-action Winchesters.

One deputy was the lanky son of Louis Pederson, a village shopkeeper. The boy had freckles that looked like splotches of oil. Beside him stood a deputy named Gene, who used to deal poker at Harry's casino. He was tall as a flagpole, with hands that together could hide a basketball, or the decks he'd used to palm cards and deal seconds.

"What've you got in mind, Tom?" the sheriff asked.

"We've gotta walk in," Hickey said. "The only way to do it is sneak up on the cabin."

The sheriff glanced up at the trees. "Maybe we oughta drive a little way. The wind's blowing off the mountain. I don't guess they could hear us till we crested the hill and started down."

"I'm not gonna risk it. We can get up there in twenty minutes or so hiking."

"You know the layout?"

"I fished Flower Lake a couple times," Hickey said. "There's only the one cabin."

Deputy Pederson offered, "What's-his-name lives on this road, doesn't he? The snowplow driver."

"Lewellen," the sheriff said. "His place is at the end of the road, about a quarter mile beyond the lake. Tom, you're sure this crony of Harry's wasn't giving you the business?"

"Sure enough."

"Okay, then, let's shake a leg."

Gene rummaged in his pocket for keys, walked to the cruiser's trunk, and got out a small duffel bag and hoisted it over his shoulder. "I'm bringing some flares. Anybody want one?"

"What for?" Roy asked.

"You'd know if you hadn't sat out the war playing your tom-tom. How else you gonna see the target, hold the flashlight in one hand, the rifle in the other? I don't think we're gonna need the snowshoes."

"Bring 'em along," the sheriff said. "And get out a Winchester and flashlight for Tom."

Roy carried the snowshoes. They started two abreast up an icy dirt road confounded by sinkholes and rivulets, bordered in second-growth cedar and fir, each tree so close to its neighbor that the branches intertwined. The trunks were thick but short, twenty to thirty feet, just high enough to make the narrow road look like a tunnel into some treacherous cavern.

Hickey startled at every footfall. No matter how softly the men walked, and whether on dirt or snow, each step crunched, grating his senses and afflicting his spirit as though it had broken a mirror. At the quietest rustling in the underbrush—probably a squirrel—he wheeled and clapped the rifle butt to his shoulder. He pulled ahead of the others and still heard them panting. His heartbeat galloped. It sounded like restless fingers drumming.

At the crest of the hill, he ran off the road, through knee-deep snow in a stand of aspen to the edge of the dropoff and stood gazing down at Flower Lake.

Maybe six hundred yards long, half that wide, deep and murky, it looked like a black hole fringed in lace. In dead center rose an island of stacked, glacier-polished boulders. There were several piers, all but one in ruins. The good one lay on the opposite shore toward the far end. Behind it, the forest made way for a log cabin, the banker's place.

Out from between Hickey's teeth came a sound he'd never heard: a falsetto whimper. Wendy was there, he knew. Dead or alive. A light, so dim it might've been shed by a single candle, flickered against the pane of the window that overlooked the water. He peered at it while trying to swallow his heart.

A volley of sharp reports sounded. Hickey's gut thought it was a gun, but his mind rebutted the idea.

Deputy Pederson marched up and stopped beside him. "Yessir. Somebody's down there, all right." He turned to meet the sheriff. "You hear? Somebody's chopping logs."

They rested for a minute before another volley sounded. Five whacks spaced seconds apart. Pederson gaped into the darkness. "Funny. The guy that's chopping, he's got a little bonfire and he ain't nowhere near the cabin. He's way down the heel, a little ways toward the cabin from the split where the road cuts up to Mister Lewellen's place. Look real close, you can see the bonfire."

"Probably run out of logs," Boggs speculated. "Had to go out and find a dead tree. Tom, let's get straight who's running things. Is it you or me?"

Hickey gave up peering at the window. He turned to the sheriff and stared as though surprised to find him there, stuck his glasses back in their case, crammed it into his coat pocket. "You and Roy and Gene, see how near you can get to the woodcutter, then wait till you hear me fire a shot. That'll be when I get to Wendy or run into trouble. The kid and I'll slide down the hill, soon as it levels some, and cut around the topside of the lake. That oughta get us to the cabin about the same time you reach the woodcutter."

"Sheriff, we supposed to take orders from him?" The Pederson kid asked.

"Might as well. I get the feeling Tom's a lot better at giving orders than taking 'em."

Hickey told Pederson to pass out the snowshoes. Each man accepted a pair, hung it by a rope loop from his shoulder, and started down the grade. About halfway, the clear swatch of a firebreak cut through the yellow pine straight down the hill from the road to the lake. Hickey and the boy turned that way, sidestepping. The path was treacherous in darkness so nearly pure, with jagged stumps and gnarled fingers of brush piercing out of the snow. Still, after a few dozen steps, Hickey found a rhythm. He might've reached the base of the hill in record time and on his feet if he hadn't tried to gaze across the lake at the cabin window and missed spotting the rock that halted his front foot and sent him toppling head first. With old football instincts, he tucked and landed on his shoulder, the rifle pressed crossways against his stomach. Snowshoes flew up and clobbered the back of his head.

He skidded and plowed into the snow. When he tried to spring up, one leg folded and he toppled forward again. This time, he only rose to his knees, gazing around to regain his sense of direction. He couldn't see the lake or cabin through the thicket of trees.

The boy caught up. He took Hickey's arm, helped him to his feet, and returned his hat. "You okay?"

Hickey growled and pushed on. About twenty yards farther, they reached the base of the hill and what had once been a logging road that circled the lake behind the trees along the high-water line. Hickey peered between the trunks. The dim light still flickered in the cabin. He took out his glasses and stood a minute watching for movement. His heart and brain throbbed with longing for even a glimpse of Wendy. A chorus of wicked voices taunted him, proclaiming he'd find her dead.

A howl lodged in his throat. Suddenly frantic to know, and to mutilate every freak who'd harmed or grieved her, he wheeled and started trudging north around the top bend of the lake.

Along the old road, which must've caught daily sunlight, the snow gave way to dry patches and mud puddles. The speed he could've made got halved by the fallen logs he and the deputy had to dodge or climb over.

Though the forest was probably muting their noise, Hickey dreaded every slapping footstep or snapping twig. Often his feet planted themselves against his will. He couldn't help but lean and stare between the trees at the cabin, holding perfectly still while listening for sounds that meant they'd gotten detected. Pederson took the lead.

Even when he'd reached the west side of the lake and lost any view of the cabin, Hickey stopped every few yards to listen. The last time, his body started quaking. For at least a minute, all he could do was press the Winchester across his middle, to keep the gun from dropping out of his hands, and lock his knees so they wouldn't buckle. In forty-four years he'd never gotten a clue that fear could be this profound.

He was standing at the last bend in the road. The deputy was running back toward him. A few muted whacks sounded: the woodcutter again. Hickey managed two steps before the deputy reached him. He grabbed the boy's arm. A handhold made standing far easier. At last he stopped quaking and gasped, "There's no sense us going in together. One of us sticks to the road, the other takes the shoreline, sneaks around behind. There's a back porch and steps going down."

"Sure. I saw it. You sick or something?"

"I'll take the road. You get to the bottom of the steps and wait. I bust through the front door, yelling like the devil. The first peep, you fly up the stairs, kick in the door, jump through the window, whatever you've got to."

"Yessir."

Hickey nodded and started up the road, planting his toes, then letting the heels fall gently to minimize the racket. He inspected every inch of the ground ahead and studied each sound. An ax bouncing off wood. A hissing noise, like a beginner attempting to whistle. The *whoosh* of a branch snapping back into place. Loosed clumps of snow falling off a tree and splattering. A rattle, like a pouch full of marbles. Feet padding on the crusty ground.

Hickey froze, stared up the hillside, and sensed the creature before he saw it: a small gray wolf skulking downhill. It made a leap onto the road and dashed across, rustling twigs as it wedged between two intertwined thickets. The boy yowled.

Chapter Thirty-one

Hickey broke into a sprint. A cabin door flew open and smacked against a wall. Somebody called, "That you, Tersh?"

"Hell, no," a distant man shouted. Probably the woodcutter.

A gunshot cracked, then another. While Hickey ran, he listened for evidence that Pederson hadn't got hit, or chomped by the wolf. All he heard were his own feet, a medley of curses and threats from voices that could've been Boggs, Roy, or Gene, and two more gunshots from the vicinity of the voices.

He had no idea how far to the cabin. The road climbed and dipped, cut in and back with every bend of the shoreline. The first clue he'd neared the cabin was another clap from a door banging open. Heavy footsteps scampered away. Either a car door squeaked or someone or something whimpered.

"Wendy!"

He'd tried to roar. But the feeble shout he'd managed seemed to collide with the air and echo back at him, while he sprinted like he hadn't in twenty-five years, since his season as a sophomore fullback, second string, at USC. Only now he was running distance with the same fury he used to rush off tackle. And he was twenty-five years older. As he crossed the last rise and saw the cabin, for an instant he caught a second wind. Then his chest seemed to burst into flames. The cabin and everything blurred. His head emptied. A drifting balloon. Still he ran and managed to lift the rifle as he jumped through the open doorway.

"Wendy!" he screamed at the empty room, and collapsed onto the floor.

◇◇◇

Deputy Pederson perched on a granite slab near the lake, holding a bead with his rifle on the man who'd tried to escape in a canoe, dragging it behind him across the fringe of ice, nosing it into the water pointed diagonally across the lake toward the northeast shore from where a firebreak led up between tall cedars to the road.

After Pederson had spooked at the wolf and yowled, and the man had shot at him, and the wolf dashed past and fled along the shoreline, the boy had scrambled up the bank onto the road out of the shooter's vision. He'd jogged down the road, following Hickey, until he heard a splash, followed by a wail so high-pitched at first he thought it was the girl. He'd peered through the trees. Spotted the canoe.

If the ice hadn't shattered beneath the man, he might've slipped away. Instead, he hung waist deep in the lake, clutching the rail of the canoe and kicking ferociously, while Pederson sat with his rifle trained. After a minute, the canoe nosed into the ice fringe and seemed to stick there. Three times the man heaved up, fell back, and sank, before he crawled over the rail and flopped between the benches.

Pederson got up, stumbled and skidded on snow, frost and beds of fallen needles. At the shore, he stepped lightly on the ice, only a few feet out before he caught the tie rope. He gripped the rope and rifle in one hand, reached under his coat for his revolver, then slung the rifle over his shoulder where the snowshoes had hung before he'd tossed them aside. Aiming the revolver at the back of the man who lay sprawled facedown, he towed the canoe ashore and jumped a few steps back. "On your feet, mister."

"Forget it," the man groaned. "I can't."

"Come on!"

"Gimme a minute."

Pederson stood grinding his teeth and skuffing the frozen sand while the man rose an inch at a time. He'd slid out of the canoe, sprawled then risen to his knees just as Hickey staggered out the cabin's back door.

Holding the porch rail, he dragged himself down to the beach. He plodded across. Things were still blurry, his chest still burned, but the dizzy light-headedness had passed. When he reached the kneeling man, he dropped beside him. He lifted his arm and loosed a vicious backhand. The tough guy caught it on the cheekbone and tumbled to his side.

"Where is she?" Hickey snarled.

"Ain't she in the cabin?"

Hickey lifted both hands and lunged at the freak's head, slammed it onto the ground, held it there. "Who's here with you?"

"A couple guys, is all."

"Name 'em."

"Tersh Gohner. Jack Meechum."

"Where are they?"

"Last I knew, Tersh was down trying to budge this damned tree that fell and blocked us in. I was up making coffee. Meechum was taking care of the girl. Then you guys showed up. That's all I can tell you, buddy."

Hickey wrenched the man's head sidewise, to face him. "You better tell me that Wendy's okay."

"Yeah. Sure she is."

Hickey let go. Slowly and warily, the man pushed himself upright. With the heel of his right hand, Hickey punched the freak's chest, knocked him back against the canoe. "Lie to me, will you?"

The man's arms had wrapped around his chest as if it were a treasure. His eyes had bugged and gone wandering, drifting toward the lake and back, before he mumbled, "She's okay, I tell you. Last I saw."

"Cuff him to a post or something," Hickey mumbled. He rose and struggled to hold himself erect, walking back to the steps and through the cabin, out the front door. He stood on the road, thinking the footsteps he heard, and the whimpering, must've been Meechum dragging her away, up the hillside. Meechum hadn't cut north on the road. He wouldn't have gone the other way, toward the gunshots. He must've dragged her into the forest.

If the hill on this shore were like the other, they could've tracked him easily, through the snow. But this was the sunny slope. Between snow patches lay clearings and trails inches deep in matted needles. Through that stuff, even with all the flashlights and flares in creation, they'd go nuts trying to follow tracks.

The footfalls sounded as close as if they were his own. Hickey wheeled and saw the sheriff about thirty yards away, loping toward him.

"You got her?"

The sheriff skidded on mud up to Hickey. "Nope. All we got's some big fella pinned down at Lewellen's place. He crawled under the lousy snowplow. Far as we can tell, only weapon's an ax. Lewellen and Gene got him cornered. Roy's scouring the woods out that way. I figured you could use me over here. What'd you find in the cabin?"

Hickey shook his head. "Pederson's got one of 'em."

"He say anything?"

"Says Meechum's got her." He paced in frantic circles. Stared into the forest of yellow pine saplings. Then he noticed a faint glow, like the palest, distant beam of a lantern. It looked about a hundred yards southwest up the hillside.

He bolted toward the light, full speed. As soon as he left the road, his feet began slipping, churning in place as though on an oil slick. He cussed himself for not having taken a minute to run home from Harry's and change to boots. He fell forward and grappled with his hands, trying to pull and run at the same time. He moaned and babbled in wild abandon, calling out endearments and assurances he'd used to comfort her after nightmares and the early times they'd made love.

Once again, his chest blazed—flames seemed to lap up his throat. Dizziness repossessed him. Any second, he knew, his heart might shut down. But if he couldn't get Wendy back, he didn't want the damned heart.

The glow had faded long before he neared it, and he'd lost sight of the spot. About ten yards before the first crest of the hill, where the saplings gave way to a rare stand of virgin tamarack—long after he thought he'd passed his destination—he saw her lying on a mat of brown needles, wrapped halfway around the trunk of a fir.

Hickey dove to his knees. He grappled and clawed at her body and face like a blind man in terror. He found the knot of a bandanna at the neck. Tore at it with his teeth and fingers. Finally it unraveled. Then her head lifted sideways.

Her eyelids trembled. The skin of her face appeared clawed and beaten. A twig looked embedded in her cheek. Dark blood seeped from her nose. The blue eyes that used to flash like tinted crystal had gone flat and murky as stagnant pools. If she saw him, she didn't let on. All she could utter were feeble groans.

Hickey dug under the small of her back and her knees. He lifted and pressed her to him until he could feel a heartbeat, and another. He struggled to his feet and started down the hill. After two steps, he wished he'd thought of kicking off his slippery shoes, but he wasn't going to let her loose for that or anything. He dug his heels into the needles and slip-stepped down about halfway before an icy patch lofted him into the air, then onto his back, where she lay sprawled across him, covering him with her legs, marvelous belly, chest, and hair.

He sat up, bent forward, and kissed her eyebrow. "You okay, babe?" he whispered desperately.

Though she didn't reply, he felt a breath on his cheek that thrilled him and roused him to spring up. But his ankle wobbled and folded sideways. Lying back down, he ran his fingers through her hair, listened to the breeze rising, and muttered, "Thank God," about a dozen times.

The sheriff stood over them. As Hickey lifted his arm to clutch the sheriff's, Wendy's head twitched, then craned upward. Like somebody who'd just stepped from noon into darkness, she peered fixedly at Hickey's face.

"Tom?"

"Yeah, babe. It's me."

"Oh!" she gasped. "Clifford wants out!"

Chapter Thirty-two

As soon as they got Wendy onto the bunk, she shuddered and pinched her eyes closed. She grasped the hand Hickey'd laid on her arm, squeezed hard. Her eyes and mouth were scrunched together as though battling to displace her nose. Her shoulders lifted, as her chest rose, then fell as her belly lifted, all the way down to her toes.

The sheriff tossed kindling into the wood stove. Pederson had found a pan and run out to the pump for water.

The twig was still embedded in Wendy's cheek. Hickey picked it out. Its image remained, like a red flower with folded petals. As her grunting quieted, through the last wavelike roll and push, Hickey bundled his coat and stuffed it under the pillow beneath her head. She sighed and lay still. Her soft moans sounded as if she were trying to run a scale but hadn't the range. Hickey got up and lifted her brown dress, pulled her panties down and off, then hoisted the dress back over her knees. He squatted beside her. Took her hand. Patted the only spot on her forehead that didn't look scraped or bruised.

"He's gonna be a big guy," she whispered. "Clifford wasn't so big. Maybe we should call him Tom instead."

"That's what middle names are for." The tip of his finger made circles on her cheek, around the flower. "Babe, will you be sad if he's a girl?"

"Not if we can think up a name. It isn't everything sounds good with Hickey, you know?"

"It isn't anything sounds good with Hickey. Let's call her Vicki. Mickey. How about Red?"

"Stop, Tom. Don't make me laugh, please. If he's a girl, maybe later we'll have Clifford, okay?"

For a minute he couldn't answer, with his throat crimped shut and his eyes marveling at the prize he'd never deserved. "Sure you wanta do this again, babe? Doesn't it hurt awfully?"

"Oh, boy. It hurts, all right."

The sheriff carried a stool over and sat. "Tom, when you first ran up the hill there, you see any sign of this Meechum?"

Hickey wagged his head. "Soon as Roy or Gene shows, send him up there. It shouldn't be hard to nab the damn fool. He's gotta be stupid, or else he wouldn't of carried a lantern or whatever it was."

"I don't think he's stupid," Wendy said breathlessly. "He didn't have any lantern."

"Sure he did, babe. It's the only reason I knew you were up there. Without the light—"

"Jack didn't have any light. Oh!" She shuddered and grunted, fiercely gripping Hickey's hand. This time she pushed so hard, it made her hips rise high, smashing her head into the pillow. Hickey reached underneath, braced his elbows against the bunk, and cradled her hips with his hands. Her body quaked like his had, on the road not long ago. She howled, then let go. He eased her down.

Pederson had run in with a pan full of water. He'd set it on the wood stove, rushed to the kitchen, and found a rag, wetted it. Now he gave it to Hickey, who dabbed at the splotches of dirt on her face, then folded the rag and held it across her brow.

"The light was Zeke," Wendy gasped.

"Huh?"

"Zeke." For a while she seemed lost, gazing around, pausing at each person or object, then passing on. Finally she opened her mouth and frowned, as if she'd done something shameful. "Zeke's an angel," she whispered.

Her head flew up and slapped back down on the folded coat. Color drained from her face. Even her lips had turned whitish blue. She sucked air mouth-deep, blew it out quickly and hard. Her body flopped and thrashed; then she fell quiet and stared at Hickey as though he were a strange and peculiar being.

Every half minute, she'd groan and launch her hips upward, let Hickey catch and hold them there while she quaked for the next half minute. Then she collapsed and rested, panting and staring at Hickey as though appalled that he didn't relieve her.

"Try making her stay flat on the bunk," the sheriff offered.

"You done this before?"

"One time. I don't much know what I'm doing. The thing is, arching up like that, all she's getting is worn out."

Wendy cried, "Oh! Oh! Oh!"

The sheriff jumped to the foot of the bunk and slung the dress back over her knees. As her hips flew up, Hickey grasped both sides of her hipbone from underneath and pulled her down close to the bunk.

"There," the sheriff yelped. "Looks like brown hair." Wendy fell back and caught a few breaths before she tried to arch again.

"Come on, kid," the sheriff cajoled. "There's steak and potatoes waiting. Apple pie à la mode. You've got a swell mama. Your old man's all right, too. A little bossy, but you and him'll get along. You're gonna like it out here."

Her shoulders, then her chest and belly, rose and fell, but her hips drove Hickey's hand and forearm into the mattress.

"Hey, look at this! The kid's got a chin. And shoulders. Whoa, not so fast!"

Hickey didn't know where to look. He couldn't stand and peer over her raised knees with his arm pinned beneath her. When he tried to glance between her knees, her legs slapped together. Anyway, he couldn't pry his eyes off her face for more than a second or two. He crooked his neck and peeked under her knees. All that got him was a view of the sheriff's elbows.

"There we go. Tom, you got a boy. Two legs. Two arms. Twelve toes. No, make that ten. Pederson, give me a towel, will you? A bunch of 'em."

Hickey eased her down, caught a glimpse of his bloody son, the tiny legs kicking, hands and arms clutching as though he saw something and wanted it badly. He made gasping sounds and small cries as the sheriff wiped him clean.

Hickey let his head fall onto Wendy's breast. He closed his eyes and listened to her tremulous, long-winded moan. It sounded miraculous. All at once there was nothing but glee, as if the world had gotten bathed clean.

His chest hardly burned anymore. His vision had cleared. As soon as he got Wendy to the hospital, he'd phone Claire. She'd tell him Leo had arrived safely. The old guy loved kids, the tinier the better.

"Look here, Tom," the sheriff said.

Hickey rose far enough to gaze at his son. He lay sucking breaths. Only scattered blotches of blood remained, on his hair, his legs, and down the umbilical cord. The boy looked perfect. Glorious.

Chapter Thirty-three

The nurse was gathering breakfast dishes when Sheriff Boggs stepped into the hospital room. He declined the extra chair and politely asked Wendy how she was feeling. In return he got her radiant smile. "Thank you for saving us, sir."

"They holding the big lug in the nursery?"

"Yep. Only for a couple days, though. He didn't get too banged up when Jack Meechum dragged me up the hillside."

"Meechum show up?" Hickey asked.

"Nope. I got a dozen boys out there, see if they can find the body before it gets shredded. Not a chance he lasted through the night. He would've had to come back to the cabin or bust into another, and we've checked every place five miles around."

"He could've circled back to the road."

"I don't believe he could. Roy got on the radio at Lewellen's place. We had cruisers on the road before he could've got there. I figure he ran scared up into the wilderness. He's not gonna find a road in eighty miles that way. If he don't freeze, and wolves or a cat don't get him, there's nothing out there but crags to fall off of and arroyos—step in one of those, some hiker'll sight him mid-August or so. By then he'll look like Jolly Roger."

"Who's Jolly Roger?" Wendy asked.

"A skeleton." Hickey kissed his finger and touched her forehead. "Like Meechum's gonna be soon enough, either way. They can stick murder one on him, for the beachcomber."

"Murder one, they'll kill him, won't they?" Wendy asked.

"Yep."

"Poor man."

"I got a better name for him," the sheriff said.

Letting her head fall back, Wendy closed her eyes. Hickey sat stroking her arm. When Claire arrived, after she greeted and kissed Wendy, the sheriff offered his hand, then pulled the extra chair close to Hickey's and seated her.

Though she'd sat with the Hickeys from midnight to dawn, Claire looked fresh and animated as though she'd just returned from a voyage in the tropics. She wore her hair up, a touch of eye shadow, a bright cotton skirt with a cashmere sweater. She rummaged in her purse, extracted a telegram, and handed it to Hickey. "There was a note on your door. I stopped by Western Union."

TOM. I GOT THE NEWS FROM WASHOE COUNTY SHERIFFS. THANK GOD. CYNTHIA SKIPPED OUT. DITCHED THE SISTER. TOOK HER SON AND DISAPPEARED. LAUREL'S DAMNED MAD. BRING THE KID FOR A VISIT, I'LL TEACH HIM TO WATERSKI. RUSTY.

Hickey blew a sigh, folded the telegram, and stuffed it into his pocket. Claire was petting Wendy's cheek. The sheriff stood, pardoned himself, and left. Hickey sat facing the women. "I got a problem."

"Leo," Claire murmured. The second it was out, she winced at her indiscretion.

Wendy stiffened up. "Leo's in a jam?"

"Naw. Don't worry, babe. I'm talking about Cynthia. See, when Meechum torched the Sousa place, he was doing the job for her. Now that he's a goner, providing they don't catch him alive, I can pin the whole rap on him if I want to. Or I can stick Cynthia with her rightful share."

"Why would you want to save her, after she burnt up a guy?" Claire asked.

"She's nuts. A purebred loon. But maybe she's only nuts about her family. Only nuts enough to kill *them* anyway." He gave her the story in brief, how the feud between sisters had begun with rivalry and escalated on account of mutual fear. "Look, either Cynthia's gonna kill Laurel or vice versa. Maybe today, maybe in twenty years, but someday. I'd make book on it."

"Well, then," Claire speculated, "if Cynthia goes to prison, it might save her. Or her sister."

"I think it'd kill her," Hickey said.

Wendy let go of Claire's hand, lifted Tom's, stared at the palm, and caressed it. "Do you think she'd hurt anybody besides her sister?"

"People get in the way," Hickey said. "Like Johnny Sousa. This beachcomber. Meechum. You don't just kill somebody clean. Every murder I've seen, it's like a pileup on the highway."

Claire nodded adamantly. "True. In a sense, she killed two people sure, maybe three, if Meechum's dead, or—" She caught herself before mentioning Leo. "And that doesn't count all she put Wendy through."

Wendy reached behind her head, straightened the pillow, and propped herself up. "I'm okay. And she's got a little boy, like Clifford. Who'd watch her boy if she goes to prison? Say, maybe we could keep him."

"Whoa. Not a chance I'm getting you or Clifford mixed up with that family. It'd be the kiss of death."

Wendy nodded pensively. "Anyhow, her boy needs his mama."

Hickey stared at his wife in awe, at the arch of her brows and her eyelashes slightly flicking. It seemed he could know her a million years and find a hundred new features to love every day: a turn of her mind, a tone of voice, a soft place or blemish of her skin. "Sousa wasn't supposed to be in the house. That part was kind of accidental. Anyway, Sousa was no choirboy."

"Right," Claire said. "And you can't really pin Meechum's killing the beachcomber on Cynthia."

Hickey wrapped his fingers around Wendy's hand, picked it up, and kissed the vein of her wrist. "Let's leave the boy with his mama."

"Okay. I think that's best."

"You know, darling, as long as you're around, I don't need a conscience. You do a way better job."

"Don't be silly." She reached around his neck and pulled herself close. Hickey rubbed her back for a long time, until Claire stood and touched his shoulder and excused herself, with a promise to return that evening.

"You know what I want?" Hickey said.

"Tell me."

"To hold you."

With a smile that turned to a grimace, she eased herself toward the wall. Hickey slipped in beside her, tunneled his arm under her neck, and flopped his head back onto the side of her pillow. He cocked his head so their cheeks touched." "Babe, are you sure the freaks didn't hurt you?" You're not just saying that so I won't sneak into the jail and mutilate them?"

"I'm sure, all right. Except when Jack Meechum dragged me up the hillside. That hurt a little. And Tersh whopped me once. Only once, though. I was singing a song he didn't like. But they couldn't hurt me bad, even if they wanted. On account of the angels."

"Yeah, how about those angels? What'd they look like?"

"I only saw Zeke, but I think there was a whole gang."

"What'd Zeke look like?"

"Oh, big. Way taller than you. It was hard to see him because he was mostly made of light, I think. I didn't see wings, but maybe that's because he had a floppy shirt that came way down. He either had hair like a girl's or he was wearing a funny hat. I think he was a redhead. That's about all I saw."

"Did he talk?"

"Nope. Didn't make a sound."

Hickey's free hand had crept over and rubbed her belly. "You're okay, sweetheart? Honest?"

"Honest. Well, I'm sore, that's for sure."

"You're not worried, about nightmares or anything?"

"Not about anything. Truly. Because nothing terrible's gonna happen, not to you or Clifford or me. Not ever. That's God's promise, Tom."

The past thirty years, Hickey'd gotten teary a few times, but if he'd sobbed in that time, he'd deleted the memory. Now he sobbed freely, and liked it. Afterward, he lay still, listening to her breathe ever more shallowly until she drifted away. Then he slipped out from under the covers, patted the wrinkles from his trousers, grabbed his coat, and walked out to the hall and down to the nursery window.

There were only two babies. Hickey stared at Clifford, who lay facedown, his head cocked the other way. From the back, he looked strong, as though any second he might do pushups. Hickey didn't need to see his face, he remembered it so vividly. A long head with puffy cheeks, ruddy skin. The kid might become a heartthrob, especially if he kept the dark hair that set off his eyes. They were blue as the shallows along Agate Bay.

Chapter Thirty-Four

Driving home, Hickey admired the sights. Streams of melted snow alongside the road, glistening blacktop, waterfalls plunging off rooftops, splattering on kerosene drums and into puddles. Even with a prize case of exhaustion trying to pound him into submission, he could've sung for joy. Except it would've felt wicked to sing when he ought to be mourning for Leo or searching for him. As he drove through the village, past Pederson's Mercantile and Post Office, a fury sparked and rushed through him.

If Mickey Cohen had knocked off his partner and oldest pal, he'd be obliged to devote whatever part of himself Wendy and Clifford could spare to ruining the freak, at least. Or else he'd live and die in shame. If Leo'd got himself killed, no matter if Wendy'd prophesied their blessed future, Hickey didn't buy it.

He made the turn and spotted Sheriff Boggs standing beside his cruiser outside the Café Rita, waving him down. Hickey pulled in, lowered his window, and watched the sheriff munch a sweet roll as he crossed the gravel.

Boggs leaned his free hand on the car door. "Tom, you ever heard of the Olive Branch Home down in Auburn? Not exactly a hospital, but I hear it's the best place for folks that're just a bit loony. It's lots cheaper than a hospital, and they got treatments can work wonders in no time."

"Who's loony?"

"Well, don't a person have to be loony to see angels? I'd figure loony was one of the requirements."

"It depends, doesn't it? If there are angels around, I guess we've gotta be loony *not* to see 'em."

"That so?" The sheriff winked and backed off a step. "Did I tell you they've got a men's wing too, at that place in Auburn?" Taking the last bite of his sweet roll, he strolled off.

Hickey backed out and pulled away. In front of him, the lake was polished silver upon which Mount Tahoe and the Rubicon shimmered. He noticed them briefly before his eyes slammed shut. He slapped his head, cranked up his eyelids and held on long enough to drive the last quarter mile.

Three times he woke to call Leo. No answer. Around dusk, Claire stopped by and chauffeured him to the hospital. They stayed a couple of hours. All of them got to hold the baby. Then Claire drove him home and made him cocoa while he tried Leo's number again. No answer. She read aloud the book on his nightstand, *Billy Budd*. One chapter put him to sleep.

Thursday morning he pulled on boots and a jacket, started out to check the mailbox. He'd just stepped off the porch when the phone rang. He hustled in and grabbed it.

"Tom?"

"Vi. Tell me he's okay, Vi."

"I can't. He's paralyzed. His spine got mashed. I don't know if he's ever coming home, Tom." She drew a long tremulous breath. From the background, Hickey heard a woman comforting her. "The doctor says he might have brain damage. I'm afraid he's gonna be one of those old men that sit in their wheelchairs drooling."

"He can't talk?"

"Some. Real slow, but he got out a description of the guys that worked him over. Mickey Cohen's boys. They tortured him and shoved the Packard off a cliff, left him for dead. I hope they burn! Tom, he can talk, all right, but it took an hour or so to describe each guy. He'll say a few words, then go off somewhere, and you think he's not coming back. His brain's goofed up bad."

Her voice had trailed off to a whimper. Suddenly it blustered. "They arrested the goons, but they're clammed up. Suppose they get convicted, so what? Six months for assault, if they don't skip town soon as bail comes through this afternoon. And all Mister Cohen gets is a laugh out of the deal. That's the hell of it, Tom. It's all for nothing. Just now, he asked for a cigaret. So I light one, hold it for him. He takes a puff and spits it out. Spits it out on the damn floor." She sobbed. "I gotta go, Tom."

"Hey, wait."

"No, I'll call back later. I'm having a rough time."

"We'll be down soon as the baby can travel. Couple days."

"Sure, I know you will. I gotta go."

Hickey set the receiver on the arm of the chair. He stood for a moment glaring at the lake. Then he reached for the nearest object, Wendy's Isak Dinesen book. He reared back and pitched as though attempting to knock down Mount Pluto. The book shattered his lakeview window.

He slumped into the chair and tried to remember the last time he'd busted something in a rage. Not counting the noses or jaws of a few guys, the last thing he'd busted like that, he was thirteen years old. Maybe he'd do it more often.

He went outside for the book, picked it up and wiped snow off the pages, and attempted to straighten the dented spine. Wrapping it protectively under his arm, he carried it to his car and put it on the front seat, where he'd remember to give it to Wendy. Then he shuffled around the car and across the driveway to the woodshed. He got out his ax. Alongside the shed lay slabs of pine about a foot thick and two feet in diameter. He singled out one. Took aim. With the first swipe, he shattered the damn thing. He tossed the ax aside. Leaned on the shed and tried to figure what he ought to do. The only answer that came was, he should ask Wendy to pray.

Before, whenever he'd been stumped, if his brain got too tangled or sore, there was always Leo. He folded his hands, placed his thumbs between his eyes and the bridge of his nose, leaned into them. "What now, old man?" he muttered.

After a minute came the vague recollection that a long time ago he'd walked outside for a reason. Though he couldn't remember what it might be, he set off wandering in search of it. He passed through the redwood grove and around back of the house, headed for the lake, but cut left before he reached the dunes. When he got to the meadow, he noticed that Claire's Pontiac was parked outside Poverman's. Briefly he questioned what would bring her there, before he received the conviction that Claire's social life hardly mattered while his partner lay mutilated and as conscious as a turnip.

The mail. That was all he'd gone out for. Murmuring curses, he wandered that way. The mailbox was beside the paved road. A pickup rattled by, spraying a tail of slush.

There was only the one envelope, with his name and address in shaky block letters. He ripped it open and stared in horror.

Tom, They're all yours, my three girls, your two, and Clifford. I'm a goner. I messed up. Drop it, that's an order.

The envelope fell into a bush. The letter stayed in his hands. He stared at it while he trudged in a stupor up the road to Poverman's mailbox and along the gravel driveway to the gambler's front porch, where Tyler sat leafing through a newspaper.

"How's the baby, Mister Hickey?"

"Swell."

Tyler pushed open the door and stood aside. Before Hickey crossed the threshold, Claire was beside him. "Mister Poverman asked for help redecorating. I had to agree, Tom. A chance to redeem this bordello—turn it down, I'd risk damnation. ..."

He passed her the letter and stood mutely until she lowered herself to a nearby sofa and whispered, "Maybe he got away."

Hickey flopped down next to her. "No, he didn't. Cohen hit him. He's alive and good for nothing, Claire. He'd be better off gone."

In slippers, woolen trousers, and a silk pajama shirt, Harry sauntered over. "So—"

Claire shut him off with a glance and passed him the letter. Reaching for Hickey's hand, she said, "Leo's right, you know.

For the girls, all of us—and especially for Clifford—you've got to let it go."

The boss paced a circle in front of the sofa, then stopped and squared off. "Yeah, Tom. I'm with her." He thrust his hands, palms out, to intercept any back talk. "I know the line: 'Who asked you. Harry?' Doesn't mean a damn if you ask me or not, I'm gonna tell you. Guys like that, Mickey's boys, they've got a knack for dying. You take 'em out, it'd be a wasted effort." He fixed a vehement glare on Hickey. "Trust me this one time, will you, pal? I *know* these guys."

Chapter Thirty-five

On Saturday a ranger found what the scavengers had left of Jack Meechum. Scraps of flannel and cotton. A hat band and alligator belt. Western boots. Feet. Car keys and a trombone mouthpiece. A skeleton in which the femur appeared so shattered, it must've dropped him when it snapped in two.

Monday morning, the Hickey family took a stroll on the beach, Clifford's first excursion. About fifty yards offshore, Mac and two females raced the speedboat *Prudence* back and forth. The sky was summer blue. The mountains all around had metamorphosed into diamonds. After four sunny days, all but patches of snow had melted in the basin.

Wendy carried the baby in a squaw blanket. Hickey wouldn't let her tromp around in slush and risk stumbling, so he towed them on the sled through the mud, bucking and lunging like a mule. By the time they got home, he needed a nap and rubdown, after which they'd drive south. Spend tonight in a Visalia motel and tomorrow with Leo.

Hickey lounged in the easy chair that faced the love seat where Wendy sat and nursed. As soon as the kid gave up sucking and burped a bit, maybe he'd doze and allow his old man a chance to get pampered for a minute. Except the phone rang. Hickey grabbed it.

"How's he doing, Tom?"

"Tops. A couple days you'll get to see him."

"Can't wait," the captain said. "What do you hear from Vi?"

"The same. Leo's a broken old man, that's all. At seventy you don't get stomped by pros, take a wild ride in a runaway car, flip a few times, splatter on the rocks, and still make a comeback."

"Yeah, I guess you're right. It's a heartbreaker....So, I hear you've been to LA. Did you stop at the hospital, visit the old man?"

"Whoa. Who's got me in LA?"

Thrapp issued a prolonged sigh. "Meaning you're not the guy who sapped a character named Gregory Kitain, aka Bass? One of the punks that did Leo. You're not the guy who brained him with a tire iron or something, five, maybe six times?"

"I'm not the guy," Hickey growled, though it seemed as if one of the boulders piled on his heart had just tumbled off and rolled away.

"Good. So, who'd you send?"

"Tell you what, Rusty. When you've got something else to talk about, give me a call."

"I'll do that."

Hickey cradled the receiver and lay back in the chair, a little dizzy, as though he'd been spinning on a dance floor and had to relearn his directions.

"Something go wrong?" Wendy asked.

He smiled grimly and wagged his head. "One of the guys that hit Leo got himself killed, that's all." He sat up, laced his boots, stood, and gave Wendy and Clifford each a kiss. "I'm going next door for a minute."

"Did Harry kill the man?"

"Maybe so, babe."

Not bothering with a jacket, he went out, shut the door quietly, and headed toward the meadow, wondering how Claire would answer when he got around to warning her to leave the gambler alone. If he argued that besides Harry's obvious failings such as cheating the public and womanizing, he also killed people when the need arose, Claire might well say, "So do you, Tom."

The porch was stacked with Formica, waiting for the Salvation Army. Though Claire had informed Poverman that to dump his furniture on the poor was to add insult to injury, he insisted on the tax write-off.

Hickey rapped on the door. It swung open. Frieda curtsied and dashed back toward the kitchen, while Harry sauntered out of the poolroom across a plush ivory carpet and the bare plywood entryway, past the fellow who knelt, laying a square of Italian tile.

"What do you think, Tom?"

Hickey motioned with his chin, led the way back across the new carpet to the poolroom, shut the door behind them. "Oh, mother," Harry said. "You're not gonna do the gun routine again, are you?"

"An LA punk named Bass got his head smashed."

"What'd I tell you? Those guys are dropping all the time."

"You send Tyler down there or hire a local?"

The boss made a grimace and a two-handed shrug. "Not me, pal. Bass is one of Mickey's boys. You think I'm crazy enough to cross Mickey?"

"Crazy as they get."

"You oughta know," Harry said. "Now scram. I was heading for the shower. Say, what kinda cologne does Miss Blackwood like best? You know, the kind that leaves her faint, makes her heart pitter-patter."

Hickey gripped his neighbor's shoulder. He scorched the man with his eyes. "I didn't ask you to whack anybody."

"So what's the deal, then? Every time somebody gets snatched or bumped off, you're gonna lay it on Harry? Okay, if that's how it is. Now beat it, will you? Go change a diaper or something."

To receive a free catalog of Poisoned Pen Press titles, please contact us in one of the following ways:

Phone: 1-800-421-3976
Facsimile: 1-480-949-1707
Email: info@poisonedpenpress.com
Website: www.poisonedpenpress.com

Poisoned Pen Press
6962 E. First Ave. Ste. 103
Scottsdale, AZ 85251